MESHUGAH

BOOKS BY ISAAC BASHEVIS SINGER

NOVELS
The Manor [I. The Manor II. The Estate]
The Family Moskat · The Magician of Lublin
Satan in Goray · The Slave · Enemies, A Love Story
Shosha · The Penitent · The King of the Fields
Scum · The Certificate · Meshugah

STORIES
Gimpel the Fool · A Friend of Kafka · Short Friday
The Séance · The Spinoza of Market Street · Passions
A Crown of Feathers · Old Love · The Image
The Death of Methuselah

MEMOIRS
In My Father's Court

FOR CHILDREN
A Day of Pleasure · The Fools of Chelm
Mazel and Shlimazel or The Milk of a Lioness
When Shlemiel Went to Warsaw
A Tale of Three Wishes · Elijah the Slave
Joseph and Koza or The Sacrifice to the Vistula
Alone in the Wild Forest · The Wicked City
Naftali the Storyteller and His Horse, Sus
Why Noah Chose the Dove
The Power of Light
The Golem

COLLECTIONS
The Collected Stories
Stories for Children
An Isaac Bashevis Singer Reader

ISAAC BASHEVIS SINGER

MESHUGAH

TRANSLATED BY THE AUTHOR
AND NILI WACHTEL

FARRAR STRAUS GIROUX
New York

Library of Congress Cataloging-in-Publication-Data
Singer, Isaac Bashevis.
[Meshuge. English]
Meshugah / Isaac Bashevis Singer ; translated by the author and
Nili Wachtel.
p.   cm.
I. Title.
PJ5129.S49M4713   1994
839′.0933—dc20   93-42785   CIP

MESHUGAH (me-shug´-a)—Yiddish word
meaning crazy, senseless, insane.

PART I

ONE

I T HAPPENED MORE than once that someone I thought had died in Hitler's camps suddenly turned up alive and well. I usually tried to hide my surprise. Why create a drama or melodrama or let the other know I had resigned myself to his or her death? But on that spring day in 1952, when the door to my office at the Yiddish newspaper in New York opened and Max Aberdam walked in, I must have looked startled and grown pale, because I heard him roar, "Don't be frightened, I haven't come from the Great Beyond to strangle you!"

I stood up and made a motion as if to embrace him, but he put out his hand and I grasped it. He still wore a flowing tie and a plush hat with a wide brim. He was much taller than I. He had not changed much since I had last seen him in Warsaw, although I noticed specks of gray in his black beard. Only his stomach had grown larger and more pointed. Yes, it was the same Max Aberdam, the Warsaw patron of painters and writers, the well-known glutton, guzzler, womanizer. He held a cigar between his fingers, a gold watch chain hung on his vest, and gems sparkled in his cuff links. Max Aberdam did not speak, he shouted—that was his style. He loudly declared: "The Messiah has come and I arose from the dead. Don't you read the news in your own newspaper, or maybe you yourself are dead? If that's the case, go back to your grave."

"I'm alive, I'm alive."

"You call this living? Holed up in a smoke-filled office reading proofs? A corpse could do this. It's spring outside, at least by the calendar. Have you noticed there is no spring in New York—here either you freeze or you fry. Come, eat lunch with me, or I'll tear you apart like a herring."

"They are waiting upstairs for these proofs. It will only take five minutes."

I did not know whether to address him by the familiar "thou" or the formal "you." He was almost thirty years my senior. His loud voice had been heard in the outer office and several of my fellow journalists stuck their heads in the open door. They smiled at me and one of them winked, perhaps thinking I had another mental case as a visitor. Since I had begun my column of advice in the paper, I often had strange types in my office—distraught wives of vanished husbands, young men with plans for redeeming the world, readers convinced they had made some startling discovery. One visitor confided that Stalin was a reincarnation of Haman. I quickly read through the proofs of my article, "Scientist Predicts People Will Live to Be Two Hundred," and handed it to the elevator man to be delivered to the tenth floor.

When we got into a descending elevator, it was crowded with writers and typesetters going down to the cafeteria for lunch. But Max Aberdam shouted over their voices: "You didn't *know* I was in America? Where do you live—in the World of Chaos? I've been trying to reach you for weeks. Yiddish papers are all the same. You call up and ask for someone and they tell you to hold the phone, but nothing happens—they've forgotten you.

Where do you live, on the moon? Don't you have your own telephone in your office?"

Outside I suggested that we too go to the cafeteria, but Max was indignant: "I haven't reached the point where I carry a tray like a waiter. Hey, taxi!" We climbed into a cab, which took us only a few blocks to a restaurant on Second Avenue. The driver told us he came from Warsaw and knew Max Aberdam and his family. He was also a reader of my column. Max handed him his calling card and gave him a large tip. At Rapaport's, the restaurant he had chosen, he was well known. We were shown to a table set with a basket of fresh rolls, a bowl of cooked peas, and dishes of pickles and sauerkraut. The waiter smiled at us because he recognized Max. For himself Max ordered orange juice and cold carp in jellied broth, and for me, a vegetarian, an omelet with vegetables. While he ate, he lit a cigar with his lighter. He chewed, blew smoke, and bellowed: "So you've become a columnist in America! I heard you last Sunday babbling on the radio, on how to subdue the emotions and other such rubbish. My friend, I may have lost everything, but a bit of sense I still have. Though I'm in debt over my head, I owe nothing to the Almighty: as long as He keeps sending us Hitlers and Stalins, He is *their* God, not mine."

"Where have you been," I asked, "all during the war?"

"Where have I not been. In Bialystok, in Vilna, Kovno, Shanghai, later in San Francisco. I experienced the full range of Jewish woes. In Shanghai I became a printer. I published the *Shyta Mekubbetzet*, the *Ritba*, the *Rasha*. I know all about proofs and typesetting. I myself have stood at the composing box, picking out type by hand. That the Jews are mad I've always known, but that they would be capable of founding a yeshiva in China, where they quibble over 'an egg that was laid on a holiday,' while their families were being shoved into ovens—that I never imagined. I escaped because an old rival of mine in Warsaw, a competitor in business, got me a visa to America. My good friends left me to stew where I was, but an enemy saved me. Nothing surprises me anymore."

He flicked his cigar ash onto his saucer. "If someone predicted I would be a typesetter in Shanghai, that Jews would have established their own state, and that in New York I would become a speculator in stocks, I would have laughed at him. But all this craziness has happened—if I'm not dreaming. Eat, Aaron, don't dawdle. In all America you cannot get a decent cup of coffee. Hey, waiter! I ordered coffee, not dishwater!"

As we continued eating, he related fragments of his experiences between 1939 and 1952. He had left his wife and children behind in Warsaw in September 1939 and, with his father-in-law and thousands of other men, fled over the Praga Bridge toward Bialystok, which was already in Bolshevik hands. There some writers he had once supported with grants and handouts denounced him as a capitalist, a Fascist, an enemy of the people. He was arrested and was within a hairbreadth of being stood against a wall and shot in the Lubyanka prison in Moscow, when a Party functionary in the KGB, a former accountant of his, recognized him and saved him. He fled east and after a series of miracles finally reached Shanghai. .

Max's wife and two daughters had died in Stutthof. Later in America he met the widow of a San Francisco sculptor whose work Max had once bought. Two weeks later they were married. "It was madness, simply madness," Max shouted. "Demons must have blinded my eyes. One day I stood with her under the wedding canopy, and the next day I knew I had fallen into a deep swamp. I was tired of roaming. In Shanghai I had a woman from Korea, an exquisite creature, but I couldn't take her with me to the United States. My present wife, Priva, is always ill and she is psychotic besides. She has convinced herself she is a medium who receives vibrations from the spirits. She converses with her dead husband through a Ouija board. She paints pictures of ghosts. In New York I found I was home again—they are all here, our people from Lodz and Warsaw.

"I even found a distant relative, filthy rich, actually a millionaire, a Mr. Wolbromer. He fell upon me as if I were his lost brother. He owns many houses as well as stocks he bought long ago, after the Wall Street crash, and nowadays they climb and climb. He arranged a big loan for me and I became a stock-market speculator. It turned out that many refugees here had received a little reparation money from Germany and had no idea what to do with it. I have become their manager. I buy stocks, bonds, mutual funds, and right now everything is going up. Of course the stock will not climb forever. But meanwhile, my clients' few dollars earn three times as much as they would in banks. Waiter, this coffee is ice cold!"

"You let it get cold," the waiter said.

Max Aberdam put his cigar down, took out a little metal box, extracted two pills, and threw them in his mouth. He raised a glass of water, took a gulp, and said: "I live on pills and faith —not in God but in my own crazy luck."

WHEN WE LEFT the restaurant I told Max I had to return to my office, but he would not hear of it. "This day belongs to me. I've been looking for you for many weeks. I even thought of putting an ad in the papers. On Sunday, when I heard you on the radio, I decided to put aside all my business affairs and next day took a taxi to East Broadway. To crawl underground into the subway in broad daylight, like a mouse in a hole, that I cannot do. Most of my clients are women, refugees from Poland who haven't learned to count in dollars. They were driven half-mad in the ghettos and concentration camps. I explain that I take a percentage off the top and they thank me as if I were a philanthropist giving them charity. I have no idea at all what these companies produce—the ones whose stocks I deal in. My broker is Harry Treibitcher, and he tells me what to buy and I buy, what to sell and I sell. I use my own head from time to time, read the financial journals and the so-called experts. I suppose I take risks. I know that sooner or later I'll disappoint my crazy clients, but disappointing women has always been my trade. I'm babbling about myself. How are things with you?" We continued to walk on Second Avenue.

"I also disappoint women, I'm sorry to say."

Max Aberdam's black eyes lit up. "The way you spoke on the radio recently made me think you've become a prude, a preacher, an American saint, or some other misfit. Everything Oswald Spengler predicted after the First World War has come to pass after the Second. Trotsky's permanent revolution is being staged in front of our eyes. Whether it is all social, or spiritual, or a result of God's madness I don't know. Let the professors decide that. I know only what my eyes see."

"What do they see?" I asked.

"The world is turning *meshugah*. It had to happen."

Max Aberdam sighed. "I am not allowed to eat much," he said. "My heart does not pump as well as it should. But when I'm served those Jewish dishes, I forget everything. In that sense I resemble our forefather Isaac. When Jacob served Isaac blintzes and knishes and kasha varnishkes, Isaac pretended to be blind and gave Jacob the blessing that was Esau's. All these women whose money I manage are a bit in love with me. I can't help it. They lost their husbands, their children, their brothers and sisters. Most of them are too old to marry again. A human being must love someone, otherwise he or she goes out like a candle. Well, so I am their victim. Don't look at me like that: I'm not, God forbid, a gigolo. I came from their towns, their neighborhoods. I knew their families. I speak their Yiddish. Why deny it? I love them also. I am the kind of man who falls in love with every woman between twelve and eighty-nine. This is how I was in my youth, and this is how I am today. How many troubles I've endured because of these infatuations, and how much sorrow I've caused, only He knows who sits in Seventh Heaven and torments us. I speak to them and tell them a joke. I assure each one of them that in my eyes she is still a girl. It is true, too. How long is it since they were all young? Only yesterday. Several of them I remember from earlier times, and with some I've slept. They don't want me to send their dividends through the mail. I have to deliver the check in person. They giggle and squirm as if I were their bridegroom. Come, there's someone you must meet."

"I have to return to my office."

"You'll go nowhere today, even if you stand on your head. Your newspaper will not fold up just because you're out for half a day. First of all, I want to introduce you to Priva. She is my misfortune, but she is a faithful reader of yours. She reads all your pieces under all your pen names. I have to buy the paper for her every morning or she'll conjure up the demons to turn me into a heap of bones. When I told her this morning that I would be looking for you, and perhaps bringing you home, she became terribly excited. A visit from Aaron Greidinger himself! For her you are only one rung below the Almighty. She told me more than once that you keep her alive. If it were not for you and your scribblings, she would long ago have committed suicide and I would have become a widower. So you must go with me. Besides, I have to deliver a check to one of my clients today. She is also a reader of yours. You know her, she used to come to the Writers' Club in Warsaw. She was what we called a 'literary supplement.' "

"What is her name?"

"Irka Shmelkes."

"Irka Shmelkes is alive!" I cried out.

"Yes, she is alive, if you can call it living."

"And what about Yudl Shmelkes?"

"Yudl Shmelkes is baking bagels in Paradise."

"Well, this has certainly been a day of surprises."

"She told me that she wrote you a letter which was never answered. You don't answer letters. Your name is not in the telephone book. Where actually do you hide yourself?"

Outside it was May, and it was already too hot. But I imagined that together with the odor of gasoline and heated asphalt, I could smell the fragrance of spring wafting in from the East River, or perhaps even from the Catskill Mountains. On Second Avenue every step was bound up with memories of not long ago for me. Nearby was the Café Royal, where Yiddish actors and writers had been steady guests. Across the street was the Yiddish Art Theater, in which Maurice Schwartz had played for years. What the Nazis had done to Jewishness in Warsaw, assimilation was accomplishing piecemeal in New York—but neither religious nor worldly Jewishness was ready to become extinct. New York still had four Yiddish newspapers and several weekly and monthly journals. Maurice Schwartz, Jacob Ben-Ami, Lebedev, Bertha Gerstin, and other Yiddish actors and actresses appeared in Yiddish plays. Yiddish books were published. Refugees still kept arriving from Soviet Russia, from Poland, Romania, Hungary. From where did they not come? Palestine was now a Jewish state, had already fought and won a war. I had gone through personal and literary crises. Since I arrived here in the thirties, I had lost my close relatives and friends both in Poland and in the United States. I had driven myself into isolation and despair. But new springs of energy seemed to have opened up in me.

Max Aberdam called a taxi. He shoved me inside and I fell across the seat. When Max himself plunged in, his lit cigar fell from his mouth. The driver snapped, "Mister, I don't want a fire in my taxi!"

"No fire on earth can burn us," Max answered with the air of a prophet. He gave the driver an address on West End Avenue in the eighties and breathed heavily as he tried to light a new cigar. He said to me, "Your name was mentioned even in Shanghai. I planned to reprint your little book—what is it called? No talent is ever completely forgotten. My memory plays hide-and-seek with me. Sometimes I think that I am becoming senile."

"Me too."

"At your age? Compared to me you are still an embryo."

"I am already over forty."

"Forty is not sixty-seven."

We got out of the taxi in front of a large building and took the elevator to the twelfth floor. Max rang the doorbell, but no one answered. He took out his key and unlocked the door. We entered a wide hallway whose floor was covered with a fine Persian carpet. The ceiling was high and carved and the walls were hung with paintings. Coming toward us was a woman with gray hair and a youthful face. She wore a flowered robe and slippers with pompons. Diamonds sparkled in the lobes of her ears. Her narrow face, her long neck, her slender figure all radiated wealth and a kind of old Jewish nobility. She reminded me of portraits one saw in museums. When she saw me, she made a motion as if to retreat, but Max shouted, "Here is your great hero!"

"Oh yes, I see!"

"This is Priva, my wife."

Priva came closer and stretched out a narrow hand with long fingers and manicured nails. She murmured, "It is an honor and a pleasure."

IT WAS HARD to believe that both husband and wife were refugees of Hitler's Europe. An air of permanence pervaded the spacious eight-room apartment. It turned out that it was loaned to the Aberdams complete with its contents by a rich woman who had been a distant relative of Priva's. When she died, her daughter had sold them everything for a pittance—the tables, the chairs, the carpets, the lamps, even the paintings on the walls and the books on the bookshelves. Priva herself had descended from a family of rabbis and wealthy merchants. Her first husband, a doctor, had published articles on medicine in the Warsaw Hebrew paper *Hatzephirah* and later in *Hayom*. During the war Priva had lost her husband, her son, who was a doctor, and her daughter, who was a student on the faculty of medicine in Warsaw. Priva had been one of those rich women who traveled abroad to various spas during the hot summer months. She spoke Yiddish, Russian, Polish, German, French. As a girl she had studied German literature with the famous Teresa Rosenbaum. She also knew a little Hebrew. Priva had brought a bit of wealthy Jewish Warsaw to New York. She told me that as a child she knew Isaac Peretz, Hirsch Nomberg, Hillel Zeitlin. As incredible as it may seem, despite her flight across Russia when she escaped from the Nazis, she managed to hold on to her album of old photographs. Every word she uttered brought back memories to me. By my calculations she must have been older than Max—perhaps over seventy. She said, "I lost everything in that terrible war. But as long as the brain functions, memory remains. What is memory? Like all the rest—a riddle. Once I had hoped to find peace in my old age, but I am surrounded with so much mystery that there can be no talk of peace. I go to sleep struck with awe, and I awaken with awe. My dreams are the greatest of all riddles."

"I am afraid that dreams will stay that way forever," I said.

"I read what you write, every word, under all your pseudonyms. You yourself are also a bit of a mystery."

"No more than the others."

"Much more."

"What did I tell you?" Max Aberdam shouted. "You, Aaron, are part of our lives. No day goes by that we don't speak of you." Max turned to Priva. "Where is Tzlova?"

"She went to the supermarket."

"We are lucky to have her as a maid," Max explained. "To find a maid here, and a Jewish one at that, is a miracle. But so many miracles have happened in our lives that we are no longer surprised. In Warsaw Tzlova was a businesswoman, not a maid. She had a shop for women's things—lingerie, handbags, lace, what have you. Here she does whatever she wants, she is virtually the lady of the house. She is our daughter, sister, nurse. She reads the articles on medicine in your paper, and every word the doctor writes is sacred to her."

"She and you, Mr. Aaron Greidinger, keep me alive," Priva broke in. "Tzlova is a primitive person, but with instincts. Men pursue her and she could get married if she wanted to, but she wants to stay with us. The shop Max mentioned was not hers, it belonged to a prosperous old couple who perished in the war. Tzlova is one of those people who are born to serve others. Such is their fate."

"Their fate is our good fortune. What would we do without her?" Max said. "On top of that, she is on friendly terms with the dead. They all come to her from the world beyond when she plays table levitation and hide-and-seek with the dead."

"So you laugh? She is a born medium," Priva said.

"Yes, yes, yes. The dead live, eat, make love, conduct business," Max joked. "All one has to do is to lay one's hands on a table and the dead flock to you from all corners of the world."

"Don't be so cynical, Max. Our Aaron Greidinger also believes in these matters. You have published scores of letters in your newspaper about them. I'll make tea. You must promise me to stay for dinner."

"Really, I cannot."

"Why not? We'll cook the old Warsaw dishes for you."

"Unfortunately I already have an engagement."

"Well, I won't insist. But you must come to us soon. Tzlova reads all your articles. When she wants to, she can cook up a meal fit for an emperor, and the Talmud says that the true emperors are those who are the learned—writers, men of spirit."

"I see that you are well acquainted with our old lore," I complimented her.

"Ah, I wanted to study since I was a child, but my father, may he rest in peace, held that girls must not be taught the holy books. Mickiewicz, yes; Slowacki, yes; Lessing, certainly. But for a girl to look into the Gemara—that is a transgression. However, I myself discovered the Haggadah and I found there much wisdom, even more than in Lessing or Nathan the Wise," Priva said.

I heard the door open in the corridor; it was Tzlova. I also heard the rustle of the paper bags she had brought back from the supermarket. Priva went out to meet her. Max Aberdam glanced at his wristwatch. "Well, this is how it is. I wanted a wife and I got an institution."

"She is a fine woman."

"Too fine. And not healthy. You can divorce a wife, but with an institution you are stuck. She swears that in Russia she stood in a winter forest at twenty degrees below zero and sawed wood. Here she has become a *grande dame*. She constantly visits the doctors, contributes to all sorts of imaginary causes, observes endless anniversaries of relatives and friends. She suffers from angina pectoris and has to be rushed to the hospital every so often. In San Francisco, where I met her, my mood was such that all I wanted was some rest. I would have been willing to enter an old-age home and lie there until I expired. But all of a sudden wild forces awoke in me. I walked into a trap from which there is no exit."

The door opened and Priva came in, holding Tzlova by the arm, as if leading a shy bride to her intended. I had imagined her to be an elderly woman, but she seemed to be young, her complexion dark, her black hair cut short; she had high cheekbones, a short nose, a pointed chin. Her eyes were slanted, like those of a Tatar. She wore a black dress and a string of red beads. Priva said, "This is our Tzlova. We have known her since our days in Warsaw. If it were not for her, I would have been among the dead long ago. Tzlova darling, this is Aaron Greidinger, the writer."

Tzlova's slanted eyes lit up in a smile. "I know you. I hear you on the radio every Sunday. I read everything you write. Mrs. Aberdam gave me a book of yours."

"I am very happy to make your acquaintance," I said.

"You wrote recently that you long to have some Warsaw browned-flour soup. I can make it for you better than you had it in Warsaw," Tzlova said.

"Ah, many thanks. Today, unfortunately, I am engaged. But I hope there will be another opportunity."

"In our house we used to eat browned-flour soup twice a week, on Mondays and Thursdays."

"Tzlova is the best cook in existence," Priva said approvingly. "Whatever she cooks tastes as if it were made in Paradise."

"There's nothing to it," Tzlova said. "All you need is browned flour and fried onions, and I add a carrot, parsley, and dill. Browned-flour soup is good served with *klops* [meat loaf]."

"Stop talking, Tzlova. Listening to you makes my mouth water," Max shouted. "The doctor told me to lose twenty pounds. How can I think of losing when you bring up all these delicacies?"

"What did people eat in China?" Tzlova asked.

"Ah, who knows what they ate—fried cockroaches with duck milk. I spoke to a Galician recently, and when the talk turned to food, he told me that in his *shtetl* they used to eat *kilishe* and *pompeches*."

"What sort of plague is this?" Priva asked.

"I have no idea whatever," Max answered. "Perhaps you, Aaron, know what kind of food this is?"

"I really don't know."

"A whole world vanished forever, a rich culture," Max said. "Who will know a generation from now how the Jews of Eastern Europe lived, how they spoke, what they ate? Come, we have to go."

"When will you be back?" Priva asked.

"I don't know," Max said. "I have a hundred things to do. People are waiting for my checks, I mean their checks."

"Don't come back in the middle of the night. You wake me up and then I can't shut my eyes for the rest of the night. You fall asleep immediately, but I lie and brood until daybreak."

"Maybe you'll think up a new invention. You might become a female Edison."

"Don't joke, Max. My thoughts at night are poison."

TWO

WHEN THE ELEVATOR took us down, and as we walked along West End Avenue, Max took my arm. "Aaron, I am in desperate straits about Miriam."

"Miriam—who is *she?*" I asked. "And why are you desperate, Max?"

"Oh, to me Miriam is still a child—young, pretty, intelligent. But unfortunately she married an American poet who is also young and now she is hoping to get a divorce. If I were not married, she would have been a blessing sent from heaven. But I can't divorce Priva. Miriam thinks she is all alone in the world. Her parents are divorced. Her father lives with some bore who considers herself an artist, one of those who dab a few smudges and smears and think they are the Leonardo da Vinci of our time. The mother, on the other hand, left for Israel with a would-be actor. Her husband, I mean Miriam's husband, fancies himself a poet. Our enlightened ones always nagged us Jews for being *luftmenschen*, people without a trade, or profession. But *luftmenschen* such as this new generation in America has produced can be found nowhere else. I tried to read her husband's poetry, but it has no coherence or music.

"These shlemiels are everything at once—Futurists, Dadaists, and Communists to boot. They don't lift a finger to work, but they try to save the proletariat. They also try hard to be original, but they repeat one another like parrots. Miriam is a dear young woman, but really still a child. Because of him, that husband of hers—what's his name? Stanley—and the breakup of her family, she left college. Now this Stanley has run off with some woman editor to California, or the devil knows where, and Miriam became a babysitter. What kind of an occupation is this for a girl of twenty-seven, to mind someone else's children? Men chase after her, but I love her and she loves me. What she sees in me, I'll never know. I could easily be her father, or even her grandfather."

"Yes, yes."

"Stop braying 'yes yes' like a donkey. I have confided this to no one but you. Since you've become a dispenser of advice, maybe you can tell me how to manage this affair."

"I can't even manage my own affairs."

"I knew you'd say that. Miriam was not born in America. She came here after the war, in 1947. She speaks an excellent Yiddish. She knows Polish and German and speaks English without an accent. What she has lived through she will tell you herself. Her father is a man without character, a bit of a charlatan. He had his office on Pzechodnia Street in Warsaw; he was a member of the stock exchange. Or so he says. He had enough sense to put away money before the war in a bank in Switzerland. Her mother convinced herself that she has a talent for acting. An uncle was killed in the Warsaw uprising of 1945. Every Jewish family in Poland has its own saga to tell. But we ourselves are mad, and we are driving the world to madness. Taxi!"

"Where are you taking me now?" I asked when we were seated inside the taxi.

"To Irka Shmelkes. I have a check for her which I've been carrying for a week now. Checks crumble in my pocket and sometimes the bank refuses to accept them. We will spend no more than ten minutes with Irka. She will insist that we stay for supper but I'll refuse with a firm no. Then we will go on to Miriam. Both women are your ardent readers. Miriam even wrote a paper about you in college."

"If I had known that we'd be going to their places, I would have worn another shirt and suit."

"Your shirt is fine, so is your suit. In comparison with what you used to wear in Warsaw, you have become a dandy. Only your tie needs adjustment. Here, like that!"

"I have not shaved."

"Don't worry, Miriam is accustomed to beards. Her no-good husband, Stanley, grew a beard recently. You knew Irka Shmelkes in Warsaw, there is no need to dress up for her."

The taxi stopped at the corner of Broadway and 107th Street, and we entered an apartment house that had no elevator. We climbed up two flights of stairs. Then Max Aberdam stopped to rest. He tapped with his finger on the left side of his chest. "My pump is acting up. Wait a few minutes."

When we continued to climb the stairs, Max complained and panted, "Why did she have to settle herself all the way up on the fourth floor? These people are careful with their money, but they are also stingy—frightened that today or tomorrow famine will spread over America."

At the fourth floor Max knocked on the door and it was immediately opened by Irka Shmelkes, a short woman with a round face, a short nose, black eyes. Her mouth was too wide for her small face. She must have been in her late fifties, since she had survived the camps, but she looked younger. Her coal-black hair appeared to have been recently dyed. She wore a décolleté sleeveless black dress. She seemed to have dressed up for the occasion. She gave me a look of surprise and said, "Ah, you brought a guest. That I did not expect." She smiled and revealed a row of false teeth. In her left cheek a hint of a dimple showed.

We walked through a long corridor. From the kitchen came the smell of roasted meat, garlic, fried onions, potatoes. She led us to a room furnished with a *tapczan*, as it was called in Warsaw—it served as a sofa during the day and a bed at night. It became clear to me that the apartment was not hers, and that the room in which we stood served her as living, dining, and bedroom. A young woman knocked on the door and said, "Mrs. Shmelkes, you are wanted on the hall telephone."

"Me? Just a minute." And Irka Shmelkes disappeared.

"Still not a bad-looking woman," Max remarked. "Her husband, the imbecile, had a yen to be a Trotskyite, and so they liquidated him in Spain. They all wanted to make a better world and died as martyrs. For whom were they sacrificing themselves? Who will reward them in the grave?"

"Perhaps the Almighty is also a Trotskyite," I said.

"Huh? What went on in Spain we will never know. Stalin had set up a full-fledged inquisition there. They came to fight against Fascism and were executed by their own comrades. Our Jews are always first in the line of fire. They simply have to redeem the world, no more and no less. In every Jew resides the dybbuk of a messiah."

When Irka Shmelkes returned to the room I noticed that the heels of her shoes were extraordinarily high. She said, "Days and nights go by and no one thinks to call. But just when two such important guests as you come, I am called to the phone. And for whom? For some old gossip who wanted to chatter!"

"Where is your son, Edek?" Max asked.

"Where? In the library. The boy makes me ill. He keeps dragging home books from every corner of the world. He goes to Fourth Avenue, where you can get them for a nickel or three for a dime, and he returns with stacks of old books. He has to know everything. The other day I found him reading a yellowed book about trains in Ohio or Iowa, full of figures and mileages. Why does my Edek have to know about the Ohio trains of so many years ago? He is sick, sick. Thank God that hunchbacked woman moved away and I could give her room to Edek. It is already filled with books."

"I have a check for you," Max said.

"That will certainly be of use. But you, my dear, and the guest you brought along are for me better than a check. What happened to you, Aaron Greidinger? Since you've become a newspaper writer you no longer want to know us little people. That young woman who called me to the phone is a reader of yours. If she knew you were here in my room, she would have turned the world upside down. Wait, I'll bring some refreshments. I've prepared more than I usually do, as if my heart had told me you two were coming. I'll be right back!" And Irka Shmelkes disappeared again.

"We'll have to taste something, whether we like it or not," Max said. "People who have known hunger consider food the greatest blessing. They make me ill with refreshments, and I keep vowing to send them their checks through the mail. What I need now is another cigar. Where is my lighter? *Nu*, I left it at Rappaport's!"

WE DRANK TEA and ate babka. Young Edek returned from the library. Short and plump, he already had a potbelly. I noticed that the top button of his trousers could not be buttoned. His round head had a shock of thick dark hair. His large eyes were crossed, and it struck me that his cheeks were as smooth as a eunuch's. He sat in a rocking chair, rocking while he spoke. He said to me, "I read all your articles and stories. I don't read your serialized novels, though. I have no patience to wait from one week to the next. Why don't you publish a book? American writers your age are already world famous. My doctor has a son who's twenty-seven years old and he sold his book to a movie company for eighty thousand dollars. If I had eighty thousand dollars I'd take a trip around the world. I read a lot of geography, and I believe there are still a great many places that don't appear on any map.

"I belong to an organization which denies that the earth is round," he went on. "There are only about forty of us, but we have been discussing the question thoroughly. There is no proof whatever that the earth is round. It is only a theory. My opinion is that Atlantis did not sink in the sea, as Plutarch reported, but that we simply don't yet know where it is. There are documents in existence from travelers who came upon a region where the earth was hollow, and they found an ancient civilization. You may consider this to be folklore, but many truths are dismissed as folklore. The witch doctors in Africa used medicines for years which were only recently discovered here. And what about the places the Bible mentions, like Ophir? Where is Ashkenaz? Ashkenaz is not Germany. Germany was still a jungle in those days. Maybe Hodu is India, maybe not, but Kush is definitely not Ethiopia. The Anakim, which the Pentateuch mentions, are not simply a legend. Giants existed in the past and they still exist today, but they live in hiding somewhere—perhaps in the Himalayas or in the virgin forests of Brazil, or maybe somewhere deep in Africa. Their footprints have been found, unusually wide and long. You'll probably ask why they should wish to hide, and I will tell you why. Many races have been wiped out since mankind came into being. The white race is incapable of tolerating rivals. Hitlerism is as old as humanity. In the last several hundred years the Indians were almost decimated. If Hitler had won the war, he would have wiped out all the Negroes. He also considered us Jews a race, and that is why he tried to wipe out every last one of us. The giants know all that, and therefore they shun other races. The spies mentioned in the Bible came back and reported that, next to the giants, they felt like locusts. Our white racists and chauvinists don't want to feel like locusts. But why the giants don't reproduce and finish us off—that is another question. It may be that nature takes a long time to produce each giant. Maybe their women carry a fetus for years instead of nine months—maybe even a hundred years. A region of Russia was just discovered whose inhabitants live for one hundred, two hundred years, maybe even more. They keep no records and their children have no birth certificates."

"Edek, drink your tea. It's getting cold," Irka said.

"It is not getting cold. We fight against prejudices, and we are immersed in prejudices up to our necks," Edek said. "Two professors at the time of Louis XIV discovered meteors, but the King declared, 'It is easier to believe that the professors are lying than to believe that stones can come tumbling down from the sky.' Why am I saying this? Because of the river Sambatyon. *The Jewish Encyclopedia* says that the river Sambatyon and the ten lost tribes of Israel are legends. But I am not at all sure that this is so. People came from there who saw the river hurling rocks into the air, and they also brought back a letter from the King, Ahitov Ben Azariah. It is clearly stated in the Bible, I don't remember where: 'The descendants of Ephraim shall mingle among the nations.' "

"If the descendants of Ephraim mingle with the nations, how can they have their own kingdom?" I asked.

"One has nothing to do with the other. Someone has claimed that the English are really the ten lost tribes. That is why they love the Bible as they do. The other day I bought a book for a nickel on Fourth Avenue and it's the best book I ever read. It's called *Spiritual Marriages*. I forgot who the author is. Someone stole the book from me."

"Who steals such old books?" Max Aberdam asked.

"People steal everything. Freud stole his entire theory out of two pages in the Gemara *Berakhot*, Chapter *Ha-Rokh*. Spinoza stole out of *Shir Ha-Ikhud*, which is recited on the night of Yom Kippur. I have a theory that spirits exist whose task it is to steal. At night I put a book down on my table, and in the morning it is gone. I have reached the point where if I find a really good book, I lock it up in a subway locker. But it is taken even from there. I also have a theory that Hitler was not a human being but an evil spirit. Where did his body vanish to? No one knows. After the war he flew away to the place where the demons dwell. I even wrote a letter about it to your newspaper, but they didn't print it."

"Enough, my child!" Irka said.

"Mama, one day you'll learn the truth, but it will be too late. How did it happen that six million Jews went like sheep to the slaughter? How did it happen that the very same nations who during the Holocaust did not raise even a hint of a protest are the nations that later voted to establish a Jewish state? I asked this of my teacher, but he had no answer for me. Mama, may I tell Mr. Greidinger about my wristwatch?"

"No, Edek."

"Mr. Greidinger writes about demons. He may find the story useful."

"Edek, it is not important."

"What sort of wristwatch was it?" I asked.

"Edek had a watch his friend had given him," Irka replied. "On the day the friend died—he suffered from tuberculosis— the watch fell from Edek's wrist and broke. I have lost more than one watch in my lifetime, and I don't blame the spirits for it."

"Mama, the watch had a metal bracelet and it was tight around my wrist. It sprang off and fell while the bracelet was still intact.

And you forgot to say that this happened at the same moment that Ilish breathed his last breath. The very same moment. It's a fact."

"It is also a fact that I must go to the kitchen and prepare some food for my dear guests."

"Mrs. Shmelkes, please, I must leave," I said.

"Me too," Max said.

"What—you both wish to run?" Irka asked. "Well, I cannot reproach the guest with whom you've honored me. I know him both from the Writers' Club in Warsaw and from his writings here, although he does not know me. And so . . ."

"But I do know you. We were once introduced in Warsaw," I said.

"I had no idea you remembered so well. Yes, we *were* introduced. You were then a very young man, a beginner. I once wrote you a letter here in America, but I did not expect a reply. Our Yiddish men of letters do not respond to their mail. Some of them, perhaps, cannot afford the postage. But you, Max, you cannot shame me by leaving!"

"Mama, I'm going back to my room," Edek said.

"Yes, my child. I'll call you later, when the food is ready."

"Mama, don't let them leave!" Edek said, already near his door.

"What can I do? I have no Cossacks at my disposal, as my father—may he rest in peace—used to say. All I can do is plead with them."

"Don't go, Max. Mama speaks about you so often. She stands by the window and looks out, as they used to do in Poland, in the small *shtetls*. Then she says, 'I wonder where Max is. Could he be lost somewhere?' In Yablona, if you stood at the window for half an hour, the whole *shtetl* would pass by. But here in New York, to spot someone through a window is—how shall I say it?—an anachronism. The odds that someone you know should walk past, even someone who lives in the neighborhood, are one to a million, perhaps even a billion. I am not a mathematician, but I am interested in statistics and in the whole realm of probabilities. What were the odds that a world should come into existence? Goodbye."

Edek closed the door. Irka Shmelkes shook her head. "The boy is ill, ill. What he's been through, what I've been through with him, no one will ever know. Not even God, if He exists."

"Irka, I have to go!" Max exclaimed.

"Don't shout. I am not deaf. When will I see you again? If you'll wait until the next check it may be too late."

"What's the matter? Are you sick, God forbid?"

"I am sick and tired of everything."

"I'll be here tomorrow. For dinner."

"Do you mean it, or are you poking fun at me?"

"I am not poking fun. You know I love you."

"What time will you be here?"

"Two o'clock."

"Well, I hope you are not making a fool of me. Mr. Greidinger, it has been both an honor and a surprise. When my boarder hears that you've been here, and that I have not kept you and introduced you to her, she will never forgive me."

"With God's help we'll see each other again," I said.

"Everyone has been calling on God recently. I am beginning to believe that the Messianic era has come." And Irka smiled at us. For a moment she looked young again, just as I remembered her from the Writers' Club in Warsaw.

THREE

THIS TIME MAX did not call a taxi. Miriam lived on 100th Street at Central Park West. Max went into a pharmacy on Broadway to telephone her while I waited outside. Refugees had settled in the neighborhood—from Poland, from Germany, from half the world. On West End Avenue there was the Paris Hotel, which the German refugees had dubbed "The Fourth Reich." Max lingered in the pharmacy for a long time, and I stood on the sidewalk and stared at the trucks streaming by. On the grassy divider in the midst of Broadway an old woman scattered the bread crumbs she carried in a brown paper bag. Pigeons flew down to her from the rooftops, flocking around her, nibbling at the crumbs. The stench of gasoline and dog excrement mingled with the fragrance of a new summer. Across the street, outside a flower shop, pots of fresh lilacs were set on the sidewalk. On benches astride the subway gratings sat people who, in the midst of New York's bustle and din, apparently had nothing to do. An old man peered into a Yiddish newspaper. A woman with a black hat over her white hair sat thumbing through the German *Aufbau*, trying to read with a magnifying lens. A Negro, his head leaning back against the bench, was sleeping. From time to time a roaring subway train passed below. From somewhere a truck appeared to sprinkle water on the dusty pavement.

I had lived in New York for years, but I could not grow accustomed to a city in which a man could live a lifetime and still be as much a stranger as on the day he landed on its shores. For no reason at all I began to read the inscriptions on the passing trucks—cement, oil, pipes, glass, milk, meat, linoleum, foam rubber, vacuum cleaners, roofing materials. And then came a hearse. It rolled slowly past, its windows draped, a wreath on the hood—a funeral, with no one to accompany it. Max came out of the pharmacy and signaled me to wait. He went into the flower shop and came out carrying a bouquet. We started out toward Central Park West. Max sighed. "Yes, this is New York—eternal bedlam. What can we do? America is our last refuge."

We continued to walk in silence along the three blocks which separated Broadway from Central Park West, until we came upon a large apartment house of sixteen or seventeen stories. It had a canopy in front and a uniformed doorman. The doorman was apparently well acquainted with Max. He greeted us and opened the door like a host, inviting us to enter. Max promptly put a tip in his hand. The doorman thanked him, noted how fine the weather had been, then quickly added that for tomorrow the radio predicted rain. The same information was imparted to us by the elevator man. Max snapped, "Who cares what tomorrow will bring! For the time being it is today. When you reach my age you must be grateful for every day you live."

"Right, sir. Life is short."

We left the elevator on the fourteenth floor, and there I saw what to me was a new phenomenon. In the long hallway, among the doors which led to the apartments, there were armchairs; on the wall there was a mirror, and paintings in gold-tinted frames, and there was also a table with a vase. Max said, "America, eh? In Warsaw all this would have been stolen the very first day. American thieves don't jump at such trash; what they want is cash. A blessing on Columbus."

Max rang the doorbell; a minute passed before the door opened. Using the fingers of his free left hand, Max meanwhile combed and smoothed down his beard. I also quickly adjusted the knot in my tie. When the door opened, before us stood Miriam. She was short, too broad for her height, with a high bosom and the face of a girl who seemed no older than sixteen. She had a youthful cheerfulness, wore not a trace of makeup, and her brown hair was somewhat disheveled. From her dark-blue eyes shone the joy of a child entertaining visiting adults. She threw me a glance which seemed to ask, "And who are you?" while at the same time assuring me that, whoever I was, I was a welcome guest. Miriam's fingers were stained with ink, as they used to be among schoolchildren in the Old Country, and her nails were clipped (perhaps bitten) exceedingly short. The dress she wore also had the cut of a Warsaw schoolgirl's dress: loose-fitting, its hem scalloped, lacking the slightest pretense to elegance. When she saw us she cried out in a Warsaw Yiddish, "Flowers again? Oh, I shall have to kill you!" Only then did I notice a wedding band on her forefinger.

"Go ahead, kill!" Max shouted back. "So many people are killed in New York, there will be one corpse more. Please take the bouquet. I am not your servant to carry your flowers for you. And open the door wider, you ninny!"

"Oh, you startled me so that I . . ."

Miriam snatched the bouquet from Max's hands and opened the door wide. We entered an apartment whose hallway was small, with space only for a table covered with notebooks and books. An open door revealed a bedroom with a large bed, still unmade, on which lay scattered dresses, pajamas, hangers, newspapers, magazines, stockings. Two raw apples rested on a pillow. The window opened onto Central Park and the room was flooded with sunlight. Through another door I saw a tiny kitchenette, a desk, a sofa. A pot sat on the floor, in front of the kitchenette. There were no rugs in the apartment and the parquet floors seemed new, freshly polished, as in a house into which one has just moved. I noticed that Miriam wore socks but no shoes. She was running back and forth, the bouquet of flowers in her hand, in search of a vase. But then she threw the flowers on her bed. She half-spoke and half-shouted, "I didn't sleep all night, that's why. We had a fire here last night. The old lady, the president of the orphans' club, forgot to turn off her stove, and suddenly there was smoke and the firemen came and we had to go down to the lobby in the middle of the night." She turned to me. "My name is Miriam."

She made a sort of half curtsy and stretched out her hand to me. But she had apparently forgotten that she was holding something in it—a pencil that fell to the floor. Good-naturedly she scolded Max, "You didn't even introduce me! You are more rattled than I am. But I know who he is. I am Miriam, that's enough." She spoke both to me and to herself. "I want you to know that I'm your greatest fan in the whole world. I read every word you write. In Warsaw I studied in a Yiddish school. We read every one of the Yiddish writers, every last one. They wanted me to speak a Lithuanian Yiddish, but I couldn't. I could read it, but to speak—no. Whenever I come home late at night and realize that I forgot to buy your Yiddish paper, I go back to Broadway and look for it. The other day I walked for almost an hour, but no one had the paper for sale. Then suddenly I saw one lying in a trash basket. Ah, I have to laugh!"

"What is there to laugh about?" Max roared. "When a person

finishes with the paper, he throws it away. New York is not Blendew or Ejszyszki, where people held on to their papers forever!"

"True, but imagine this: I was walking and searching—as if with candles—for the sequel to his novel, and here it was lying in a trash basket, as if it were waiting for me. I immediately began to read it in the street, under the lamppost. Generally I notice that you don't make an issue of words. You write the way people speak."

"That is what a writer should do. A writer should not be a puritan," I said, "in any sense whatever."

"Yes, right. I read recently that the errors of one generation become the accepted style and grammar of the next," Miriam said.

"How do you like that?" Max said. "Born only yesterday, and already she speaks like a perfect *mensch*."

"I'm twenty-seven and for him it is yesterday. Sometimes I feel as if I were a hundred years old," Miriam said. "If I told you what I've lived through, both during the war and here in America, you would understand. A whole world collapsed before my very eyes. But you, my favorite author, are bringing it to life again."

"Are you listening?" Max shouted. "This is the greatest compliment that a reader can pay to a writer."

"I thank you a thousand times," I said. "But no writer can resurrect what the wicked have destroyed."

"When I buy the paper and read your stories, I recognize every street, every courtyard. Sometimes I feel as though I even know the people."

"Love at first sight," Max muttered, as if to himself.

"Max, I never kept it from you," Miriam said. "I love you for what you are, and I love him for what he writes. What does one have to do with the other?"

"It does, it does," Max said. "But—I'm not jealous. I like him myself. He knows even less than one hundredth of what I know about Poland and Warsaw. How can he? He was born in some poor little *shtetl*, in some impoverished village. He is truly a provincial creature. He sits at his desk and he fabricates. But his fabrications are worth more than my facts. The Gemara tells us that after the Temple was destroyed, prophecy was taken from the prophets and given to madmen. Since writers are known to be mad, prophecy was given to them as well. How else would a young squirt like him know how my father used to speak, or my grandfather, or my aunt Genendele? You can be sure that he will write us all up, inventing things which never happened, making us idiots."

"Let him. He has no need to invent—I'll tell him everything," Miriam said.

"Everything?" Max bellowed.

"Yes, everything."

"Well then, I am done for already. What do they say in America—my goose is cooked. Let him say about me whatever he wants. After I'm dead you can both cut me up and feed me to the dogs. But as long as I'm alive and I bring a guest to meet my girl, I want her to receive him properly. Put on some shoes, and take away the pot you left sitting on the floor. Why did you leave it there—for the mice?"

"I was going to water the rubber plant."

"You were going to, eh? Come, I'll help you clean up. This is an apartment, not a pigsty, you wild creature."

"And what are you, Count Potocki?" Miriam asked. "You didn't even give me a kiss."

"You don't deserve a kiss. Come!"

Max spread out his arms and Miriam fell into them. "So!"

———

I COULD SCARCELY believe my eyes. In a matter of ten minutes
Max and Miriam cleaned up both rooms, put everything in place,
and soon the apartment was neat and clean. Miriam combed her
hair and put on high-heeled shoes, thereby becoming taller.
When she had kissed Max, she had to rise on her toes while he
bent his head down to her. As she stood locked in his arms, and
he in hers, she threw me a smiling, flirtatious glance. I imagined
that there was something mocking and promising in her eye.
God in heaven, this day has been uncommonly long and rich in
events, the writer in me was thinking. This is how literature
should be, packed with action, with no space left for clichés or
sentimental brooding. I had heard much praise of Joyce, Kafka,
and Proust, but I had decided I would not follow the path of
the so-called psychological school or the stream of consciousness.
Literature would have to return to the style of the Bible and
Homer: action, suspense, imagery—and only a modicum of mental play. But was such a decision workable? Wasn't my reality,
and the reality of others like me, too paradoxical?

I felt I was growing intoxicated on Max's cigars, on the coffee
Miriam served us, on our conversation. I questioned Miriam
about her life, and she answered willingly, briefly, with childlike
simplicity. Born?—In Warsaw. Studied?—In a Jewish school, a
private Gymnasium, in Havatzelet—a Hebrew-Polish high
school. Her father had belonged to the Folvist Party. He had
been a Yiddishist, not a Zionist. But he had nevertheless contributed a shekel every year to the Jewish National Fund. Her
father's father was a landlord; he had houses on Leszno, Grzybowska, and Slota Streets. Her mother's father was a Hasid of
the Rebbe of Gur, and the owner of a wine shop. How many
children had there been? Only two—an older brother, Manes,
who had died in the Warsaw uprising, and Miriam. Her girlfriends had called her Marylka, sometimes Marianna. At one
point, when the conversation turned to the Warsaw Writers'

Club, Miriam said, "I was there only once. My mother went to buy tickets for a lecture and she took me along. A teacher of mine was a member and he happened to be eating in the front room when we arrived. When he saw us, he dropped everything and showed us around as if it were a museum. I was nine at the time and was already reading Yiddish books. Not only school-books, but books meant for adults. My mother scolded me. She said, 'If you keep reading these books you'll grow old before your time. You may also forget Polish.' I promised not to read them, but as soon as she left my room I returned to them. Whom did I not read? Sholem Aleichem, Abraham Reisen, Sholem Asch, Hirsch Nomberg, your brother, Segalovich. We used to subscribe to *Literarishe Bleter*, and when I grew older I read that as well. The daily papers we read and discarded, but the literary journals—those my father always kept. A novel you translated was included as a bonus to the *Literarishe Bleter* and we kept all the issues in our home. My teacher—Shidlovsky was his name —introduced me to everyone at the Writers' Club. I was so naive as to believe that all of them had died long ago. But that day I met many of my favorites alive and not old. They were sitting and eating noodles with chicken soup. I became acquainted with your work only later here in America. As soon as I read the first chapter I said . . ."

"Don't praise him so much!" Max interrupted. "He'll feast himself on these compliments until he swells and bursts. A writer is like a horse: you feed it a sack of oats and it eats a sack of oats; if you give it two, it'll gorge itself on two. On my father's farm more than once a horse would stuff itself on wet grass and soon it was dead."

"Oh, the things you say!" Miriam said reproachfully.

"It's the truth! Aaron may think that I begrudge him his praise, but I wish him success a thousand times over. Over the years there were many things that I wanted to be, but never a writer—scribbling never attracted me."

"What is it that you wanted to be?" I asked.

"Look here, if you keep addressing me by this formal 'you,' I'll grab you by the scruff of your neck and roll you down the stairs. Such politeness! Say 'thou' plain and clear, or go to the devil! If our little schoolgirl here can be informal with me, you certainly should. I tell you quite openly, you and she are as close to me as if you were my brother and she . . . Well, I'd better not speak nonsense. I seem to remember that you asked me a question, but I don't remember what it was."

"I asked you what it was that you wanted to be?"

"What did I not want to be? Rockefeller, Casanova, Einstein, even simply a pasha with a harem filled with beauties. But to sit with a pen and scratch on paper—that is not my cup of tea. To read—yes. A good book is as important to me as a good cigar."

"I had no idea you dreamed of having a harem," Miriam said.

"I used to dream of it thirty years ago, before you, Miriam, wriggled out of your mother's womb. But now that I have you, I no longer want anyone else. That's the bitter truth."

"Why is it bitter?" Miriam asked.

"Because it means that I've grown thirty years older, not younger."

"Poor Max. We all grow younger every day, while he alone grows old. Do you want to grow steadily younger, until finally you are an infant once more?" Miriam asked.

"No, but I wish I had stopped at thirty."

"Ah, idle dreamer," Miriam said in Polish.

It was growing dark. Shadows filled the room but no one rose to turn on the light. From time to time Max drew on his cigar and the reddish glow illuminated his face. A light shone in his eyes, and suddenly I heard him say, "When I am with the two of you, I am young again."

———

I HAD HEARD these stories countless times before, but coming from Miriam they seemed somehow different. The facts were more or less the same—in Warsaw trenches had been dug, even barricades erected. Just the same, the outbreak of the war in September 1939 came as a surprise to many. Many houses had already been struck by German bombs. Hunger by then was also widespread. Miriam was a girl of thirteen, and her mother and she had been left at home alone. Miriam's father had gone with thousands of other men in the direction of Bialystok.

So familiar were these tales to me that occasionally I corrected Miriam when she erred on a date or the number of a house. I knew it all by heart—the hunger, the disease, the dragging of Jews to forced-labor camps, the fires, the shootings, the brutality of the Germans, the indifference of the Poles. Amid a ghetto lying in ruins actors tried to stage Yiddish plays. In a cellar someone had fashioned a sort of cabaret in which well-to-do women whiled away their time, while outside people were killed. Later, when Miriam's apartment was seized, her mother was taken to a concentration camp, while Miriam was smuggled out of the ghetto to the Aryan side. A former teacher of hers hid her in a dark alcove, where old furniture was stored with rags and bundles of newspapers.

The concierge's son, a vain and bragging youth, a *shmalovnik*, had learned of her hiding place. She was forced to pay him bribe money obtained from selling her mother's jewels, which her teacher had managed to sell. He had also forced her to submit to him, and when he came to her he held a knife to her throat. The teacher, an old maid, had suffered a nervous breakdown from grief and fright. I heard Miriam say, "Why I did not commit suicide I don't know. Actually I do know. I simply could not burden my teacher with a dead body. How long could she have hidden a corpse? The Nazis would have shot her and all her neighbors as well."

"Yes, yes. This is how the human race behaves," I said. "This has been its conduct throughout the ages."

"But my teacher belonged to the human race," Miriam said.

"Yes, true."

"The other day I read a piece of yours about a religion of protest. What did you mean by it?" Miriam asked. "Don't laugh, but someone had torn out a part of the page and I was unable to finish it."

I hesitated for a moment and Max broke in: "He probably forgot what he meant. He has a dozen pseudonyms and he has to deliver copy constantly. He writes whatever comes into his head."

"Oh, hush, Maxele. Let him answer."

"No, I certainly did not forget. What I meant was that one may believe in God's wisdom and yet deny that He is the source of goodness only. God and mercy are not absolutely synonymous."

"Why bother with God altogether? Why not simply ignore Him?" Miriam asked.

"We cannot ignore God any more than we can ignore time or space or causality," I said, more to Max than to Miriam.

"How is protest going to help us?" Max asked.

"We will no longer be flatterers and masochists; we will no longer kiss the rod that whips us."

"I don't know how it is with you, but I am quite willing to do without God, His wisdom, His mercies, the whole religious paraphernalia that goes with Him," Max said.

"On what would you base ethics?" I asked.

"There is no base and no ethics."

"In other words, might is right?"

"So it seems."

"If might is right, then Hitler was right," I said.

"Inasmuch as he was defeated, he was not right. If he had won, all the nations of the world would have joined hands with him, the entire world."

"Really, Max, you are wrong," Miriam said. "We Jews must never entertain the notion that there is no morality in the universe and that man may do whatever he likes."

"And what does Jewishness consist of?" Max asked. "When we Jews had might, four thousand years ago, we fell upon the Canaanites, the Girgashim, the prizim, and we wiped them out, every man, woman, and child. Only a few short years ago our boys were forced to fight the very same war. What, Aaron Greidinger, is your definition of God?"

"The Plan behind evolution, the Power which moves the solar bodies, the galaxies, the planets, comets, nebulas, and all the rest."

"That power is blind and has no plan," Max said.

"How do we know this?" I asked.

"If you ask me, there is nothing but chaos. Even if there is a plan, it concerns me as little as last year's frost."

"Yet you're always speaking of God, Max," Miriam said. "You even fasted on Yom Kippur."

"Not from piety. I did it in remembrance of my parents and my heritage. One can be a Jew without believing in God. What sort of religion is this religion of protest? If God does not exist, there is no one to protest against. And if He does exist, He may very well afflict us with another Hitler. Those who are moved to kiss the rod do it from fear. God Himself has put it concisely and clearly—you must love me with all your heart, all your soul, all your might. If you do not, all the calamities of the Book of Curses will be visited upon your head."

"No one can be forced to love," Miriam said.

"Apparently one can. Not all at once but gradually . . ." Max said.

MAX TURNED ON the light and proposed that we dine in a nearby restaurant, but Miriam insisted that she would prepare supper. Max went into the bedroom to telephone, speaking in a loud voice, and I heard him mention stocks. Miriam opened the door to the kitchenette and busied herself at the refrigerator.

She said to me, "I still can scarcely believe that you are here in my apartment. Being together with you and Max makes me feel as if I were still in Warsaw, and what came later was a nightmare. If God were to grant me one wish before I die, I would ask that you and Max move in with me, so that we three could be together."

She said it so simply, and with such a childish innocence, that several moments passed before I could answer. I blurted out, "You are too young to be speaking of death."

"Too young? I have stared death in the face for years. I began to think of it long before the war. Somehow I knew that my brother would die a violent death. He always tried to enlist in the Polish Army. My father used to say that if the Nazis captured Poland, my brother would give us all poison to drink. Ah, there was no reason for us to have stayed in Warsaw. My father could have gotten visas for us, but he was too immersed in business affairs. Before he crossed the Praga Bridge that day, he took along a satchel filled with bank notes and stocks. It all went down the drain, but when he returned from Russia in 1945 and we left for Germany, he began to rake in the money again. He became a smuggler. To this day I do not know what he smuggled. My mother told me that once when the German police arrived to search our house—they poked in every hole—he had more than seventy thousand marks hidden. We are a peculiar family. My father is a maniac. My mother is muddleheaded, and my brother, Manes, was not quite right in his head. I am the maddest one of the lot. It is our luck that we are each peculiar in some way. I love Max because he is perfectly insane. And I love you because you write about madmen. Did you actually meet the people you describe, or did you make them up?"

"For me the whole world is an insane asylum."

"For these words I must kiss you!"

She ran up to me and we kissed. I was afraid that Max might walk in and see us, but instead I heard him shouting, "Texaco? How much? Wait, Hershele, I will write it down."

"Who is Hershele?" I asked, moved not by curiosity but by a wish to smooth over what had just transpired.

"His name is Harry Treibitcher, not Hershele; he is American-born. Max insists on calling him Hershele. He is a speculator, an adventurer, he plays the horses. Max has given him power of attorney—and that is sheer madness, because Max handles other people's money, the money of Hitler's victims. Harry is a brilliant money-maker, but should the stock market crash again, it will be catastrophic for the hundreds of refugees Max represents. How do you say *power of attorney* in Yiddish?" Miriam asked me.

"Really, I don't know. In the Holy Tongue you could say *power of permission* but it is not the same thing. In Israel today they have lawyers and courts, and I'm sure they have found suitable names in Hebrew. *Power of permission* was used in my father's court, his *Bet Din*, when, before Passover, he would draw up a bill of sale turning over to the janitor all the leavened dough on our street. But you probably understand nothing of what I am saying."

"I understand perfectly. I am studying Hebrew," Miriam said. "My grandfather used to sell our leavened dough before Passover. There were rabbis in my family, Hasidim. My father considered himself a heretic, but our kitchen was kosher. My mother would light the Sabbath candles, and then she would sit across from them and smoke cigarettes. I think it was her way of showing spite, or maybe this was her version of what you call protest. I read everything I can find about Jews and Jewishness. I am especially fond of Yiddish. It is the only language in which I can express exactly what I want to say.

"I read Lermontov's *A Hero of Our Times* and found it absolutely entrancing. When I met Max in America I thought he was a Jewish Pechorin: Perhaps you are, too—no, you are a blend of Pechorin and Oblomov, and maybe Raskolnikov, too. You always keep yourself hidden. In my unfinished dissertation I call you 'the Hider.' I wrote in English, naturally. Ah, I've given my life a goal—to make you famous. Don't laugh, someone has to do it. I have still one other ambition—actually two."

"What are they?"

"To tell you all that I have lived through—everything, leaving out nothing, not even the most foolish things."

"What is the second ambition?"

"That one I'd better not mention today."

"When?"

"Sometime in the future. Do you remember a story you once wrote about a man who had several wives, a polygamist? Was this fiction or was it based on someone you knew?"

"It was a true story," I said.

"Max said it was your own invention."

"No, it really happened."

"Why should a woman want to stay with a maniac like that?"

"Women are even crazier than men," I said.

"You left Poland in the thirties, but I went through all the seven hells, as my grandmother used to say. If I could tell you what I experienced, you would not need to invent things."

"Please tell them to me."

"I could not tell you even a thousandth part of it. I didn't even tell Max. I love him more than my own life, but he likes to talk, not to hear someone else talk. What goes on between us could fill a book of a thousand pages. He has a wife and she is completely manic—mad as a hatter, as they say in English. Why is a hatter mad? Languages themselves contain elements of madness. I quote your own words."

"What? I never said such a thing."

"You wrote it in an article about Esperanto, and you said that an international language would miss all the idiosyncrasies of ordinary languages created by a natural process."

"Really, you have a wonderful memory."

"You even mentioned that you once lived on Dzika Street, a part of which was later called Dr. Zamenhof Street, after the man who created Esperanto. Do you remember now?"

"Yes, yes, you have a remarkable memory."

"I wish I didn't. It depresses me, especially when I am alone. Max comes to see me often, but he is always terribly busy. He has a wife, Priva, who owns him, and a flock of other women. When I read your story about this polygamist I thought you were describing Max. He assures every one of them that she alone is his true love. He speculates with their money and he is bound to lose all of it. He feels compassion for them, but he will be their Angel of Death," Miriam said. "There is even a name for it in English, mercy killing."

Max returned to the room. "The market is going up. We are reaping shovelfuls of gold in the land of Columbus. And what are you two doing? She probably told you every possible evil about me. Don't believe a word of it. She takes after you, a born storyteller. I've just learned that I must travel to Poland. My father left me a house in Lodz and the Poles are finally letting me sell it—for one-tenth of its true value, naturally."

"Did you speak to Harry?" Miriam asked.

"Yes, all the papers are ready. He's been trying to reach me all day, but I was busy with our young writer here."

"When are you leaving?"

"Soon. If the whole affair is a trap and the Communists are bent on liquidating me, you two will know what to do."

"You must be drunk," Miriam said.

"I was born drunk. *Pif-paf!* A world full of wonders! And what became of our supper?"

FOUR

I T WAS PAST midnight when I took my leave of Max and Miriam. Miriam kissed me on both cheeks, and on my lips as well. I gave her my address and the number of the house telephone in the rooming house where I lived. In Max's presence she promised to call me the next day. She used an expression often used in the Warsaw underworld: "I've got you on my list!" When Max announced his intention to stay a while longer, it was clear to me that he meant to spend the night. I rode the elevator down to the lobby and stepped outside. Not a soul could be seen on Central Park West and traffic lights blinked in the darkness. I had promised Miriam to take a taxi, but the many hours of sitting had stiffened my body and I longed for a walk.

I strolled slowly along the park, and although the streetlamps were shining, I walked in a darkness that no amount of light could dispel. I had developed a knack for injecting suspense not only into my writing but into my life—entanglements without exit. I seemed to attract a variety of lost souls—melancholics, would-be suicides, people obsessed with manias, missions, prophetic dreams. Those who sought my counsel at the editorial office often returned with further questions and to complain that my advice had not helped them. Readers kept sending me lengthy or complex letters which I only glanced at. I even received correspondence from inmates of insane asylums. One such writer insisted that the whole of modern medicine was alluded to in the Pentateuch, and another had discovered a machine that worked forever—perpetual motion. Refugees wrote describing their ordeals in concentration camps in Nazi Germany, in Soviet Russia, in postwar Poland, and even in America. A staff of secretaries would be needed to answer all my mail.

It was not long before I reached the corner of Seventy-second Street and Broadway. Exactly as I had before in Warsaw, I occupied not one but two furnished rooms—the main one on Seventieth Street and the other, which I used infrequently, an alcove in the East Bronx apartment of my *landsman* Misha Budnik, who now earned his living as a taxi driver.

I knew I could always rely on other friends for an overnight stay in an emergency, especially Stefa Kreitle, who had been one of my girlfriends in Warsaw. She and her husband, Leon, had spent the war years in London and now lived in New York. Leon, who was approaching eighty, had lost his two daughters in the Holocaust and had suffered a heart attack. Nevertheless he was still doing business in New York and also speculated in stocks and bonds. Stefa's daughter by her previous marriage, Franka, was married and lived in Texas with her husband, an engineer who was a Gentile, and their baby daughter.

God in heaven, in my late forties I remained just as I was at twenty—lazy, disorganized, immersed in melancholy. No success I had, small though it was, seemed to end my depression. I lived by the day, by the hour, by the minute. I stood for a long time at the corner of Seventy-second and Broadway, contemplating what remained of the night. I longed to boast to some male acquaintance of my new conquest, as I felt it to be, perhaps to arouse his envy. If only I could assure Miriam that, whatever the future might bring, I would be true to her—in my own fashion. But the hour was too late for such foolishness, and I began to walk toward my room on Seventieth Street.

I climbed up the three flights and entered my room. A narrow cubicle, it held a small table and two chairs. When I opened the window I could glimpse a small length of the Hudson River and a neon sign in New Jersey which cast a reddish glow on the water. It awed me to think that the river had flowed in just this way for millions of years, and that it carved its path through the rocks of the Palisades, which were themselves as old as the earth. If I strained my eyes I could see a single star high in the heavens above the Hudson.

In my room I read the papers and turned, as always, to the obituary page with photographs of men and women who only yesterday had lived, struggled, hoped. "Oh, what a dreadful world!" I murmured to myself. "How indifferent was the God who created all this. And there is no remedy." I was aware that at the very moment I browsed through the papers, thousands of people languished in hospitals and prisons. In slaughterhouses the heads of animals were being cut off, carcasses skinned, bellies ripped open. In the name of science countless innocent creatures were being subjected to cruel experiments, infected with harsh diseases.

Without undressing I threw myself on my unmade bed. How much longer, God, will you look on this inferno of yours and keep silent? What need have you of this ocean of blood and flesh, whose stench spreads across your universe? Or is the universe no more than heaps of dung? Are trillions and quadrillions of creatures tortured on other planets as well? Have you created this boundless slaughterhouse merely to show us your power and your wisdom? Are we commanded to love you with our hearts, our souls, for this?

Every night my fury raged in me anew. I had to find a way

to dull the pain of my rebellion. How well I understood those addicts who lulled themselves to sleep with alcohol or drugs! For some fortunate reason it was not in my nature to resort to such means of escape. I fell asleep and my dreams were filled with shrieks and cries. I was not in New York but in Poland, where Nazis pursued me. I scrambled over graves which Jews had dug for themselves. The mounds of earth were moving and muffled cries rose from below. I shivered and woke up. The rusty springs in my mattress squeaked and my shirt was wet with perspiration.

For a brief moment I could not recall what had happened the day before, but gradually my memory returned. Max Aberdam had risen from the dead and dragged me along to Rappaport's restaurant, to Priva, to Irka Shmelkes and her son, and then to that young girl—what was her name? I could see her standing before me, but I could not remember her name—yes, Miriam.

IT WAS LATE when I arose. Outside, the sun was shining and the bit of the Hudson I could see through my window shimmered like a fiery mirror. The air smelled of trees, grass, flowers. The washroom in the hall was not occupied, so I showered and shaved and put on a fresh shirt. I was ready to leave for the cafeteria where I had my breakfast. Just as I reached the ground floor, I heard the house telephone. I picked up the receiver, and on the other end a young voice asked in English, "May I speak with Mr. Greidinger?"

"Speaking," I said.

There was a pause. Then the voice said, "I hope I didn't wake you. This is Miriam, remember me?"

"You didn't wake me. Yes, Miriam. It's good to hear from you."

As a rule I spoke on the telephone softly, but this time I fairly shouted. Then she said, "I think Max told you I'm a babysitter. By the way, how do you say babysitter in Yiddish? The mother of the child I'm looking after lives on Park Avenue. She is an American, not one of our refugees. I told you last evening of the dissertation I'm writing about you. It occurred to me that you might meet with me, since I have a great many questions to ask you. I know it is presumptuous and if you have no time or patience for me today, I won't feel insulted."

"I have both—time and patience."

"Have you had breakfast?"

"No, I was on my way to the cafeteria."

"May I meet you at the cafeteria? I don't know whether Max told you that I drive a car."

"A car?"

"Yes. I've become a real American. It's an old car but it runs. What cafeteria is it? Where?"

"The Broadway Cafeteria," and I gave Miriam the address.

"I'll be there in five minutes. I keep my car parked in the street, not in a garage. By the time you reach the cafeteria I'll be there."

"Where is Max?"

"Max will be busy all day. He's having lunch with Irka Shmelkes. He and I spoke about you for a long time last night. That I love you is not altogether astonishing, but Max said last night that you are like a son to him. I told him I would call you this morning. Ah, I have so much to tell you and I don't even know where to begin. Bye!"

Miriam rang off. I stood by the phone for some time, as if waiting for it to ring again. Then I ran up the three flights of stairs to my room. I put on my new suit—a lightweight summer one I had bought recently. I had had several loves during my lifetime, and other relationships which could be called half-loves. But on that morning a certain exhilaration came over me which

I had not felt for years. "Could it really be love?" I asked myself. "Or is it merely thirst for new adventure?"

The Broadway Cafeteria was nearly nine blocks away, closer to Eightieth than to Seventieth Street. I had developed a fondness for the place because the tables were wooden, not metal, and the chairs were comfortable, more *haimish*, than elsewhere. There was a European air about the cafeteria and Yiddish was often spoken there, sometimes Polish. I did not want to enter the cafeteria breathless and perspiring. The moralist and pragmatist in me warned that I might be sinking into a quagmire of complications from which I could never climb out. I heard my mother saying, "This Miriam of yours is no better than a whore, and Max Aberdam is a deranged libertine, a depraved lecher." I heard my father saying (how many times had I heard it?), "Thou shalt utterly abhor it and utterly reject it!"

There was a time when I would have answered my parents in my thoughts, reasoned with them—but not now. I reached the cafeteria at the very moment that a car pulled up in front and Miriam sprang out, nimble, her face a schoolgirl's face. She was resplendent in a white dress. She smiled at me and waved her hand. Had she contrived in so brief a time to cut her hair short, like a boy's? She seemed taller to me, slimmer, and more elegant than on the evening before. She carried a white bag and white gloves. She gave me a mischievous, worldly-wise smile. She took my arm and we entered the cafeteria in such haste that for a moment we were stuck together in the revolving door. Our knees touched. We both began to laugh at our eagerness. I pulled two tickets from the machine that dispensed them near the door, and the machine gave two rings. I saw an empty table by a window, looking out on the street, and I grabbed it at once.

Miriam assured me she was not hungry, and that she wanted nothing more than coffee. But on my way to the counter I decided to bring back breakfast for the two of us. Though I often felt awkward and lost on the street, in the cafeteria I knew all the rules—where the trays were stored, the spoons, the forks, the paper napkins, and so on. I knew where to get in line for food and where for coffee. When I returned to our table with scrambled eggs, rolls, butter, cereal, marmalade, coffee, Miriam again said that she had eaten, but she tasted the eggs, had a spoonful of farina, and bit into a roll.

We sat at our table like two refugees, but it was Miriam who was Hitler's victim, not I. She had faced countless perils until she found a haven in this blessed land where a Jewish girl could drive a car, rent an apartment, study at a university, even write a dissertation on an unknown Yiddish writer. I was enjoying the first stage of a love affair, the beginning, when the lovers-to-be owe nothing to each other, when all that is exchanged is pure benevolence, unspoiled by demands, complaints, jealousy.

Soon Miriam Zalkind (she told me this was her family name) was confiding her secrets to me. Her mother had been a Communist in Warsaw in the thirties—the sort dubbed "salon Communists"—and contributed money to help political prisoners. She had had an affair with a Communist functionary, as they were called. Miriam's father was a member of the People's Party, but when that party failed, he turned to Poale Zion, both on the right and on the left, and supported the central Yiddish school organization. Miriam's brother, Manes, had become a revisionist; he belonged to the Jabotinsky faction and advocated an end to the British Mandate over Palestine, even if it required terrorism to achieve. The Moscow trials, Stalin's anti-Semitism and his pacts with Hitler cured Miriam's mother of her Communism. When Fania, her mother, ran off to Palestine with an actor, Miriam's father, Morris, moved in with an artist named Linda McBride. Miriam said, "She is a McBride like I am a Turk. Her real name is Beila Knepl, she is a Galitzianer. Her first husband was a Gentile and she kept his name. I tried to read her poems once, but I had to laugh. She wants to be modern and futuristic. She also paints and her paintings are like her poetry—smudges. How my father could be fired up over a *yente* like her I will never understand.

"I am not, as you know, a moralist. I have had men in Poland as well as here and I always had the illusion that I loved each man, or at least that he loved me. Everything that happened to our family is a sort of suicide. Instead of committing suicide in Russia or in the concentration camps, many refugees waited to kill themselves here in America after they became rich, fat, secure. A day does not go by without my hearing of another friend who died. Do you believe all this to be coincidence?"

"I don't know what to believe. There is such a thing as a death wish."

"I have it, too," Miriam said. "At the same time that I study, read, become inspired by you and others, dream of happiness, travel, of having a child—and then I become tired of this cursed game and want to put an end to it. In Max this wish is even stronger than in me. He always speaks of death. He wants to provide for everyone, all the refugees, and especially for me. Every few weeks he changes his will. He is optimistic enough to believe that he will leave behind a fortune, but I am sure he will lose everything sooner or later. He probably told you that I have a husband, Stanley Bardeles. He's a maniac, a compulsive scribbler without talent. He refuses to grant me a divorce and creates all sorts of difficulties. Max has convinced himself that I am a helpless little girl, a child, but in fact I often have the feeling that I am old, very old."

"How many men have you had?" I asked, immediately regretting my tactlessness.

A smile began to play in Miriam's eyes. "Why do you ask?"

"Ah, I don't know. Foolish curiosity."

"I had many."

"Twenty?"

"At least."

"Why did you do it?"

"Perhaps because of that wish for death. My teacher had a brother who became my lover in Warsaw. He died in the uprising of 1944. When one is lying in a hole for many months and can barely stretch one's legs—and one's life is threatened—every encounter with someone from the world of the living is an exciting event. That was part of the price I paid for my wish to live. When I finally came out to freedom and saw a city of ruins and graves, I felt as if through some miracle I had risen from my grave. You wrote a story like this—what is its name?"

" 'In the World of Chaos.' "

"Yes, I read it. All refugees have stories to tell and some of them lived a life worse than death. We sneaked into Germany. The roads teemed with murderers of every kind—robbers, Fascists, all sorts of fanatics. We spent nights sleeping in barns, in stables, in potato cellars. Sometimes I would sleep near a man who, without a word, would climb on me. There was no sense creating a scandal. We all expected to die soon. I am sure that you find me repulsive, now that I've told you these things. But since you asked, I wanted to answer."

"I had no right to ask. And it is the murderers I find repulsive, not the victims."

"Agents from Israel, members of the Brikha, came to help us. They were also men, not angels. What does a woman have in such circumstances? Nothing but her body. When we reached Germany we were placed in a camp again, to await our visas for America or Palestine. My father became a smuggler and made a small fortune, but we were still inmates of a camp. I became thoroughly cynical and began to doubt that love or loyalty really existed. In America I came across Stanley Bardeles, who flattered me. I convinced myself that I had found true love and saw too late that he was a fool. My God, it's a quarter to eleven. Do you still want to come to Park Avenue with me?"

"Yes, if you like."

"If I like? Every minute with you is pure joy for me."

"Why do you say that?"

"Because you and Max are brothers, and I want to be a wife to both of you. Ah, you still blush! You are still a child—that is the truth."

I sat next to Miriam and watched her as she steered the car, smoking a cigarette. She said, "I want you to know that in my first *gilgul* I lived in Tibet, where a woman can marry two or three brothers. Why not here, then? First of all, I love both you and Max. Second, Max wants to provide me with a husband. I often ask, Why is everything permitted to men, and to us women—nothing? Our relationship is quite open. The other day Max asked me whom I would like as my future husband or lover—and I answered immediately, Aaron Greidinger. I hope you don't find it insulting to be number two. But Max is older than you are. He is my number one and will always be."

"Miriam, I would be delighted to be number two."

"Are you serious?"

"Completely."

Miriam gave me her right hand and I took it in my left. Both our hands were damp and shaking and I managed to find her pulse, which was rapid and strong. She was driving along Madison Avenue now and I asked her why, since Park Avenue was our destination. Miriam answered, "I can't bring you upstairs when the child's mother is at home. As you can see, I have planned everything. Here, I've written down the telephone number. Wait ten minutes and then call. The child's mother leaves almost as soon as I arrive. In her way, she is also in love."

Miriam stopped the car and I climbed out. She gave me the

slip of paper and said, "Look at your watch and call me in ten minutes." And before I could utter a word, she sped off.

"Where is the slip of paper Miriam just gave me?" I asked myself. It always happened this way—as soon as some good fortune was granted me, the imps and demons began their pranks. Suddenly I realized the slip of paper was being held in my left hand. "Why am I so excited?" I asked myself. And again I heard my father's voice: "Lecher!"

Ten minutes passed and I found a phone and dialed the number. Miriam answered immediately. "She's gone," she said. "Come on up!" I was sure that Park Avenue was to my right, but instead, I found myself on Fifth Avenue. I retraced my steps. Why was it that I always took the wrong way? Meanwhile, I reached the apartment house—a large building, apparently for the rich. The doorman was decked out like a general, complete with gold buttons and epaulets. He eyed me with doubt and suspicion. The elevator was furnished with a bench and a mirror, and the operator waited until Miriam opened the door. I entered an apartment that seemed like a palace. Miriam took my arm and guided me, as if we were in a museum with Oriental carpets, richly tapestried walls, large hanging lamps, carved ceilings. Quietly she opened a door, which led to a child's room cluttered with expensive toys. In a little bed slept a pale boy with reddish hair. Nearby I saw a bottle and a thermometer. The thought passed through my head: He could be my child.

As if she had read my mind Miriam said, "Didi looks like you."

"What gives you this idea?" I asked, surprised by her telepathic powers.

"There are still several red hairs left on your head. His mother's hair is fire-red. She is a lesbian, separated from her husband. This is where she now lives with her lover. Both come from well-to-do Jewish families in Brooklyn. Theirs is a passion I will never understand. I saw her husband once. Tall, handsome as a picture. He holds a doctorate from Harvard University. Why did she marry and have a child if she preferred someone of her own gender? For some reason she trusts me and confides in me. Ah, it is all so tragic and comic. I know the other one, too—ugly as sin and her voice is a deep bass."

The living room was a mixture of old and new: a grand piano decorated in gold and paintings by modern artists whose names I did not know. Miriam said, "And that is not a bookshelf but a bar." What appeared to be gold-leaf-decorated volumes by Shakespeare, Milton, Dickens, and Maupassant was in reality the door of a cabinet which held bottles of wine, whiskey, champagne, and dozens of liqueurs. Miriam said, "If you want to drink and forget your troubles, you may."

"No thanks, not now."

"Max has been here several times. He drinks like a fish. He can down a whole bottle of cognac and not become drunk, only cheerful. My employer has given me a free hand in her apartment: I can eat here, drink, invite guests. She has poured out her heart to me. What is this madness which took hold of her? When I remember the time I spent in that dark hole in my teacher's house, it seems like a fantasy. And now I have—at least temporarily—everything I want. But for some reason I am not happy."

"Why not?" I asked.

"You tell me. Perhaps I ask for too much. Is there such a thing as happiness?"

"What exactly do you lack?"

"That is what I myself would like to know. Now that Max's trip to Poland is definite, he asked me to go with him, but the thought of being there again, of walking among the graves, makes me shudder. But he is everything to me: my father, my lover, my husband, everything I have on earth. From the time

my mother went off with that crook I lost all feeling for her. I
see her now as she is, a cheap woman who can love no one but
herself. My father is made of the same stuff. You are thinking,
Of course, the apple does not fall far from the tree. And you are
right. How can I be different when I am their daughter? I know
exactly what you think of me."

"No, you don't."

"Yes, I know. I love Max, but since he has other women and
since he gives in to all his lunacies, why should I not do the
same? He always urges me to find another husband and even
proposed to find one himself. Is it because he feels guilty, or
does he want to be rid of me? Perhaps you see the truth better
than I."

"How can I see the truth? I've known you less than twenty-
four hours. Yesterday at this time I did not know you existed.
I even thought Max was dead."

"You are right. You may know me for less than twenty-four
hours, but I have known you for five years. Was a novel ever
written about a woman who knew a man for five years while he
knew her for only a day? The hero would have to be a writer
like you and the heroine someone like me."

"He could be an actor," I said.

"True, but I could never love an actor, who only parrots
someone else's words. I can only love a man who speaks his own
words, be they untrue or insane. The truth is that we, you and
I, are birds of a feather."

"And yet you don't want children."

"I want you," Miriam said.

We embraced and faced each other, pressed closely together.
Our eyes seemed to ask, Are you ready? But the question re-
mained unanswered because the telephone began to ring loudly.
It awoke Didi and we heard him crying.

"Wait!" Miriam called out, and tore herself from me. It was

her employer on the phone, explaining that she was coming back unexpectedly. I knew of course that I would have to leave. Miriam went into Didi's room, quieted the child, and came out to kiss me goodbye. Waiting for the elevator in the hall, I glanced back; Miriam, looking sad, was standing in the doorway. We stared at each other, astonished at our own lust.

FIVE

THE NEXT MORNING I was called to the telephone at the newspaper, and when I picked up the receiver, a voice, speaking in Polish Yiddish, said, "Are you the writer Aaron Greidinger?"

"Yes, may I ask who is speaking?"

"Chaim Joel Treibitcher." I knew he was a friend of Max, as well as the uncle of Max's associate, Harry Treibitcher.

"Recently someone sent me your novel," he went on, "and I read it from cover to cover. How does a writer remember such things? There were words and expressions in your book I have not heard since my grandmother Tirtza-Meyta died, may she rest in peace."

I wanted to tell him what an unexpected honor it was for me to hear from him, but I was not able to interrupt his stream of words. He spoke so loudly that I held the receiver away from my ear. He half-spoke and half-sang in tones and half-tones from the *Bet Midrash*, the Hasidic *shtibl*, the black-market stock exchange, and a hint of the Germanized Yiddish that was spoken in the halls of Zionist congresses.

"How do you remember so much?" he went on. "Have you persuaded Pura the Angel of Forgetfulness to have no dominion over you? Do you intone '*armimas, rmimas, mimas, imas, mas*' at the close of the Sabbath, after the *Havdalah*? And did you never, as a boy, drink the water which your mother—may she rest in peace—left behind after kneading dough? And did you never eat tendons, and take care not to put on the sleeves of your robe together with the *arba kanfes*?"

"You yourself have quite a memory," I managed to throw in.

"What is man without a memory? No better than a cow. The Gemara tells us: '*Thou shalt observe* and *thou shalt remember* came down from heaven together.' Now the story is this: My good friend known in these parts as Max Aberdam and my wife, Matilda, have decided to fly to Poland together. Let me be brief. We are preparing a bit of a party for them, a get-together or a farewell party, call it what you like. And inasmuch as I know that you and Max were friends in Warsaw, and have only recently renewed your friendship here, we invite you to join us at supper. Have no fear, meat in my house is *glatt* kosher—*lemehadrin min hamehadrin*—suitable even for the most observant. You won't have to write about it in your newspaper, although a little publicity never hurts. America, after all, lives on publicity. I live on West End Avenue, not far from you."

"How did you know about my friendship with Max Aberdam?" I asked.

"I've already spoken to Max, and he promised to bring his dear wife, Priva, and perhaps also that secretary of his, Miriam. We will be a small group, one table only. Be so good as to write down the date and my address . . ."

I thanked Chaim Joel Treibitcher and told him that I knew how much he had done for Yiddish, Hebrew, Jewish art. And he answered in his own style: "*Eishe besheishe polevine.* It's not worth a pinch of gunpowder . . ."

For this distinguished man to invite me to his home was a
sign that my stock had risen. And yet I had always shied away
from dinners, banquets, and receptions, since I never had the
proper clothing. During my years in America I shunned people's
company. "Have no commerce with men," the misanthrope in
me muttered. Yet a single meeting with Max Aberdam was dragging me into countless complications. My old shyness returned,
a shyness that had never fully left me. Matilda was a snob, and
a tuxedo was probably required for her party, with a stiff shirt
and a black tie. I telephoned Max at his home, but no one
answered. I rang up Miriam, who had also been invited. She
said, "What's the sense of it? I have neither the right dress, the
right shoes, nor the patience. You know of course that Matilda
was Max's mistress for over thirty years?"

"So it was rumored in Warsaw."

"Everyone knows it. It's an open secret. I am beginning to
think that I won't go to their party. Matilda likes to play the
grande dame. I'll feel like a fish out of water." Then Miriam
asked, "What are you doing now?"

"Ah, nothing at all."

"Come over!"

"When?"

"Now, this minute."

Yes, we already addressed each other with the informal
"thou," but we had not gone further than kissing. I had been
warned by Otto Weininger's writings against becoming ensnared
in the web of a woman—The Feminine—a creature without
ethics, without memory or logic, the purveyor of sex, the affir-
mation of materiality, the denial of the spirit. Nevertheless I
said, "I'm coming."

"When? Take a taxi. Don't make me wait. I need you now
more than ever," Miriam said.

"I need you, too."

I wondered why Max had permitted our relationship to happen. Otto Weininger called woman a purveyor, but in our case the real purveyor was Max. Jealousy has its opposite—"coupling," as Otto Weininger called it. A will to share, a desire for sexual community. I had observed it in both men and women —and especially among the members of the Warsaw Writers' Club. Actually, I first encountered this phenomenon in the Pentateuch, when I was a *cheder* boy: Rachel had given her maid Bilhah to Jacob, to be his concubine, and Leah had given him Zilpah. All the peculiarities of modern man had their roots in the very dawn of civilization. On the phone I heard Miriam ordering me, "Take a taxi!" She almost shouted the words. There was in them a commanding note, an impatient urge which could no longer be restrained.

I WAS NOT accustomed to hailing taxis, but I found one. "Has anyone ever been in my predicament?" I asked myself in the taxi. "Has anyone ever written a novel about a person like me, about loves and entanglements like mine?" Compared with my situation, the fiction I read seemed to me simplistic and devoid of complications. As far as I could tell, no one in these books was as poor as I was, with the possible exception of the hero of Knut Hamsun's *Hunger.* But he did not engage in love affairs, he only fantasized. The taxi stopped and I paid the fare. As it pulled away, I realized I had given the driver a five-dollar bill instead of one dollar. Poor as I was, I was fated to lose money.

I rode the elevator to the fourteenth floor. As I stretched out my hand to press the bell, the door opened. Miriam was apparently standing there, waiting for me. We embraced without a word. My bony knees struck against hers, pushing her back into the apartment. The door slammed behind us, perhaps driven by a gust of wind. We wasted no time on misgivings or conscience. We fell on the bed. Miriam wore a robe over her naked body. We surrendered to each other silently, biting into each other's mouths, with the force of passion. Twilight fell, and still we wrestled, trying to wrest every last bit of pleasure from our bodies. In my mind I implored the telephone to keep from ringing—and it was silent. Strangely enough, the moment we sat up, the phone started to ring furiously, as though unable to suppress itself any longer.

I heard Miriam saying "Hello, Max," and I retired to the bathroom. I did not want to eavesdrop on their conversation. I did not turn on the light, and in the mirror against the reflected light of a glowing New York sky, I saw a wraithlike silhouette, disheveled, unkempt. I was as flushed as Esau must have been when he returned from the kill of the hunt, weary, ready for death, willing to sell his birthright for a mess of lentil soup. I had betrayed all my former loves, betrayed myself, betrayed those powers which warned me I would bind myself in a knot from which I could never extricate myself.

The bathroom door opened and Miriam slipped in in her stockinged feet, half-naked. I took her in my arms again and we stood silent in the darkness. In the gleam of her eyes I recognized that sense of contentment which comes between the sexes when they acknowledge a *fait accompli*.

I finally spoke. "Did you tell Max I was here?"

"No."

Thank God, I murmured to myself.

We returned to the bedroom, which was still dark. I was reminded of the oft-repeated saying "The night is made for love," which expresses a profound truth. The sexes had not yet lost the shame mentioned in the book of Genesis, and their sense of touch served them better than their sense of sight. We lay on the bed, a small distance between us, as if leaving space for each other's thoughts. I realized I could not remember now exactly how Miriam looked. In truth, we were still strangers, as our pious grandfathers and grandmothers had been when they united in the darkened *ichud-shtibl*, where they were taken after the *mitzvah* dance. I asked, "Does Max know you and I have had breakfast and discussed your dissertation?"

"Yes, I told him."

"Where is he?"

"At the Treibitchers'. He is having supper with them."

"What did you and Max talk about for so long?" I asked, uncertain whether I had the right to know.

Miriam did not answer. I began to wonder whether she had heard my question, but then she said softly, "Max and Matilda would like to stay in Poland longer than they had originally planned. Then they want to travel through Europe. They want us to join them in Switzerland."

"What's the sense of that?" I asked.

"There is no sense, no sense at all."

Miriam uttered the last words half in her sleep. I wanted to ask another question, but she was already fast asleep. I had forgotten how quickly the young could sleep. For a while I lay still. Am I happy, I asked myself, or am I unhappy? But my question remained unanswered. I half-dozed, half-daydreamed. We would not keep from Max what had happened this day. He was not betrayed, because it was he who had brought us together. Miriam loved him. Even in the midst of our passion she had spoken of her love for him. When I assured her that I would never be jealous of that love, I knew the words I spoke were not empty. We had silently sealed a pact between us.

I fell into a deep sleep, a sleep without dreams. When I opened my eyes and gaped in the darkness, I could remember nothing: where I was, who I was, what I was doing. For a moment I thought I was in Poland again. I stretched out my hand and touched hair, a throat, breasts. Was it Lena? Sabina? Was it Gina?

But Gina was dead. Suddenly everything came back to me, and at the same moment Miriam awoke and said, "Max?"

"No, it's me."

"Come!"

And we fell upon each other with renewed lust.

MIRIAM AND I told Max we had decided not to attend Chaim Joel Treibitcher's party, but he stubbornly insisted that we should go. "What's the sense of hiding like a worm in horse-radish?" he pleaded with me. "Even one who 'seeks shelter among the vessels' must sooner or later stick out his nose. If you want to be a writer, you must associate with people. You are not a youngster or a beginner. Pushkin and Lermontov at your age were already world-famous. How much longer will you keep your head down like a goat in a cabbage field?"

And to Miriam he said, "If you, Miriam, don't take him in hand and make a man of him, then he will be a *shmagege* forever, and you two can put away your teeth and be prepared to starve."

He spoke to her not as her lover but as if he were the father of the bride. One of his eyes glared, and the other winked. "I will not be your nursemaid forever," he said. "Since my own children were taken from me, you are my children now. If you, Aaron, are dispensing advice far and wide, you can't remain a *shlimazl*. If something should happen to me, you'll both be left without support."

"Max, what is the matter with you?" Miriam asked.

"I'm not crazy. I know what I'm saying."

"You'll live to be a hundred and twenty."

"Maybe yes, maybe no. I can't give you guarantees."

"Max, don't go to Poland."

"Nanny goat, be quiet!"

"Nanny goat" was one of Max's nicknames for Miriam. He

had given her seven nicknames—or "Jethro's names," as he called them—Tiny, Crumb, Witch, Panna Marianna, Little *telisha*, Etl-Betl, and Nanny goat. He had heard that in Warsaw I was nicknamed *Tzutzik*, so he promptly applied it to me here. He also added Donkey, Scribbler, and *Katva raba*. Miriam called me Arale, *Yeshiva-bucher*, and Butterfly. I in turn gave Miriam the name my mother had given me, *Oytzerl* [Little treasure]. That evening Max had invited us to a restaurant on Fifty-seventh Street. I watched with alarm as he smoked one cigar after another. He ordered a beefsteak and two types of schnapps. Miriam reminded him, as she had countless times before, that his doctor had forbidden him to smoke more than two cigars a day. He was also ordered to go on a diet and to drink no more than one cocktail. But Max exclaimed, "Not today, my dear, not today." And from his breast pocket he drew a little box and tossed a white tablet in his mouth.

As we sat at the table, Max related some particulars of Chaim Joel Treibitcher's life. He remained a wealthy man. His business empire in America exceeded the one he had had in Europe. He slept exactly four hours at night, and three-quarters of an hour during the day—not a minute more or less. As he lay in bed, hardly a night passed without his lighting upon some new scheme for increasing his wealth. In the thirties in America he had bought up houses and factories, as well as stocks and securities, all of which rose in value. In Miami Beach he had purchased lots which now were worth a fortune. Long before Israel became a Jewish state, he had bought lots and houses in Jerusalem, in Haifa, Tel Aviv. Everything he touched turned to gold. His wife, Matilda, was rich in her own right. His nephew Harry, who acted as a stockbroker for Max, had been born in New York.

Recently Chaim Joel Treibitcher had embarked on a new project—the translation of the best in Yiddish and Hebrew literature into a series of European languages. He also planned to publish a journal and an academic Yiddish-Hebrew dictionary. So highly had Max praised Miriam to Matilda that she asked him several times to bring Miriam to her home. The Treibitchers were eager to help gifted refugees develop their talents. They would gladly award Miriam a scholarship so that she could finish the dissertation she had begun on my work. Max demanded that we both promise to attend the party—not together, naturally. He, Max, would attend with Priva, his wife. But we both said nothing.

After supper Miriam asked Max to come back to her apartment. But Max answered, "Not today, my dear, not today." And to me he said, "You go with her. A man my age should have a stand-in. I also promised Priva to come home early. Aaron, how did you ever have the presence of mind not to marry?"

"No one wanted me," I answered.

"She wants you," and Max pointed to Miriam.

"I want both of you. That is the truth," Miriam said.

"You brazen girl!"

"What is good for the gander is good for the goose."

"You are a man's wife."

"First of all, Stanley is not a man but a *golem*. Second, we were married in City Hall, not by a rabbi."

"So we have a scholar to boot, eh? If our grandparents could hear you, they would tear their clothes in mourning and sit shiva not seven days but seven years."

"And what would that accomplish?" Miriam asked.

"Inasmuch as the Almighty has kept His silence for eternity and a Wednesday, how can we know anything?" Max asked. "He wants us to see the truth, and we are like blind horses who have wandered into dark ditches. Sometimes, Miriam, I call you a cow. But the real cow is my wife, Priva. She sits at her séance table, turns on a red light, and invokes all kinds of spirits, like the witch at Endor—Spinoza, Karl Marx, Jesus, Buddha, the

Baal Shem Tov. She orders them to come, and so they come, and they bring messages from the Other Side."

As we left the restaurant, Max muttered, "I need the trip to Poland like I need a hole in my head. Give me your word, both of you, that you'll come to the party." Max took our hands in his; his hand was uncommonly warm. He said, "Arale, don't be a fool. You'll come out a winner, as they say here. Taxi!" A taxi pulled up, and Max shouted back at us, "See you at the party!"

WE HAD DECIDED, Miriam and I, to say nothing to Max of our affair. Perhaps he already knew and it needed no confession. If he was ignorant, or unsure, why upset him before his journey? We spoke of him as children are wont to speak of their fathers. I told Miriam that a father complex was hidden in her (I did not mean an Oedipal complex), and she did not deny it. She snapped, "And what daughter doesn't have one?" She admitted that she often called Max *"Tatele,"* the childish word for papa.

Until that time I believed that I could not love a woman knowing that she loved another. Yet in truth I now realized it had often happened before. I had loved women who had husbands. I loved them for themselves and never envied their husbands. In fact, I took every opportunity to tell a woman that her husband should always be number one. I wondered whether my attitude toward the husband was purely pragmatic or whether it masked a peculiar ethic. In those years I believed that the sexual awakening of modern times would lead to unofficial but accepted polygamy and polyandry. Rarely would a modern man consent to live out his years with one woman, and rare would be the woman who consented to be one man's possession. Society would be forced to create a sort of sexual cooperation in place of the prevailing sexual deception and adultery. I often thought the essence of betrayal lay not in the fact that two men shared one woman, or two women a man, but in the lies that both sides were forced to tell, in the subtle deceptions which the law foisted upon those who were merely true to their natures and to their physical and spiritual needs. For the first time I loved someone I did not want to deceive, nor did she want to deceive me.

How pleasant it was to keep company with a young woman without having to assure her that she was and would continue to be my sole love! How pleasant to know that I need not demand of my beloved what I was not prepared to ask of myself. During the days we spent together, usually in the apartment on Park Avenue where Miriam looked after the child Didi, we spoke of the Eskimos, the Tibetans, of others like them who had not developed a sense of sexual ownership. I told Miriam about the group of anarchists, followers of Proudhon, Sturner, Madame Kollontai, and Emma Goldman, who regarded free love as the foundation of social justice and the future of mankind. The only question was: What would become of the children? I myself had not the least desire to father a new generation. But Miriam repeatedly spoke of her awakening longing to have a child.

I spent the day before the party in Miriam's company, and for the first time I spent the night in her apartment. Two weeks had passed since Max had first introduced us, but to me the time seemed uncommonly long. That evening, when we left the cafeteria and walked along Broadway, I felt for the first time the peace which true love could bring. I had no other wish than to be with Miriam. It was summer and we walked arm in arm. There was a pensiveness in Miriam's young face which to me captured the very essence of life. We turned from Broadway to Central Park West on 100th Street, which we passed through as if in a dream. We came to Miriam's apartment house and the elevator man took us upstairs in silence. We entered her darkened apartment, whose windows looked out on the park. We were tired and we lay, fully dressed, on Miriam's wide bed, as though listening to the fullness in our hearts. Miriam touched her lips to my ear and whispered, "This is your home."

I often thought about animals and their ways in love. Mighty as some of God's creatures were, they did not—so far as I knew—reveal particular prowess in sex. I had witnessed the mating of horses and oxen, and of lions in the zoo. They did what they did, and then returned to their animal pursuits. The reason for this, I told myself, was that animals lacked speech, unlike men and women, for whom language is an instrument of lust. With words, men and women expressed their longings, their needs, all that had actually come to pass and all that might have happened. That night the theme of our foreplay, our afterplay, and the act itself was Max. We promised never to deceive him and to hold him as a kindred soul. I had experienced stormy outbursts before, but it seemed to me that Miriam and I outstripped them all. We turned in early that evening, and later, when, half dozing, I glanced at the luminous dial on my watch, I saw that it was half past two.

As I closed my eyes again I thought I heard Miriam murmur some words to me, but I could not make out their meaning. Suddenly she let out a muffled scream. I awoke at once, prodded to life by terror. Someone was fumbling at the front door, trying to pry it open. Miriam rolled over, half falling out of bed. The thief, or murderer, or whoever it was, had managed to come inside. Suddenly the hall ceiling light was on and I saw a young man, short and stocky, with long hair and a black beard. He was dressed in a pink shirt and a pair of dirty trousers. In his right hand he held a revolver, and in the left a small satchel. It reminded me of a scene in a grade B movie, although I knew all the while that my end might be near. In a second I became composed, alert. Miriam, stark naked, made a motion as if to strike the man, but she stopped in her tracks. "Stanley!" she exclaimed.

"Yes, it's me," the young man said. "Please try not to scream or do anything foolish."

I sat up in bed, also naked, and watched the scene without the terror it should have aroused in me but with curiosity. I knew Stanley was Miriam's lawful husband. She had spoken of him before—of his sexual ineptness, his sloppy sentimentality. He said, "Who is this, your newest lover?" and he pointed his revolver at me.

Miriam glanced behind her, looking for something with which to cover herself. But her nightgown lay beyond her reach, and I did not dare hand it to her. She asked, "What do you want?"

"You."

"You see that I have someone."

"Finished with Max, did you?" Stanley asked.

"No, I did not," Miriam answered.

"Hey, you." Stanley turned to me. "If you want to live a few years longer, better get out of here. Otherwise they'll carry you out."

Only then did I notice that Stanley spoke with an accent. It was as if he was translating his words from another language. Was it Yiddish? Polish? German? I said, "May I get dressed?"

"Yeah. Take your rags and go into the bathroom. Make no attempt to get help or I'll . . ."

"Just a moment."

"Find your things and get out of here. Quick!"

I put my feet down on the floor and they almost buckled under me. My knees bumped against the radiator. I had hung my jacket, my trousers, and my shirt on a chair which stood between the bed and the bathroom. It was as though my eyes were blinded. Where did I leave my shoes, my socks, my hat? As I picked up my jacket, my reading glasses, keys, and a bunch of loose bank notes fell on the floor. I turned to go to the bathroom, and Miriam asked in Yiddish, "Did you drop something? I heard keys hit the floor." Her voice held not the slightest note of fear.

I answered, "Nothing of any importance."

"You speak Yiddish?" Stanley asked.

"Yes, I come from Poland."

"From Poland, huh? Wait a minute. I think I know who you are," Stanley said. "You're that Yiddish writer. I've seen your picture. What's your name?"

I told him my name.

"I know you, I know you. I read your book. In English, not Yiddish. What is it called?"

I gave him the title of the book.

"Yes. I read your book. I am a poet. I write in English, not Yiddish." He called out to Miriam, "Don't move! Stay where you are!"

"I'm staying, I'm staying, you idiot!"

"Mr. Stanley," I said, "I am acquainted with your situation and I can understand your feelings. But there is no need to point a gun at us. We are not putting up any resistance. I am not a young man, I am close to fifty. After all, we are all Jews," I said, ashamed of my own words.

"Huh? You may be a Jew, but she is worse than a Nazi," Stanley answered. "What sort of Jew are you to keep company with a slut?" And Stanley raised his voice.

"Stanley, don't make a fool of yourself. Put down the revolver," Miriam said.

"I'll do as I like, not as you tell me to. Stay where you are or you'll be dead. What happened to Max? Are you through with him?"

"No, not through," Miriam said.

"I have come to put an end either to your stinking life or to mine," Stanley said. "I will not kill this man," pointing at me, "but you, you filthy whore, soon you'll be dead and gone. Mr.—what's your name?—Greidinger, I think you should know that you have been keeping company with a whore. She was a whore at fifteen, she told me so herself. In 1939, when her parents left for Russia, she refused to join them because she was the mistress of a pimp. Later he brought her over to the Aryan side and put her in a brothel, a bordello. Is this the truth or is it not?"

Miriam did not answer.

"May I use the bathroom?" I asked.

"Wait. Let her answer my question. Is it or is it not the truth? She herself has told me this. Answer, or you're dead!"

"It's not true," Miriam answered.

"You told me so yourself, with your own filthy mouth. Nazis were your clients, murderers of Jews. They brought you the gifts they seized from murdered Jewish girls. Am I lying? Answer me, or this will be your last moment!"

"I didn't want to die at sixteen."

"You could have crossed the bridge with your parents, instead of taking up with a pimp. In Germany, in the camp, you were the mistress of a German. And here, in college, you did the same with your professors. Am I speaking the truth?"

"At sixteen I wanted to live. Now I no longer do. You can shoot me this instant, you psychopath!"

"Go use the bathroom," Stanley ordered me. "And make it quick!"

I tried to open the door to the bathroom, but it seemed to be stuck. I pulled on the doorknob, but my hand had lost its strength. I turned my head and looked at Miriam, who was still naked, and at Stanley. The scene seemed unreal to me, the sort of caricature life makes of us. I heard myself saying, "Excuse me," and the words were foolish, cowardly. In my predicament I was seized with something like shame—for myself, for Miriam, even for Stanley—short, with stubby legs, a protruding belly, a face half hidden by his long hair and black beard. The revolver shook in his hand, threatening to fall. Something welled up in my throat and started to choke me—a mixture of coughing and laughter.

As soon as I entered the bathroom I felt faint. My scalp pressed down on my head, circles danced in front of my eyes, a bitter fluid filled my mouth. Stumbling, I managed to sit down on the toilet seat. The walls, the sink, the faucets, the frosted window, the ceiling whirled around me as if I were riding on a carousel. I wanted to vomit, but I was afraid to soil the floor. No sooner did I stand up than a stream of bitter fluid shot out of my mouth into the sink. With one hand I held on to the radiator, while with the other I pressed against the wall. I did not want the two people outside to become aware of my discomfort, and so I turned on the faucets and washed out the sink. With an effort I pushed open the frosted window and let the cool night air revive me. I had managed to escape the indignity of fainting, as well as the danger of cracking my skull in a fall. But I was smeared with stains from an evil-smelling fluid from my own body. Let him shoot me, it's all the same to me, I thought to myself.

The bathroom door flew open, and I saw Miriam, now no longer naked but clad in a bathrobe. Close behind her stood Stanley, without his gun. Both Miriam and Stanley were speaking to me, but my ears had turned deaf, as though they had filled with water. Shame overcame me for my own nakedness and for the stench that arose from my body. "Shut the door," I blurted out, "I'll be out soon."

"Wipe yourself off," Miriam called out, and pointed to a towel.

"He will be all right." I heard Stanley's voice. "Shut the door."

I began to busy myself with the shower, but apparently it did not work. Outside, dawn was breaking and the crimson light of the rising sun fell on the tiled bathroom walls. I caught a glimpse of my face in the mirror—pale, drawn, unshaven. I began to wash myself with cold water. I opened Miriam's medicine cabinet and looked for a razor. My fear of Stanley had passed and I was eager to appear in his eyes less old and unkempt than I did in the mirror. My jacket and trousers were with me in the bathroom, but I had neither my shirt nor my shoes.

So I had embarked on a love affair with a whore. Her husband had barged in during the night with a gun. We were a hairbreadth away from being shot. It was not merely a thought, but a voice I literally heard, as if my mother's soul were always with me, following my every step. "Mother, where are you? Forgive me," something in me pleaded. And she answered as if she were alive: "You can sink no lower than this. Promise me that you will flee from this harlot, before it is too late . . ."

"Yes, Mother, I promise."

"For her house inclineth unto death and her paths lead unto the dead." My father chanted the verses from the Book of Proverbs in his own voice and with his own *nusekh*. "None that go to her return again, neither do they choose the paths of life."

Somehow I managed to wash myself, and I put the jacket over my naked body. I opened the door a crack and cautiously peeked out. There was no one in the bedroom, but I thought I heard the sound of muffled laughter from another room. I looked for my shirt and shoes, but they had vanished. One of my socks was lying on the bed. I called out, "Miriam!"

She immediately appeared in the tiny corridor, pale, disheveled, still dressed in a buttoned-up bathrobe. Stanley followed her close behind. "Where are your shoes?" Miriam asked, searching the floor with her eyes. In the bedroom it was still night and the venetian blinds blocked the light of the rising sun. Our eyes were searching the floor when suddenly I realized that Stanley still held the gun to Miriam's back. At the same moment I saw my shoes atop the radiator. "There they are!" I exclaimed.

Stanley also saw them and his face turned stern and embittered. He spoke to me over Miriam's shoulder: "Get dressed and be on your way. Miriam is still my wife, not yours."

"Yes, thanks," I answered submissively.

"Where will he go so early in the morning?" Miriam asked. "It will not do for the elevator man to see him leaving my apartment at this hour."

"Let him use the stairs."

"The door to the staircase is locked," Miriam said.

"No, it must be left open in case of fire," Stanley answered.

I hurriedly put on one of my socks. The other sock had vanished and I put the shoe on over my bare foot. I tried to arrange the shoelaces, but in the dim light I could not see the holes and soon gave up the effort. I heard Stanley say, "Make it quick and be on your way. But remember: if you say a word to the police or even to that old idiot, Max, you'll pay for it with your life. I know where your office is."

"I'll tell no one."

"Do it for your own sake. My life is worth nothing to me."

I wanted to ask him what would become of Miriam, but I said nothing. Then I heard myself saying, "I feel sure that the two of you will be reconciled." Again I felt ashamed of my words. My throat was so dry that I could barely speak.

"Reconciled, huh? I treated her honestly. I did not force her to marry me. She pursued me, not I her. Isn't that true, Miriam?"

"It's much too late for these discussions."

"It's never too late. Since you took him into your bed and told him, I presume, how good you are and how evil I am, and how much you love him and what a devoted wife you would make, he has a right to know the truth."

"No one chased anyone."

"You chased me. I was in no rush to be married. Already I realized that a holy virgin you were not, ha-ha. But you demanded that we go to City Hall and make it official. Is that true or isn't it?"

"Let it be true. Nothing can harm me anymore," Miriam said haltingly.

"It is all true. This man is a writer, a Jewish writer. The book jacket mentioned that he is a son of a rabbi. He should know what you are and with whom he has taken up."

"He already knows everything."

"No, not everything. Even I don't know all there is to know. Whenever I meet someone who knows you I learn of more lovers, more affairs, more lies."

"I told you the truth right from the beginning."

"Put on your tie," Stanley said to me. "Before you go I want to ask you a question. Is it true that you believe in God?"

"I believe in His wisdom, not in His mercy."

"What do you mean by that?"

"Everyone can see His wisdom—whether you call it God or Nature. But how can one believe in His mercy after Hitler?"

"God is evil?"

"At least to animals and men."

"How can you live with this sort of faith?"

"I can't, really."

"I'd like to talk with you someday, but not now."

"Stanley, may I say something?" Miriam asked.

"You keep still! I warn you again: if you say one word more, you'll be in trouble."

"I give you my sacred pledge not to speak again."

"Well, go," he said to me. "If you read in the papers that we are both dead, you will know why."

"Don't do it. If she is as you say, she is not worth dying for."

"And what is worth dying for? Goodbye."

I opened the door to the hallway and Miriam called after me, but I did not hear what she said. By the dim light of the night lamp I saw that the door to the staircase was not locked. A middle-of-the-night warmth pervaded the hall, a remnant of the night's stillness, a stagnation made up of garbage, undissipated gas fumes, sleeping bodies. I began to feel my way down the stairs with the caution of someone half-blind. I had salvaged my own life, but I had left Miriam's in the hands of a murderer. Again I heard my father's hoarse warning: "Thou shalt utterly abhor it and utterly reject it . . ." And something in my brain added, "This world and the next world are the same world."

I had walked down half the flight when I stopped in my tracks. What was it that Miriam had called out after me? Did she say goodbye? Did she ask for something? She had almost shouted the words, but in my agitation I could not make them out. Well, what difference did it make? Everything between us was finished. I felt a bitterness in my mouth—in the gums, the throat—in my intestines, my eyes. A bare light bulb threw shadows on the blackened ceiling. I heard footsteps, and soon a worker came walking up the stairs carrying a broom and a huge trash can. For a moment he stared at me, uncertain whether he should ask me to explain my presence. Then he continued to climb the stairs, accompanied by the clatter of tin cans and lids. If Stanley were to kill Miriam and run, this man would testify to the police that he had seen me on the stairs. I would be suspected of having committed the murder myself. Something in me laughed. I had become a bit of trash tossed out at night and left to be swept up by day. I leaned against the wall to keep from falling.

According to my calculations I had descended a sufficient number of stairs to be on the ground floor. I tried to open the door which led to the lobby, but it was locked. There was no strength left in my legs and I had to sit down. What would I say to the police if I was arrested? I had given Stanley my word to say nothing. The air reeked with coal, with decay, with other pun-

gent subterranean odors. Only now did I notice that the walls
were brick red and smudged with soot. I had walked down too
far. I needed to gather my strength and climb up. Stanley's words
began to ring again in my ears—the mistress of a Gentile, a pimp
. . . he put her in a brothel . . . Nazis were her clients, murderers
of Jews . . . They brought her gifts which they had snatched
from murdered Jewish girls . . .

I climbed up one more flight, saw a door, and pushed it open.
I found myself in the lobby. The pointer on the dial above the
elevator rested on 14, the floor of Miriam's apartment. The
doorman was nowhere to be seen. I stood in the street and
breathed deeply, taking in the cool morning air, the moisture
rising from the trees and grass in the park. An early-rising sun,
fresh from its dip in the ocean, hung in a clear blue sky. Flocks
of squawking birds flew across the park. Pigeons milled on the
sidewalk and on benches outside the park, hopped on little red
feet, pecked at invisible morsels of food, cooed, flapped their
wings. Only now did I realize that my weakness was bound up
with hunger. I had vomited days' worth of food; everything
inside me was hollow. There were no restaurants on Central
Park West, and no taxis or buses passed in the street. I put my
hand to my back trouser pocket and found it empty. I remembered that while carrying my clothes to Miriam's bathroom, my
money and my keys had fallen out. I put my hand into the breast
pocket of my jacket and found that my checkbook had vanished
as well.

I continued to walk slowly, because I had no strength to run
and no place to run to. In my room on Seventieth Street I kept
neither money nor food. I kept my traveler's checks in a safe-
deposit box in the bank, but the key to the box hung on the
ring I had lost at Miriam's. That evening I was supposed to be
at Chaim Joel Treibitcher's party with Miriam, to see Max off.
But all this belonged to a distant past.

SIX

I WALKED, AIMLESS and confused, unaware whether my feet were taking me uptown or downtown. Finally, overcome with weariness, I sank down on a bench that was damp with dew. I was without money, checkbook, and keys. Unnerved by the truths Stanley had revealed about Miriam, I swore by God and by the souls of my parents, by all that was sacred and dear to me, that I would never gaze upon her wicked face again. I also vowed to see no more of Max Aberdam.

I was too tired to continue on to Seventieth Street, to find the superintendent's wife and ask her for the key to my room. I had no change at all, not even the few coins required for a bus or the pay telephone. My address book was also at Miriam's and I could remember none of the phone numbers in it. I did not even have a handkerchief with which to wipe the perspiration from my forehead. I felt a gnawing in my stomach, and a nauseating fluid filled my mouth. Although I had taken a beating, I could not help marveling how clever Providence—or whatever one calls that force which rules the fate of men—had been, in arranging for my downfall. As in Job's days of yore, everything happened with extraordinary speed, one blow after another.

I had to find a place to rest, to wash up, to shave. Fortunately, I remembered that Stefa Kreitle lived nearby, in an apartment no more than ten blocks away. During the war years we had lost contact and I was sure that she had perished. Suddenly in 1947 she showed up in New York with her husband, Leon Kreitle, and her grown-up daughter, Franka, and again it was a case of a resurrection from the dead. I was forty-three then, and she was close to fifty. Leon was seventy-five, an old man. They had managed to flee to England only a few days before Hitler entered Poland. Leon's two daughters had died in the camps. Of course he had lost his entire fortune. Stefa had become a chambermaid in London, and later a nurse. We had stopped corresponding even before the war. I had gone through a personal crisis in New York at the time and fallen into melancholy. I had stopped going to the editorial office and had practically severed my connections with the Yiddish language, Yiddish literature, the Yiddishist movement.

Between 1947 and the beginning of the fifties, major changes took place both in Stefa's life and in my own. Leon had found friends in America and a partner with whose help he built low-cost houses on Long Island, and almost overnight he was affluent once again. Stefa's daughter, Franka, had married a Gentile. During her childhood years in Danzig, Franka had absorbed the Nazi hatred of Jews, and in America she adopted the Catholic faith of her husband, an engineer. She broke off all contact with her mother and stepfather.

My life had changed as well. I had begun to write again. I had published a novel and a collection of stories in Yiddish, and found a translator and a publisher in English. I had become a steady contributor to the Yiddish paper, writing essays, reviews, and various columns. I also dispensed advice on the Yiddish radio. I had now reestablished contact with Stefa, and whenever I saw her I had the uncanny feeling that I was with a ghost, one of those I used to write stories about. Our years apart had built a kind of wall between us. Stefa spoke English with a London accent, and what little Yiddish she had learned in Warsaw she had forgotten. She had apparently had affairs in London, although she never discussed them. This was not the same Stefa who used to quarrel with me, call me "Literatnik," and correct my Polish. This Stefa was a well-mannered lady, the grandmother of a small child. Her knees were no longer pointed, they had rounded out; her bosom was higher now and her hips were fuller. Only her treatment of Leon remained the same, and she murmured that she would never know what he was. Sometimes she added, "The whole masculine gender is a riddle to me."

Leon, on the other hand, had scarcely changed. He had no hair on his head, his face was so bony and the skin so taut that he had no wrinkles, and he still weighed no more than one hundred pounds. Eighty years old, Leon still conducted business, had houses built, bought lots, speculated in stocks and securities. They had an apartment in a skyscraper at Central Park West and Seventy-second Street. Leon still reproached me for my infrequent visits. He had begun to read the Yiddish paper in America, perhaps because he never fully learned English. He was curiously fired up about my writings. He never ceased to ask questions: Did everything I wrote really happen? Did I invent it all myself? How was it possible to make up accounts which seemed so real? And when did I do my inventing—at night, daytime, asleep, awake? He assured me that in Warsaw he had known characters and types exactly like those I portrayed—I had only changed their names, he would smile at me and wink. Other times he would complain, "Where do you find these words and expressions? I have not heard them since my grandmother Chaya-Keyla died. And how do you remember the streets of Warsaw so well when I have almost forgotten them. What sort of a creature is a writer? Tell me, I want to know."

"Mostly a liar," Stefa said.

"A liar, huh? Yes, it must be so. But still, when I wake up in the morning I go straightaway to Broadway to buy the Yiddish paper. I want to know what happened next. But then again, in your novel, how could a man such as Calman—prosperous, wise, a clever merchant—allow himself to be so deceived by that Clara? Couldn't he see that she wanted his money, not himself? Did you really know such a person? *Nu*, that Clara is a sly one. She is—how do they say?—worth a sin or two, he-he-he. Above all, a person needs luck. I myself knew a woman like that who had all the virtues: pretty, clever, a fine piece of goods. But if things didn't go as they should for her, everything went topsy-turvy."

The day before Max Aberdam had first dropped into my office, I had promised to have dinner with Stefa and Leon and to spend the night in their apartment. Then weeks had passed and I had forgotten to ring them up. Leon had actually visited my office, and when he did not find me he left a message consisting of a single, badly misspelled Hebrew word which meant "Can it be?" He signed it, "Your sincere friend and ardent admirer, Leon Kreitle."

Luck was with me this time. The doorman on duty at Stefa and Leon's apartment knew me and let me in. He even signaled the night elevator man to take me to the eighth floor. I rang the bell and Leon, after peeking through the peephole, opened the door. He was wearing an ornate robe and plush slippers. He looked at me with curiosity and mockery. He spoke in his ironic manner: "Imagine! A guest so early! Has the Messiah come? Or did you run away from Sing-Sing?"

"Both."

"Come in, come in. Stefa is still asleep, but I, as usual, woke up at five. Why didn't you phone? I am preparing breakfast and you are cordially invited to join me. Forgive me for giving you a Jewish compliment, but you don't look well. Has something happened?"

"No, but . . ."

"Come with me to the kitchen, where the coffee is brewing. There is no better remedy for every woe and affliction than a good strong cup of coffee. You look sleepy, probably been up all night saying *slikhes*. I understand, I understand."

Leon took my arm and led me into a sort of dining area, separated from the kitchen by a room divider. Slices of bread and a bowl of fruit were already set out on the table. Leon pointed to a metal chair and said, "As you can see, I have kept all my old habits. Only the wine with which I used to wash down my food is missing. But giving it up didn't help at all—I've already had two heart attacks. One cannot outsmart God. But who knows? Maybe if I had not stuck to my diet I would have had three heart attacks, or perhaps died. At eighty one should have no complaints against God, especially when He does not exist. You probably take me for an ignoramus, but in my youth I studied. My father was a pious Jew, a learned Jew. What will you have? I can make eggs for you, even an omelet."

"Whatever you give me will be fine. I am grateful to you."

"Ah, I forgot your orange juice. Just a second!"

I sat down, again feeling the weakness in my legs. Leon handed me a glass of orange juice.

"Drink. *L'chaim*. You used to be a frequent visitor to our house. Lately for some reason we rarely see you. Ah, here is Stefa!"

Stefa entered the kitchen looking sleepy, her gray hair somewhat in disarray. She was wearing a lace nightgown and had pompommed slippers on her feet. She looked healthy for her age and would have looked even younger had she dyed her hair, but to Stefa this would have meant giving in to Americanization and vulgarity. She looked at me, surprised, smiling with the mocking reproach one shows to a close friend or relative who suddenly turns up unannounced. She said, "Am I dreaming, or is it you?"

"No, Stefele, you are not dreaming," I said.

" 'Stefele,' huh? You haven't called me that in decades. What happened? Someone sent you packing in the middle of the night? Did her husband suddenly show up with a gun?"

Hardly believing my own ears, I said, "Yes, exactly so."

"Well, I am not surprised. As usual I lay awake for half the night. At daybreak I finally fell asleep. All at once I heard voices in the kitchen. I asked myself, Has Leon reached the stage where he speaks to himself, or have I gone senile?"

"Let him eat, let him drink his coffee. As far as I can remember, this is the first time that I have served your lover breakfast. If one waits long enough, one is rewarded. Sit down, Stefele, I'll serve you, too. Let's live it up, 'There is a fair in Heaven'."

"Well, all right. All I want is a cup of coffee. But make it strong."

Stefa spoke to her husband in both Polish and English. Sometimes she threw in a Yiddish word. She sat at the table and said, "It's strange, but we spoke of you last night. Leon is reading your serialized novel to me. We always wake up at five minutes before two. Leon wakes me up because he begins to hum to himself, and I am a light sleeper. What will be the end of this Clara of yours? Whenever I try to guess what's next in the novel, you turn the plot upside down. Is this a method of yours?"

"It is life's method."

"That's what I told her," Leon chimed in. "Life is more thrilling than novels can ever be. Thirty years ago if someone had told me that in my old age I would be an American and the co-owner of a hotel in Miami Beach, I would have thought him mad. Your lover once wrote an article in which he said that God was a novelist and the world His novel. It is precisely so. And if not God, then some other force runs our little world."

"Perhaps you'll stop referring to Aaron as 'your lover,'" Stefa said angrily.

"What is he, then? Your father, Leibush-Meir?" Leon asked.

"He is everything, but not my lover. A lover loves, but he does not know what love is. Look at him now. What was it my mother used to say: 'At least he's better-looking than he'll look in the grave.'"

"Wait, I have to make a phone call. I'll be right back!" Leon sprang from his chair and hurried out of the kitchen in small tripping steps.

Stefa said, "He keeps complaining how old and sick he is, but he has the energy of a young man with all his business affairs. Really, what did happen to you?" Stefa's voice changed. "As far as I can remember, you and I never did have breakfast together before."

"Yes, we did. Once."

"When was it? In King Sobieski's days?"

"When I lived with Lena in Otwock. I telephoned you from the Danzig train station and you told me you had a pack of letters for me. I had already had my meager breakfast that morning, but you forced me to eat once again with you."

"My God, the man has an uncanny memory! Yes, you are right. How long has it been? Eternity twice over?"

"I remember it as if it happened yesterday."

"Yes, yes. You dragged me to that idiotic Hebrew teacher's apartment, and he unceremoniously showed us out. For some reason that particular breakfast slipped my mind."

"That particular breakfast saved my life."

"You were no good then and with the years you have grown worse, not better. You even write about me in your stories, using

all sorts of strange and false names, but I recognize myself. Even
Leon recognizes me and himself as well. In the midst of his
reading he says: '*Your* appearance, *your* words.' Arale, your own
appearance this morning worries me. Are you ill or what?"

"I am not ill."

"What, then? Mad?"

"So it seems."

"Well, you have made your own bed. Believe me, I don't
begrudge you your women. When I returned from England and
you told me of your life here I said to you, 'Let us be friends,
no more than that.' We cannot be complete strangers because
what had taken place between us God Himself cannot erase. I
endured enough in England and had no desire to enmesh myself
in new complications. To become involved with you and your
women is to condemn a healthy body to a sickbed. Nevertheless,
for the sake of our friendship I ask you, Why are you killing
yourself and destroying your talent? What is the sense of it?"

"No sense at all."

"What happened to you?"

"I cannot stay at home, I mean in my room, and I cannot go
to my office. I need a few days' rest."

"You know you can rest here as long as you like. Franka's
room is free and it's yours now. You can eat and sleep here.
Have no fear, I won't rape you."

"I have no fear of that."

"Is someone after you, threatening you?"

"No, but I need to hide out for several days."

"My home is your home. Leon is even more devoted to you
than I am. Why, I will never know. This may sound strange and
wild, but I can renounce you, whereas he cannot. Today he
called you my lover. Sometimes he says 'your second husband.'
He has convinced himself that once he is gone we will rush to
stand under the wedding canopy."

"He will undoubtedly outlive me."

"I believe so, too. What can I do for you now?"

"Nothing. I need nothing more than rest."

"Go into Franka's room and rest. I'll ask you no more questions."

"Stefa, you are the finest person I know."

"Liar, scoundrel!"

"I must kiss you!"

"If you must, you must."

I retired to Franka's room, where the window opened out on the park and the sun shone in. The room had a bed, a desk, bookshelves. Franka had hung up photographs of film stars, as well as portraits of her grandfathers, her grandmothers, and her aunt who had died young from too much dancing. On one wall I saw a photograph of a young Polish officer riding a horse—it was Mark, Franka's father.

That day it was as good as decided that I would come to live with Stefa and Leon. Despite my protests, Stefa announced that she planned to add a sofa to Franka's room, as well as a cabinet for my books, my manuscripts, and the installments of my novel clipped from the newspaper. Leon was going to present me with a gift—a new Yiddish typewriter. At every opportunity he repeated the same thing: since it was ordained that after his death I should become Stefa's new husband, why not begin now? "You'll be spared from praying for my death," Leon said, and Stefa retorted, "If these foolish fantasies give you pleasure, go ahead and dream."

I had prerecorded tapes of my radio talks weeks in advance, but by Monday I knew I had to return to my office at the newspaper. I telephoned the young man who was the receptionist and he informed me that many advice seekers had come to my office in my absence. He had assigned numbers to them, after the fashion of a busy bakery. Monday, after breakfast, I also

planned to go to my own room on Seventieth Street and retrieve
the manuscripts I had left there. I promised Stefa to give that
room up and move in with them. I said I would at least pay for
my meals, but both husband and wife told me I was insulting
them. Just when I had begun to earn good wages and had even
managed to put some money in the bank, I felt I was becoming
a parasite. Leon began to drop hints about rewriting his will,
making Stefa and me the executors. I protested, but he answered
me shrewdly, "It is *my* will, not yours."

Stefa muttered, "At eighty he is beginning to act like a child."

THE DAY PROMISED to be a hot one. I was still without my keys
and my checkbook. At least I knew Miriam was alive. I had
dialed her on Sunday and hung up when I heard her voice. It
was possible that Stanley was with her, holding her captive in
her apartment. Perhaps he had forced a reconciliation on her.
Again I vowed to have no more to do with Miriam—neither with
her nor with Max Aberdam, who was probably in Poland by now.
I could easily obtain another checkbook and a new key to my
safety-deposit box. Fortune had smiled upon me—no sooner did
I lose one pillar supporting my existence than another took its
place. True, it had happened only because I was never able to
terminate any of my relationships. Whatever I began seemed to
trail behind me forever, both in my writing and in my life.

When I came to my rooming house on Seventieth Street, the
entrance door was open, apparently to let in the air. I began to
climb the stairs to my room when I heard the telephone ring in
the hallway. I quickly ran down, grabbed the receiver, and
shouted into it, "Hello!" There was a murmuring at the other
end, the rustling of someone who could not decide whether to
answer or not. Finally I heard Miriam's voice, weak and quiv-
ering: "It's me, the whore."

I made a motion as if to hang up the receiver, but it was as if it clung to my hand. I either did not want to or could not speak, and Miriam continued, "You left your keys in my apartment, also your checkbook and some money. Like the whore whom Judah visited, I want to return 'thy signet, thy bracelet, and thy staff.' "

Miriam spoke the words in English, and I realized she had taken them from the Pentateuch. Some forty years had passed since I learned these phrases in Yehiel the Melamed's *cheder* on Krochmalna Street. Miriam had apparently found the story in the Bible in English. I said, "Tamar pretended to be a prostitute but you *are* one."

"Then how was it that a man as saintly as Judah went to her?" Miriam asked.

"Miriam, this is not the time to discuss tales from the Pentateuch."

"When is the proper time? I want to give you your things. I may be a whore but I am not a thief."

Again I wanted to put down the receiver, and again some physical power restrained me. I heard myself asking, "Where are you?"

"Near the Broadway Cafeteria, where we ate together," Miriam said. "I have your things with me. If you are ashamed to be seen with a whore, I can bring them to your room."

"Miriam, everything is finished between us."

"I know, but I want to return your property."

There was a pleading in her voice. I finally said, "Meet me at the cafeteria."

"Good. I'll be there in five minutes."

As I put down the receiver, I began to murmur a vow never, never, never again to have any dealings with this harlot.

I went out in the street and for a while walked away from the cafeteria, in the direction of the Hudson River. Then I reversed

myself and began to walk back. The fact that Miriam had telephoned the moment I entered the house meant that she had
phoned repeatedly before. The thought that Stanley might follow her and shoot us both also entered my mind. I was glad I
could recover my keys and my checkbook without the usual red
tape. I knew I had been neglecting my work. A writer whose
novels appear in installments is never free. If he takes his work
seriously, his own existence begins to occur in installments. He
must continuously seek out the surprises, the twists, the unexpected events that correspond to what Spinoza called the order
of things and the order of ideas. I told myself not to hurry. Let
Miriam wait. But my feet hurried on just the same, as if of their
own accord. Perhaps they were eager to know how that early-
morning visit with Stanley had ended. When passersby walked
toward me, I tried avoiding them by steering to the right, but
they steered to the left and we almost collided. This happened
several times. We either did a sort of dance with each other or
we blocked each other's way. When I reached Eightieth Street,
I saw Miriam on the opposite corner and waited for the red light
to turn green.

Yes, it was Miriam, but she looked different. She wore a short
red dress and a pair of red boots. Her stockings, too, were red.
Her cheeks were thickly painted with rouge, and her eyelashes
were blue and black with mascara. From her scarlet lips a cigarette dangled at the end of a long cigarette holder. Instantly I
understood what she had done. She had decked herself out in
the manner of the Warsaw prostitutes. Even the cigarette in the
long holder was typical of Warsaw. She had planned it all—the
quote from the Pentateuch and the clothing she now wore. I
saw passersby following her with their eyes, shrugging their
shoulders, smiling. The thought, Surely I will be arrested if I
walk with her, flitted through my brain. The traffic light changed
and I was ready to cross the street. Just then a giant truck ap-

peared from Seventy-ninth Street and obstructed Miriam from view. I was forced to circle around the monster, which was as high as a house. I heard honking, and a car suddenly darted out of a nearby side street and nearly ran me over. I could feel the heat of its engine and smell the fumes of gasoline as the car sped by. Was I going to be killed because I was overly zealous to meet this girl, who spoke not a word of truth, who made fools of Max, myself, Stanley, and the devil knew who else? "Filth! Filth! She is utterly immersed in debauchery and deception," I said to myself. And once again I vowed that this would be the last time I saw her vile face.

WE SAT IN the cafeteria, although this time our table was not near the window but tucked away in a corner. Several patrons glanced at us with surprise, but no one approached us or spoke to us. After some time Miriam wiped the rouge and the mascara off her face. We were drinking coffee and she spoke: "Yes, this is what I was and what I shall always be. I don't feel guilty, not for a minute. It was foolish at sixteen to fall in love with a scoundrel like Yanek and to endure all I have endured. But what is the sense of feeling remorse, which is a religious concept. If one does not believe in a personal God or in sexual morality, how can there be any repentance? I endured the whole sordid game, and I must add that I had my good moments, too. I was almost always drunk during those days. It was better to be where I was than to roam among the ruins of the ghetto. I was prepared to die, and the fact that I survived and emerged at least physically sound is something I cannot explain. If I have any regrets, it is that I kept the truth from you and Max. But the truth surfaced anyway; as they say—like oil on water."

"A person like you should not even breathe the word 'truth.' "

"You wrote once that behind every lie there hides a truth. Not in the Freudian sense, but clearly and objectively."

"The truth is that you are the greatest scoundrel I have had the misfortune to meet."

"Maybe so. But it is still a fact that I have lived, suffered, hoped. You once quoted Spinoza, saying that there were no lies, only distorted truths. Even a worm has its own small truth. It is born, it lives briefly, then it is trampled under someone's foot. Those are your words, not mine." An expression akin to victory appeared in Miriam's eyes.

I heard myself asking, "What happened that morning after I left?" And immediately I regretted my words.

"You want to know, huh?"

"You are not obliged to answer."

For a while Miriam did not speak. "Things happened. Stanley stayed with me that whole day and the following night. I did not expect to live out the night, and I was prepared to die. You don't have to believe me, but I have lived for years with death. I know it as well as I know my own body. Stanley was not the first to threaten me with a revolver. That same Yanek for whom I had sacrificed my life amused himself by shooting a glass tumbler which he put on my head. He brought his colleagues— Poles, not Germans—and they played the same game. This is but one of hundreds of true stories, whether you believe them or not. Don't think that I have come to you to cry or to apologize. I owe you nothing—not you, not even Max."

"Where is Max?" I asked.

"Max is in Poland."

"Did you see him before he left?"

"No. How could I? The telephone rang, but Stanley forbade me to pick it up. I found out that the morning after the party Max left for Poland together with Matilda Treibitcher."

"How did you get rid of your husband?"

The beginning of a smile appeared in Miriam's eyes. "My husband, huh? Since he didn't kill me, sooner or later he had to be on his way. Before he left he said that he was ready to divorce me. It was funny, really funny."

"Why was it funny?"

"He couldn't decide whether to kill me or not. He kept talking about it and finally he asked my advice. Have you ever heard such a thing? The murderer asks his victim for advice. In the midst of my so-called tragedy, I simply had to laugh."

"What was your advice?"

"My advice was: Do what you like."

"Is this one of your fabrications?"

"No, it's the truth."

"What happened then?"

"He said goodbye and left. One minute he spoke about killing and the next he babbled about a reconciliation. He even proposed that we have a child together. I would not have believed it to be possible, except that after what I have seen in my life, I am no longer astonished. Nothing can shock me anymore. If the heavens were to split open this very moment and God were to walk into this cafeteria surrounded by a host of angels or demons, I would not even blink. You may be a writer, you are a writer, but what the human race is capable of I know better than you do."

"What about your teacher and the dark alcove in which you allegedly spent the war years—was that also a lie?"

"It was not a lie. I didn't struggle hard to stay alive—what for? But a sort of ambition grew in me to overcome everything and to come through those swinish times alive and strong. I would say it became a sort of gamble or sport for me: will I make it, or will I not? You often write that life is a game, a wager, or something similar. I had decided to slip out of the hands of the Angel of Death at any cost. When it became clear to me that any day I would be grabbed and sent away with one of the transports, I fled, and my former teacher took me in."

"When was that?"

"The end of 1942. No, it was already 1943."

"Did your teacher know of your conduct?" I asked.

"Yes; no. Who knows?"

"And it was at her house that you read all those books?"

"Yes, at her house."

"And then what happened?"

"In 1945 I crawled out, like a mouse from its hole, and another chapter began—wandering, sneaking across borders, sleeping in barns, in ditches, and all the rest."

"What happened to your pimp?"

"Yanek is dead."

"Killed in the uprising?"

"Someone gave him his due."

"That's exactly what men do, they kill one another to show that Malthus was right," I said.

A smile played on Miriam's lips. "Is this your theory?"

"As good as any other theory."

We sat in silence for a long time. Miriam picked up her cup, took a sip, and said, "The coffee is cold."

We went outside and began to walk toward Central Park West. People passed by, staring at us. Men smiled at Miriam's strange appearance, women shook their heads with disapproval. Miriam said, "Look, I forgot to give you your things. I have them here in my bag—your money, keys, checkbook."

She made a motion to open her bag but I said, "Not here in the street."

"Where did Tamar return his belongings to Judah?" Miriam asked.

"She sent them with a messenger. Earlier he wanted to send her a little goat, but the messenger could not find her. When she was taken to the pyre to be burnt, she sent him back his *mashkones*."

"Ah, you remember everything. I read the story only a few days ago, and already I forgot it."

"You read it, but I learned it in *cheder*."

"Children in *cheder* were taught such things?"

"Sooner or later, children know everything."

"A goat in exchange for one visit with a prostitute is not a bad bargain," Miriam said, and laughed.

"Evidently Tamar was a good-looking woman."

"How was it that an important figure, after whom all Jews were later named, found it necessary to visit a prostitute? And why does the Bible tell us about it? And why did Judah send her the little goat? Would you ask someone from your office to take a goat to a prostitute?"

This was so outlandish that I had to laugh. Miriam also burst out laughing. After a while I said, "Those were idolatrous times. The prostitute was associated with the temple. She represented an institution, not unlike that of the geisha in Japan."

"Why can't the institution exist today? Pretend that you are Judah and I am Tamar. You left as your *mashkon* with me your checkbook, your money, your keys. If you have no one by whom to send me a goat, pay me yourself."

"What is your price?"

"Still a goat."

Suddenly Miriam began to sing:

> *Taigelekh, migele, kozinka,*
> *Red pomegranates.*
> *When Papa begins to beat Mama,*
> *The children all dance.*

We had come to a bench outside Central Park and we sat down. Miriam turned serious again. She said, "What has really changed from ancient times? The idol worshippers are still with us and so are the idols. What was Hitler if not an idol? And Stalin? And what are the actors and actresses of Hollywood who receive sacks of love letters and whose photographs circle the globe? It's the same Yentl in a new mantle. Whores are certainly the same, even if they graduate from college or write dissertations about you. What would restrain a person like me? While we were in Warsaw my mother flitted about with all sorts of riffraff. She was ostensibly a Communist and an actress. She was as much an actress as I am a *rebbetzin*. It was all a pretext for her to have affairs with men. My father was no better. Heaven knows how many mistresses he had. He sent me to a Gymnasium where I was taught Hebrew and Bible, but he took neither one seriously. He insisted that a Jewish girl like me must observe the Sabbath, while he himself broke all the Sabbath laws. All worldly Jews are like that. In Germany my father was a smuggler. My mother carried on a love affair with a journalist who was half Jewish. And what do you think goes on in the Jewish state? Except for the religious ones in Mea Shearim, they are all far from saintly. And you yourself? And Max? And that idiot Stanley? None of you has a right to point a finger at me. How am I worse than the girls in my college? Heaven knows how many men my class-mates had. And what of the women whose husbands lavish furs and jewelry and Cadillacs on them while they while away their own time with all sorts of trash? I, at least, was trying to rescue my stinking life. Most of the Jewish girls who fell into Nazi hands would have done the same had they been given the chance."

"I preach no morality, and there is no need to explain yourself to me," I said.

"You *do* preach, you called me a whore. How am I a whore any more than you are a lecher? What are all you writers, you artists? If there is no God and man has evolved from a monkey, why can I not do as I please?"

"If all women conducted themselves as you do, no man would know if he was the father of his children. You know yourself what happened in Russia after the Revolution, when prostitution became a proletarian virtue. Hundreds of thousands of thieves, criminals, murderers appeared on the streets. They came near to destroying Russia. What would become of our Jewish remnant if Jewish girls became as licentious as you are?"

"They are already licentious. All the Jewish girls in my college had affairs with Gentiles. Even those who got married or joined synagogues were thoroughly assimilated. Jewishness in America consists in sending checks to Israel or belonging to Hadassah. And I hear that things are no different in the Jewish state."

We sat for a long time without speaking, looking straight ahead. We had apparently walked uptown, because the bench on which we sat was not far from the Treibitchers' apartment building. Miriam suddenly stirred.

"Here are your *mashkones*." She opened her handbag and handed me my keys, my checkbook, and the dollars she had put in an envelope. She said, "You can tell Max everything that happened. Just remember that I can manage without men, too. If you like, this can be our last meeting."

We rose from the bench and entered the park, walking in silence until we reached the pond. The morning had been sunny, but now clouds covered the sky. There was a hint of rain in the air and a trace of approaching autumn. Flocks of birds flew and squawked across the water. I could not continue to meet with Miriam, but neither could I bring myself to part from her.

What was the next step? I often had the feeling that whatever one would say or do, the future would merely be a repetition of the past. Stefa had offered me a home and I had accepted. She had grown plump, middle-aged, and often bitter. She bore a grudge against her married daughter and brooded over her unceasingly. "Franka loathes Jews," she would say. "She resents me. What harm have I done her?" No, I could not go to live with Stefa and Leon. I could not bear Leon's strange discourses, the hints about his will, the endless chatter about my writings. He managed to praise me and, in his primitive way, to sting me. Somehow he understood my passions and illusions, and derided them with the derision of an old man who has seen the vanity of life.

Twilight came and Miriam and I were still walking. The park gradually emptied of people and soon we were alone. The day had been a long one. The red sun hung in the sky, like a huge ball of fire. It did not shine, it glowed. To me it seemed as if, because of some error of astronomy, the sun had forgotten to set and hung in the sky lost and confused. I often fantasized about a cosmic change taking place before my eyes. The earth would tear away from the sun—and then? Could God cause some sort of renewal in the world? But why would it be any different when the people were people as before?

Miriam took my arm, but the touch of her fingers on my skin annoyed me and I removed them one by one. She spoke of the destruction of Warsaw, the Polish uprising, the Nazi atrocities, and I wanted to hear no more. For some reason she clung to me. Could such a woman feel love? I noticed that she continuously changed the subject of her conversation, probably from fear of boring me. I wondered selfishly if I had gained the upper hand over Miriam, that biological power which exists in all species, all genera, among men, women, animals, birds—a sort of universal pecking order. I no longer needed to please her, I could spout out every variety of nonsense and absurdity. I heard her asking, "What do you think will become of Yiddish?"

Had she just cooked up the question, or was it connected with something she had said that I had not heard? I decided to answer seriously. "The language will become progressively richer, but those who speak it will be poorer. The Yiddishists will become a band of beggars and will write poems that no one will read. The writers will carry backpacks of manuscripts so heavy that they will stagger under the weight. They will plot a revolution to take place not on earth but in—"

Miriam suddenly interrupted me: "Look at that!"

We had reached the southern border of Central Park. The windows of all the skyscrapers were reflecting an eerie glow, as if an immense wall of glass were glowing of and by itself. It was a beautiful sight, except that the light made the buildings seem empty and devoid of humankind. I was reminded of a story told by Rabbi Nachman of Bratzlav about a palace in which a long table had been set for a royal feast, even though the palace had been abandoned for scores of years.

Miriam said, "Don't laugh, but I'm hungry."

"That's no cause for laughter."

"Butterfly! May I *still* call you Butterfly?"

"You may even call me Nachbi ben Vafsi."

"What sort of name is that?"

"It's from the Pentateuch. There was also a writer who used the name himself—I forget if he wrote in Yiddish or in Hebrew."

"Butterfly, I can no longer live without you. That is the bitter truth."

I halted, as did Miriam. "So soon?" I asked. I actually felt that it was not I who spoke. I had granted a sort of autonomy to my mouth and it worked of its own accord.

"With me everything happens quickly. Either quickly or not at all," Miriam answered.

"And what about Max?"

"I miss him, too."

"And Stanley?"

Miriam shivered. "Don't mention his name, may it be cursed!"

"Where would you like to eat?"

Miriam did not answer. She took my arm and pressed it hard enough to hurt. She said, "Butterfly, I have an idea. But promise not to laugh at it."

"I will not laugh."

"Since you already know the truth about me, let everything remain as it is."

"Let what remain as it is?"

"I will be a prostitute and you will be my client. My apartment will be our brothel. You will pay me—but I will be cheap. A dollar a week, or ten cents a night. There were cheap prostitutes of that sort in Warsaw, in fact on your street, on Krochmalna. Am I less desirable than they? You will get yourself a real bargain. I will even cook for you. People grab bargains in all sorts of places. I will be your bargain. You can call me whore; that will be my name from this day on."

"What about Max?"

"He will call me that, too. I no longer want to play deceptive games. I want to be an honest prostitute."

Something in me wanted to laugh, and I also felt a stinging in my eyes.

"And what of the others?" I asked.

"What others? There will be no others."

"A prostitute with two clients only?"

"Yes, you and Max. If Max does not want me, I'll be yours alone. I remember a story in the Bible about a prophet who married a whore. But I don't want to be married, I simply want to be a whore."

"What shall we do now?" I asked.

"Give me ten cents."

"In advance?"

"In Warsaw they always paid in advance."

"Wait."

I dug in my trouser pocket until I found a dime. Miriam stretched out her hand.

"Here!" I put it in her palm.

She held the coin for a while and stared at it. Then she took it with her other hand and held it to her lips. "This is the happiest night of my life," she said.

PART II

SEVEN

TWO WEEKS PASSED and we heard nothing from Max. Could he have been arrested in Communist Poland? I phoned Chaim Joel Treibitcher, but no one was at home. I spent the night with Miriam, not in her own apartment but in the Park Avenue apartment of the lesbian whose child Miriam looked after. Miriam had introduced me to the lady of the house—Lynn Stallner—a tall woman with green eyes and fiery red hair cut in a masculine style, and with freckles sprinkled on her face and hands. Her nose was short, her lips full. Her companion, Sylvia, was short and dark. They had both divorced their husbands. The couple had gone for a summer vacation to Martha's Vineyard and Miriam was to care for the child. In the plush apartment on Park Avenue Miriam prepared meals for herself and me. We drank wine from Lynn Stallner's bookish wine cellar. During the day, while Miriam took the boy Didi to the park and the playground, I sat in Lynn Stallner's library and read her books. I also made notes of new themes and ideas. Sometimes I leafed through the Yiddish newspaper which Miriam would bring up in the morning.

There was a telephone in every room of the apartment and I often telephoned Stefa. Our conversations were almost always the same. Where was I hiding myself these hot summer days? She wanted to know why I didn't come to see her. She and Leon were preparing for a month's stay at a hotel in Atlantic City. They would gladly take me along. Stefa complained, "I am disappointed in you, Arale. Instead of concentrating on your work, you are prancing about with all sorts of riffraff. I believed in you and your talent, but you are doing everything you can to ruin yourself. Leon is enthusiastic about your Yiddish writing, but who reads Yiddish in America? You are stuck in a swamp and you will never get out of it. Scribblers twenty years younger than you are growing rich and famous while you cling to something that is sick, decaying, more dead than alive. Leon offered to pay for someone to translate your work into English. Others would jump at the chance he gave you, but you do nothing to extricate yourself from the fix you're in."

"Stefele, literature is not so important to me that I should become a beggar for it."

"What *is* important? I could understand if you were a pious Jew, as your father was, or a Zionist who wanted to rebuild the Jewish land. What you are doing, your entire conduct, is sheer suicide. Where are you speaking from?"

"From my office."

"Liar, you are not at your office."

"How do you know?"

"I called you at the office and they told me you were not there."

"Why did you call?"

"Because Leon concluded his business earlier than he expected and we are leaving for Atlantic City tomorrow. I called to say goodbye."

"Goodbye, Stefele. Have a good summer."

"Where are you?"

I waited and then I said, "I have become a babysitter for a lesbian mother."

"Are you poking fun at me, or what?"

"I am not poking fun."

"Wait a second, someone is ringing the doorbell. I'll be right back."

Stefa went to her door and I remained sitting with the receiver at my ear. Earlier I had put the morning paper on my lap, and now I had a chance to leaf through it. Suddenly I saw a headline spread over several columns: HARRY TREIBITCHER COMMITS SUICIDE. Something in me shuddered. Harry Treibitcher, or Hershele, was the stockbroker whom Max had entrusted with his refugee clients' money. The paper reported that Treibitcher had hung himself while in detention for the misappropriation of stocks and securities. It stated that he was the nephew of Chaim Joel Treibitcher, an eminent philanthropist long active in community affairs. I heard Stefa's voice, "Arale."

"Yes, Stefele."

"It was the mailman with a registered letter for Leon. What were you prattling about a babysitter and a lesbian? Are you drunk, or what?"

"I am not drunk, but I just read in today's paper that someone who speculated with the money of Polish refugees, people from my parts, has taken his own life. This is simply a catastrophe."

"You entrusted him with money?"

"I didn't, but a good friend of mine did. Perhaps you have heard of Max Aberdam?"

"No, who is he? Where are you calling from? Who is the lesbian?"

"Max Aberdam is a friend of mine from Warsaw. He has a mistress here in New York, a student. She is the lesbian's babysitter."

"What has that to do with you?"

"The student is writing a dissertation about my work. She invited me to see what she has written. She made a great many errors and I am trying to set them right."

"Really, I am beginning to believe you have lost your mind," Stefa said. "No university will accept a dissertation about the work of an unknown Yiddish writer. You always involve yourself with people who do nothing but take up your time. I cannot bear New York summers and we are leaving for Atlantic City tomorrow. But as you are well aware, to spend a month with Leon day in and day out is quite unbearable. Here in New York he has his business affairs and he leaves me alone. But once we are in the country he has only me, and it is difficult to shake him off. If you were to come with us, we would all enjoy ourselves. I want you to have our address so that if you grow bored with your lunatics and the hangers-on who sap your energy, you can call and join us. Find a pencil and take this down . . ."

Stefa dictated the name of their hotel, the address, the telephone number, and then asked, "What was his name, your friend, the one you mentioned before?"

"Max Aberdam."

"Is he the one who took his life?"

"No, his broker, his stockbroker."

"I never heard of him, but Leon will know who he is. What does all this have to do with you and the lesbian?"

"It's all bound up together."

"Well, so be it, goodbye. Only God can help you!"

No sooner had I put down the receiver than the telephone rang again. It was Miriam. She asked in an agitated voice, "Why were you speaking with someone so long?"

"It was someone in my office."

"Arale, Max is ill!" she cried out.

"Ill in Poland? How do you know?"

"I wheeled Didi in his stroller to my own apartment and the super had a cable for me from Warsaw. My heart told me that something was wrong. Max is in the hospital. He had an operation!"

"God in heaven, what happened?"

"All it says is that he had an operation. I know that he had a kidney problem. I was afraid of this trip of his. As soon as I heard he was going to Poland I knew he was heading for disaster. Here in New York he has a doctor who knows all his problems, who looks after him. But the doctors in Warsaw, especially after the war, are probably all youngsters, students."

"What does the cable say exactly?"

"That he had an operation and that he will cable me from Switzerland. And warm regards for you."

"Where in Switzerland?"

"He gives no address. He is probably going there to rest. I know that Matilda Treibitcher has a villa somewhere in Switzerland. You know, of course, that she is with him."

For a moment we were both silent. Then I said, "Miriam, it seems that with us one calamity follows on the heels of another. Harry Treibitcher, or Hershele, as you call him, committed suicide."

"What? I can't believe it!"

I read the account in the paper to her. Miriam began to speak in a singsong Warsaw lament. "This will kill Max! This is the end of Max—my life, too. Without him I don't want to live. Arale, my punishment has come at last. Max entrusted Harry with all his money—not only his own but his clients' as well. When it comes to money, Max is exceptionally honorable. When he hears this, his heart will break. Ah, I don't want to live any longer. Butterfly, you have just put a knife through my chest."

"Miriam dear, I couldn't keep this news from you."

"No, no, how could you? This is a calamity, a catastrophe.

Priva will have nothing, nothing. I warned Max, I told him. The very first time I met you I told you that Harry was a swindler and a gambler. He played the horses and drove around in a Rolls-Royce. He chased after prostitutes, not cheap ones like me but those who demand a high price for their services—actresses, models, opera singers, the devil knows who. Max knew all about Harry's escapades, but he considered him a financial genius, like his uncle Chaim Joel. For all his faults, the uncle is a Jew of the old school, but Harry was a charlatan, a libertine, a thief. Someone told me he had a private airplane. What does anyone need an airplane for? What a scoundrel! This was not simply money"—Miriam's voice grew louder—"this was gut money, blood money, reparation money which mothers received for their children. Ah, wait a minute . . ."

Through the telephone I could hear coughing, wheezing. I also heard Didi's sobs. "Miriam, what is the matter?"

"Nothing, nothing. Wait. *Sha*, Didile! *Sha, oytzerl*, sweet *ne-shome*. Here, drink. Arale, as soon as I calm the child down I'll bring him back. I want to tell you only one thing more."

"What?"

"Butterfly, fly away, run! If you are not completely blind you must have seen the muck I've dragged you into: theft, robbery, prostitution, an ocean of filth. You were a hairbreadth away from being shot by Stanley. What do you need this for? You are a creative person, you need rest, peace. Why should you be roasting in my inferno?"

"Tell me these things later, Miriam, not on the telephone."

"I'll see you very soon." And Miriam hung up.

I was too restless to remain in my chair. I stood and moved to the sofa across the room. True, of what real concern to me was the health of Max Aberdam? Why did I fret over Chaim Joel Treibitcher's swindling nephew? Or Priva, or Tzlova, or Irka Shmelkes and her mixed-up son, Edek? I had to put an end to this tangle of personalities and return to my work. But how was I to free myself, what precisely should I do? It was impossible to work in my room on Seventieth Street. All day long the sun streamed in until I could no longer abide the heat. Perhaps I should join the Kreitles in Atlantic City? Of course, I could not afford the charges demanded at a first-class hotel, and a few weeks in such an establishment would wipe out my savings. I was not even sure that I could work there in peace. The truth was that I liked the mountains, not the sea. My pale skin did not fare well in the broiling sun. I had never learned to swim. Besides, the shyness I still retained from boyhood prevented me from stretching out half naked on the sand or splashing with women and girls in the ocean.

I began to doze, and when I opened my eyes I saw Miriam. She had returned and had already managed to put Didi to sleep. An astonishing change had come over her. She was now a mature woman, her hair disheveled, her eyes red. In her gaze and in her pursed lips I could see the despair of those who suffer from permanent melancholy.

Miriam tried to telephone Chaim Joel Treibitcher, hoping for the latest details of Max's condition, but she learned that the old man had also gone to Europe. To me Miriam said, "I would go to Poland, but I don't have Max's address and I have no money."

"I'll give you what I have," I said.

"Why should you do that? I could scrape up the money somehow—my father would give it to me. But I don't want to set eyes on that country again, after they wiped out the Jews. Somehow I knew that this trip of Max's would end in a fiasco. How can I go to him? He may be on his way to Switzerland to live in Matilda's house. I am sure that Chaim Joel Treibitcher is also on his way to Switzerland. I would be a fifth wheel. They wouldn't let me near Max anyway. All I ask for is that he continue to live, but this business with Hershele will kill him. Butterfly, what should I do?"

"Do nothing."

"Irka Shmelkes called up. They all know of my involvement with Max. Irka's tone when she spoke to me implied that *I* had taken her money. She was simply hysterical and spoke as if Max had squandered her savings on me. Who knows what those old hags are capable of? When it comes to money, people lose their minds."

"It's understandable when money alone protects them from disaster."

"They'll all come knocking at my door. Irka said that Max had left his wife, Priva, penniless. It's a lie. She has money of her own. But she also hates me and incites the others against me. That Tzlova is also a mean one. They will all form a clique and vent their rage on me. Butterfly, I have but one way out—death. I want to ask a favor of you, but don't laugh, I am quite serious."

"What is it?"

"Several times during the dark periods in my life I wanted to end it all. But I am a coward, I have no courage. I tried to take some pills once, but I threw them up. You must help me to die."

"Miriam, enough!"

"Don't shout at me. I have nothing to live for. I've failed in everything I've tried to do. I disgraced my parents and I even managed to drag you down. You look pale and ill. All this trouble is harmful to your health, certainly to your writing."

"What exactly do you want me to do? Chop off your head?" I asked.

Miriam's eyes lit up. For a moment she looked young again. "Yes, my dear, do that. I am not brave enough to do it myself. But if you do it for me, I'll kiss your hands. I'll stretch out my throat for you like a dove."

"A dove?"

"My grandmother used to say that, when one prepares to slaughter a dove, it stretches its neck out for the knife."

"You know you are playing a comedy."

"No, my dear, I mean it seriously. I have a cleaver at home, I'll give it to you. I will leave a note stating that I did it myself."

"Miriam, not even Al Capone could chop off his own head."

"Strangle me, then. You have two powerful hands. In your hands I'll die happy."

"A kiss of death, eh?"

"What is that?"

"According to legend Moses died having been kissed by God."

"You be my God."

"You mean your Angel of Death."

"It's all one and the same."

Miriam threw her arms around my neck. She began to kiss me, to bite into my mouth. I had known for a long time that talk of violence, murder, and death aroused lust. In moments of passion I have heard shrieks of "Kill me! Tear me! Stab me!" Atavistic cravings tore out of throats, cries from the primeval forest, from the cave. We threw ourselves down on Lynn Stallner's sofa, and we wrestled, rolled, embraced, kissed, bit. Miriam began to howl like an animal: "I want to have your child! I want to carry your child!"

It was all part of the love game. Night fell. Didi awoke and began to whimper in his bed. Miriam tore herself from me and ran to his room to change his diapers, to give him his bottle. His mother was bedded somewhere in New England with her lesbian partner. When Miriam returned, she turned on the lights. She was carrying Didi in her arms—a red-haired tot with blue eyes, a pale little face, wearing a nightie over his diapers. He rested his little hand on Miriam's breast and she pointed to me with her finger and said, "Didi, this is your daddy."

The child watched me, his face earnest and calm. A quiet

wisdom was reflected in his eyes. Somewhere, I said to myself, in all that exists there is a power that knows and understands all the complications of body and spirit. I had never had a child, never wanted to bring a new soul into this accursed world, but that evening I felt a fatherly love for this little creature who was entirely helpless, wholly dependent on human responsibility and kindness. An animal at his age possesses teeth, nails, sometimes even horns, and can already provide itself with food. But *Homo sapiens* is born a helpless invalid and must remain so for many years until he learns to cope and accumulates experience. The period of childhood seems to grow longer with the passing generations. Miriam lowered the child to me. "Give your hand to Daddy."

I took Didi's little hands in mine and kissed them. I played for a while with his toes. Miriam's voice grew thick and moist. "A darling, isn't he?"

"For the time being."

"What do you mean?"

"He may grow up to be a thief, a crook, a murderer."

"He is more likely to be an honest man, an artist, a scholar," Miriam said. She glanced at me with friendly reproach and said, "We might have had a little boy like Didi if things had not gone so wrong."

WHEN LYNN STALLNER telephoned Miriam to say she would return to New York the next day, Miriam suggested that I move to her, Miriam's, apartment. But Miriam's apartment terrified me. Stanley still had the key to the door and he could barge in at any time. We parted and I returned to my room on Seventieth Street. I had forgotten to roll down the shade before I left and the sun had warmed the room all day. It was as hot as an oven. Books, journals, newspapers lay scattered on the floor, on the bed. It was a wonder that the heat had not set them on fire. I was too tired to get undressed. I threw myself on the bed in my jacket, my trousers, my shoes. I had bought the morning paper, but I had no strength left to read it. Although the hour was late, the clattering, chattering, clapping of the subway drifted over from Broadway. In the summer months New York was an inferno. I slept through the night in my clothes.

In the morning I showered in the bathroom in the hall and then took the subway to my office. I had neglected my work. On my desk I found a list of the people who had come to pour out their hearts to me and seek my advice. Some of the names I had seen before—the Communist who had become disillusioned with Russia and sought a new interpretation of Marxism; the woman who had tried three times to take her own life; the betrayed man who sought comfort in alcohol and drugs; the young man driven to madness by rays beamed at him by enemies; the girl who sought a way to God and to a renewed Jewishness. I assured them all that I had no help to give them. I was a lost soul myself. But they had made up their minds that I alone could rescue them, and they clung to me and to my words of comfort. They had clipped out passages from my articles, and underlined words. Sometimes they showered me with undeserved praise; at others they heaped bitter criticism on my head. And they all wrote me long letters.

I had written a series of articles about telepathy, clairvoyance, premonitions, daydreams, and other occult phenomena, and many letters arrived with data that astounded me. Occasionally I received a love letter from a female reader with a photograph enclosed.

I longed to give up my post, but my bosses refused to let me abandon the role of adviser either on the air or in the newspaper. For years I had been unknown and suddenly all the readers knew me, and even discovered all my pseudonyms. I acquired detractors, too. There was no end to the complaints lodged against me: I was too pessimistic, too superstitious, too skeptical of humanity's progress, not devoted enough to socialism, Zionism, Americanism, the struggle against anti-Semitism, the activities of the Yiddishists, the problems of women's rights. Some critics complained that a Jewish state had sprung up before my eyes while I busied myself with the cobwebs of folklore. They accused me of dragging the reader back to the dark Middle Ages. *Nu*, and why such interest in sex? Sex is not in the tradition of Yiddish literature.

Someone knocked on my door, then pushed it open—slowly, cautiously, with the sly smile of an intimate who suspects that he will not be recognized. He was slight in build, thin, with a sharp nose and a pointed chin. He wore a plaid suit and what is known in Warsaw as a bicycle cap. He looked me up and down and said, "Yes, it's you. Does the name Morris Zalkind mean something to you?"

"Zalkind? Yes, of course."

"I am Miriam's father."

I sprang out of my chair. *"Sholem Aleichem!"*

He extended to me not his hand but two fingers. He was wearing a yellow tie with black dots and a pearl in the knot. His fingernails were manicured. He reminded me of the Writers' Club dandies. I blurted, "Miriam's father? You look like a youngster!"

"I'm already over fifty. That is, going by the number of years I've lived. Going by what I've lived through, I'm already a hundred and fifty. Miriam probably told you about me. I hope she does not deny that she has a father." He winked, smiled, exhibiting a mouthful of false teeth. I noticed that he wore a signet ring with a jewel on one of his fingers. From the front pocket of his jacket protruded a handkerchief and a gold fountain pen.

"Sit down, sit down. It's really a pleasure. Your daughter speaks of you very often."

"Do you mind if I smoke?"

"Absolutely not. Make yourself at home."

He took out a silver cigarette case and lighter, and lit a cigarette. His movements were rapid and precise. He blew the smoke out through his nostrils. He said, "I live on Long Island, but I have an office in the Astor building. I began to read your work in Warsaw. I also read all the papers—*Haynt, Moment, Express*, even the *Volks-Zeitung*. I used to attend the meetings at the Writers' Club, and you were pointed out to me. 'See that red-haired young man?' someone said. 'There grows a talent.' In Russia the mere mention of your name was forbidden. Their Jewish critics—the *shmageges*—considered you an imperialist. I know, I know. My wife, Fania—she is in the Holy Land now, with her *lyubovnik*—was one of them. In Warsaw she gave them money, for political detainees and the devil knows what else. They dropped it all into their own pockets. Books were written about those years, but not one-thousandth of what actually took place. Stalin had already condemned them all to death. One had to be blind not to know it. Come down to the street with me. I have a matter to discuss with you, and it cannot be done hastily. We'll have a cup of coffee. I won't take up much of your time. At most, fifteen minutes."

The fifteen minutes grew into an hour and more, and still Morris Zalkind was talking. We ate lunch in the cafeteria. Morris Zalkind repeatedly said he wanted to pay for our meal, but I had stuffed my ticket into my back pocket, and I was determined not to surrender it. He was reciting in detail his whole family history: "You know, I presume, that my son, Manes, was killed in the uprising of 1944. The Jew has his own kind of microbe, which unfortunately lives forever. Now comes the story of Miriam. Wait, I'll bring us more coffee and cake. Give me your check."

"No, thanks."

"Stubborn, eh? I'll be right back."

Morris Zalkind returned with two cups of coffee and two egg cookies. He started to speak as soon as he sat down: "Yes, Miriam. It is because of her that I came to see you. I know everything and I assume that you also know everything. She is writing a dissertation about your work. She thinks the world of you. Max Aberdam, a friend of yours, is a great braggart. She is twenty-seven and he sixty-seven, or perhaps even seventy. He has a weak heart, and to top it off—a wife. He also keeps a former mistress of his in his house. What's her name? Yes, Tzlova. For a girl Miriam's age, with her talents, to involve herself with such a good-for-nothing is suicide. I can offer only one justification: her mother is much the same, completely insane. The story is this. I can no longer talk to her, I mean to Miriam. Why is she angry? She is permitted and I am not? If my wife could live with another man in the Jewish state, openly, for all the world to see, why can't I? Miriam has as good as crossed me off as her father.

"I would like, first of all, for you to have a talk with her. You probably know that Harry Treibitcher went bankrupt after stealing the money of scores of victims of Hitler and committed suicide. Max Aberdam was the middleman; they trusted him, not Harry. Max Aberdam went to Poland with his old flame Matilda Treibitcher and became seriously ill. I hear that Matilda is also ill and that Chaim Joel, the idiot, rushed to her bedside. For my child, my only daughter, to be mixed up in this scandal is a shame and a disgrace. My daughter plays a part in this adventure and dirt is heaped on my head as well. Someone told me that Miriam is preparing to go to meet Max abroad. Of course you are busy with your own writing but since you seem to counsel everybody—and I must say sensible counsel it is—why not my

daughter, who is a fervent admirer of yours, who literally worships you? You probably already know that my daughter committed an outrageous folly and married some slob from a vulgar
home, an imbecile. Miriam is altogether her own worst enemy.
She has done things for which there is only one name, masochism. It reached the point that we wanted to send her to a
psychiatrist, a certain Dr. Biechowsky, who was one of Poland's
greatest experts in the field. But Miriam would not hear of it.
To her twisted mind it appeared as though we wanted to send
her to an insane asylum. *Nu*, there's a great deal more to say.''

Morris Zalkind was parked on East Broadway and he insisted
that I go sightseeing with him in his new car. He wanted to take
me to the Café Royal, to Lindy's, or to a seafood restaurant in
Sheepshead Bay. "Why must you sit in sweltering New York?
Where I live now, on Long Island, the air is cool. Fresh breezes
blow from the sea. Since you don't believe in the world to come,
why not enjoy this world a bit more? Come, let's spend a few
hours together. Where do you live?''

"I have a furnished room on West Seventieth Street.''

"Does it at least have a bathroom?''

"In the hall.''

"What's the point of that? Don't you intend to pour all your
energies into literary immortality?''

"Not really.''

"I asked Miriam what kind of a living a dissertation on Aaron
Greidinger would give her when her subject is a pauper himself.
She retorted that my soul cared only for money, not for idealism.
What good, I ask you, does idealism bring? But my daughter is
stubborn, a real mule. I've paid plenty for her and I still pay
today, although she doesn't know it. A girl her age should be
married instead of running around with a man who is gravely ill,
who is married, and is bankrupt to boot. What is the sense of it
all, huh?''

"Love does not ask for sense,'' I said.

"But what does she see in him? To me he is loathsome."

"She sees him with her eyes, not yours."

"It's easy for you to say. You have no wife, no daughters."

I WAS DIMLY aware that we had crossed over the Brooklyn Bridge and that Morris Zalkind's car was traveling toward Coney Island. I had not seen Coney Island in years. We passed Sheepshead Bay, Brighton, and we came out on Surf Avenue. It was Coney Island and yet there were visible changes—many new houses had been built. Only the noise and bustle and the sunny beaches filled with bathers were the same. I estimated that the boys and girls who frolicked at the oceanside when I had lived in this area were now mature and that the half-naked and deeply tanned youths playing there now were probably their children. But their faces were the same—the blazing eyes, the frenzied expressions betraying a thirst for pleasure, and a readiness to grasp it at any cost. One youth was carrying a girl on his shoulders. She held on to his curls, licked an ice-cream cone, and laughed the triumphant laugh of youth. Airplanes flew low over the water advertising meals, but rarely did I see the word "kosher." On benches along the boardwalk old people sat leaning on their canes, arguing, talking.

"I want to ask a question," Morris Zalkind said, "but don't be offended. You don't have to give me an answer. It's simply curiosity on my part."

"What do you want to ask?"

"What sort of relationship do you have with my daughter? I understand that she is enthralled with your writing. But you are some twenty years older than Miriam. And second, if she already has that old idiot Max, what is your role in this affair?"

Morris Zalkind stopped the car. He had driven up to a restaurant. For a while I sat in silence, stunned by the turn of our

conversation. Then I heard myself say, "Your daughter is charm-
ing, clever, erudite, and she has a rare appreciation for literature;
she is altogether a wonderful girl."

"It is good for a father to hear his daughter so highly praised.
But I've already told you that the immigrants' New York is a
small *shtetl* and spreading gossip the chief occupation. According
to them it seems that Miriam has two lovers, Max Aberdam and
you. I can't believe it. Why does she need *two* old men? Forgive
me for saying this to you. I am already over fifty. But for a girl
Miriam's age you are not young. If what I'm told is true, it is
sheer madness."

"It isn't true."

"And in addition, she has a husband. True, she is not living
with him, but now he does not want to divorce her. He is apparently in love with her, head over heels, but he drifts around
with a revolver, and he confided to someone that he is prepared
to kill us all—her, me, Max, and who knows who? I have informed the police of his threats. Why should a man with your
intelligence be mixed up in these intrigues and scandals?"

"Miriam has read parts of her dissertation to me, and that is
how we became acquainted," I said. I could barely pronounce
these words. My throat and palate were dry.

"That I can certainly understand, but spending the night with
her is something else again. I know for certain that you spent
the night in her apartment. One of the tenants in the building,
a customer of mine, saw you leaving the building at five o'clock
in the morning. When he told me what he saw, it was like a slap
in the face. I want to be completely frank with you. If your
relationship with Miriam is serious and you both come to a certain
understanding, then no one would be happier than I. It's true
that Jews don't make their writers rich, but I see that you are
already appearing in English. You come from a good family and
it would be an honor for us all. My own life does not give me

the right to preach morality to you, but a father is a father. Come, let's have a cup of coffee. Whatever your answer might be, we'll still be friends. Here's the restaurant!"

We sat at the table while a waiter brought us lemonade and rolls. It was curious but when I unwittingly called him Max, Morris Zalkind gave me a forgiving smile. "I am Morris, not Max. I understand that he is able to deceive women, even my daughter. But that he should take you in—this is hard for me to grasp."

"He has charm."

"What does his charm consist of—flattery?"

"You could say that. It is a talent to say something pleasant to every person."

"And to cheat them out of their money."

"He never cheated me, nor did he cheat your daughter."

"That's where you're wrong. I gave my daughter five thousand dollars and he bought stocks for her in the name of his crooked agent who is now dead. She will never see a penny of it."

"I didn't know that."

"There is a great deal you don't know."

We spoke together for a long time. I heard Morris Zalkind say, "It's no longer the style to give dowries, especially in America. But since she is my only daughter I am prepared to give you a handsome dowry, no less than twenty thousand dollars. Actually everything I own is hers. I am even ready to give you a house, so that you'll be able to do your literary work in peace. Give me an answer, clear and honest."

I felt heat in my neck and head, and my mouth answered of its own accord: "It all depends on her. If she agrees, then so it shall be."

"Do you mean it seriously?" Morris Zalkind asked.

"Yes, seriously."

"Well, this is a historic day for me. She will agree, she'll agree.

She worships you. We'll extract a divorce from that Stanley by hook or by crook."

"I hear that you are now living with an artist," I said.

"Yes, yes, yes. Linda. She signs herself Linda McBride—McBride was her husband's name—but she is a Jewish girl, a Galician. It's not good to be alone. Our people have a saying: 'To be one is to be none.' I'll tell you the truth, I don't understand her poems. She also paints and I don't understand her paintings. Yes, we live together, Linda and I. But to divorce my wife and marry Linda—that I don't intend to do. Eat, don't leave food on your plate."

"Thanks. I can't eat so much."

"Perhaps you want to take a look at Sea Gate? I know you once lived there."

"Where did you learn that?"

"From you. You write these things and then you forget that you wrote them. But we, the readers, remember. Waiter!"

Morris Zalkind paid the waiter. I wanted to pay for my portion of the meal, but Zalkind would not hear of it. We climbed back into the car and soon we were in Sea Gate. I told him I wanted to find the house in which I had once lived. They had torn down the house in which rooms were rented to Yiddish journalists and writers—that I knew. A hotel now stood in its place. But I wanted to see if the house with the two wooden columns in front still existed, the one in which my brother had lived. But I found that it, too, had vanished.

We began to walk toward the sea, and Morris Zalkind abruptly took my arm. A fatherly warmth streamed from his arm and a feeling akin to love overcame me for this man who wanted to give me his daughter for a wife. It struck me that he himself resembled Max, not a physical resemblance, but a spiritual one.

We stood at the railing and Morris Zalkind said, "Look at this sand and these seashells—they are millions of years old. I read that the place we know as Africa was once the North Pole—a cold region, at any rate. In what are now cold regions traces of palm trees and tropical plants have been found. The world once turned itself upside down, and perhaps it may do so again—who knows? As long as one continues to breathe, one must think about a *takhles* for oneself and one's children. What does God want? There has to be something He wants."

EIGHT

As SMALL AS my world was, it was filled with excitement. Suddenly I heard that Matilda Treibitcher was dead. It had happened on the airplane going to Switzerland. Taken ill in Warsaw, she had refused to enter a hospital. Chaim Joel Treibitcher, who had flown to Poland to be at his wife's bedside, was on the plane with her and Max when she died.

Max sent Miriam a cable from Switzerland. Miriam responded with a long cable which must have cost her nearly one hundred dollars. She assured Max that she and I were devoted to him, that we missed him, and that everything remained the same. We would both take a plane just as soon as we received word from him. I had informed my editor that I was taking some vacation. The newspaper owed me not one vacation but several. I had worked virtually the entire year, sent articles without keeping score, never failed to present copy even when I fell ill with the flu. I was publishing a serialized novel and I could not, nor did I want to, resign from the paper while the novel was still unfinished.

I was spending part of each day and all night with Miriam. For the first time in my literary career I was dictating some of my journalistic writing and even some fiction. Miriam had created for herself a kind of Yiddish stenography. She typed on the Yiddish typewriter with extraordinary speed. I discussed the themes of various articles with her and together we planned the remaining chapters of my novel—the final third. The cogency of her advice astounded me.

Soon she heard that Stanley had found himself a new love, ostensibly an actress, with whom he had gone to British Columbia. Miriam's father was now traveling in Europe with Linda McBride. I had told Miriam about my meeting with him and she said, "There is no power in the world which could tear me away from Max—not twenty thousand dollars, not even twenty million—especially now."

I assured Miriam I would be true to both her and Max as long as I lived. We toyed with the idea of my writing a novel entitled *Three*, the story of two men and a woman, the theme of which was that the emotions heeded no laws, no religious, social, or political systems. We agreed it was the mission of literature to express the emotions with honesty—savage, antisocial, and contradictory as the emotion might be.

In the evening I usually invited Miriam to a restaurant for supper. We never had too much love or too much conversation. There was no subject I could not discuss with her—philosophy, psychology, literature, religion, occultism. All our discussions sooner or later turned to Max and to my strange partnership with him. But there was no word from Max. Was he lying in a hospital in Switzerland?

We heard that several refugees who lost their money had broken into Priva's apartment and smashed furniture, dragged clothing and linen out of her closets and jewelry out of her bureau drawers. One woman had struck Tzlova, who wanted to call the police, but Priva said no. Apparently Irka Shmelkes had tried to take her own life by swallowing scores of sleeping pills but Edek called an ambulance and took her to a hospital, where they pumped out her stomach in time.

Max's silence plunged Miriam into melancholy. She began to drop hints about committing suicide herself. If Max was dead she might as well be dead, too, she said. That night I felt as though a ghost was lying between us, preventing us from coming together. Several times she called me Max, and then apologized and corrected herself. I fell asleep and was awakened by the telephone ringing in the living room. The luminous dial on my watch showed a quarter past one. Miriam had taken a sleeping pill and was fast asleep. Who could be calling in the middle of the night? Was it Stanley again? In the darkness—I still did not know where the light switch was—I grabbed the receiver and put it to my ear. No one spoke, and I was ready to hang up when I heard a murmur, a cough. A man's voice asked, "Aaron, is it you?"

It was as though something broke within me. "Max?"

"Yes, it's me. I returned from my grave to strangle you."

"Where are you? Where are you calling from?"

"I am in New York. I just flew in from Europe. The airplane was late and we couldn't land for an hour. Arale, I am here incognito. Even Priva doesn't know I've arrived. If my refugees find out I'm here, they'll tear me limb from limb and they have a right to do so."

"Why didn't you write to us? We sent you a cable."

"I didn't know until the last moment whether or not I could take the plane. Matilda is dead and I am half dead. All the curses of the *Toykhekha* rained down on my head during this trip."

"Where are you now?"

"In the Empire Hotel on Broadway. How is Miriam?"

"Miriam took a sleeping pill and she is sleeping soundly now."

"Don't wake her up. I became seriously ill in Poland, and for a while it looked as if I might die. Matilda suffered a heart attack and died on the plane. After many difficulties Chaim Joel managed to take her body to Eretz Israel. She will lie there with other righteous men and women. As for me, it seems that I'll have to make do with a grave in New York. Those quacks in Warsaw operated on me and botched the operation. My urine is bloody."

"Why didn't you go to a hospital in Switzerland?"

"I was told that the best doctors for this are in America."

"What are you planning to do?"

"In Switzerland I was given the name of an American doctor, a world authority in the field. I cabled him, but have received no answer. I don't want to die among strangers."

"Shall I wake Miriam up?"

"No. Come over tomorrow quietly. No one must know I am here. I've taken another name for myself—Sigmund Klein. I am on the eighth floor. I've grown a white beard and I look like Reb Tzotz."

Suddenly the living-room light went on and Miriam, in her nightgown and bare feet, tore the receiver out of my hand. She screamed into it with a mixture of laughter and tears. I had never before seen her in so hysterical a state. I returned to the bedroom; more than half an hour went by. She had never made a secret of it—Max was her number one. Suddenly the door flew open and Miriam turned on the light.

"Butterfly, I am going to his hotel."

I decided not to go with her and she asked, "Are you angry or what?"

"I am not angry. I am twenty years older than you are and I lack the strength for these adventures."

"You have plenty of strength. I'd rather die than leave him alone and ill!"

I lay back and watched Miriam put on her clothes. She finished dressing and was soon gone. I asked her to call me as soon as she reached the Empire Hotel, but I was not at all sure she would.

I began to doze off and dreamed that it was Passover and I was in Warsaw. My father was in the midst of a Seder and my younger brother, Moshe, was asking the four questions. I saw everything clearly: the *heysev* bed, my father in a *kittel*, my mother in her Sabbath dress, the one she had first worn on her wedding day. On the covered table I saw the silver candlesticks, the wine, the wineglasses, and the Seder plate containing the *kharoses*, the bitter herbs, the egg, the shankbone. The matzoh lay wrapped in a silken matzoh cloth which my mother had embroidered in gold for her bridegroom when she became his bride. I heard my father lift his voice as he chanted, "Said Rabbi Eleazar, the son of Azariah: See, I am almost seventy years old, and I have never been privileged to have the Exodus from Egypt recounted in the nights until Ben Zoma so expounded it . . ."

"Father is alive!" I said to myself. "There was no Hitler, no Holocaust, no war. It was all a bad dream." I shivered and woke up. Was the telephone ringing? No, I only thought I heard it ring. Suddenly something made me realize I had made a fatal error in the installment of my novel slated to appear in Friday's paper. I had written that the heroine went to the synagogue on the second day of Rosh Hashanah to recite the memorial prayer for the dead. Only now did I remember that the *Yizkor* was not recited on Rosh Hashanah. I was astounded by my blunder and by the fact that a dream about Passover and my father's Seder should remind me of an error connected with Rosh Hashanah. Had my brain been aware of that error all along? The blunder was not a mere oversight, a typographical error committed by the young typesetter. It occurred in a lengthy paragraph filled with descriptions. I would be a laughingstock with the paper's readers. Was there still time for me to rectify it? The metal frame containing the text was still on the printer's stand in the composing room, and the type would probably be cast first thing in the morning. There was one way to save my literary name from disgrace—get dressed, go down to the editorial offices, and pluck out the entire paragraph with my own hands—something a mere writer was not permitted to do under the laws of the printers' union.

I was tired and weak. I could barely keep my eyes open. How would I find a taxi to take me to East Broadway? Was the building open and was the elevator running? I remembered the words of Rabbi Nachman of Bratzlav: As long as the flame of life burns, anything can be rectified. I started up and began to get dressed. Somehow I managed to get into my suit and my shoes, but my tie had vanished. I searched for it, but it was gone. Just as I was walking toward the door, the telephone rang. In my haste I put the mouthpiece to my ear and the earpiece to my mouth and I called out, "Miriam!"

"Butterfly, I have a room for you!" Miriam was shouting. "Here in the hotel. Two doors away from Max. Come right over. Max is ill, gravely ill, and he wants to talk to you."

Miriam burst into tears and could not bring herself to speak. I asked, "What is it that ails him?" And I felt a lump forming in my own throat.

"Everything, everything!" Miriam wailed. "Come over right away. The doctors in Warsaw murdered him! Arale, he must be taken to the hospital immediately, but I don't know where to turn. I tried to call an ambulance but got nowhere."

Miriam tried to repeat why the ambulance wouldn't come, but her words were swallowed up in a new flood of tears. I could hear her choking on her own words and I muttered, "I'm on my way."

I went out to the elevator. "Well, let them print the blunder and make a laughingstock of me!" I said to myself. For the second time that summer I left Miriam's apartment in the middle of the night. A cool breeze blew from the park, but from the sidewalk rose the vapors of yesterday's heat wave. The sky over-head was colored red by the city's lights, without a moon, without stars, a sort of cosmic sore. The lampposts threw their lights on the trees in the park.

I waited at the corner for ten minutes, but no taxi came. Then two passed by that refused to stop, even though I signaled them. I began to walk downtown toward the Empire Hotel. Now sud-denly taxis began to appear, but I no longer wanted to hail one. Then a taxi came by that pulled to a stop near me. Perhaps the driver meant to rob me? I heard him address me in Yiddish and call me by name. It was a man I knew from childhood, Misha Budnik, my *landsman*, who had lived in Bilgoray at a time when the *shtetl* was occupied by the Austrians. I still went to the *Bet Midrash* in those days, and had already begun to write. Misha was some five years older than I, a free spirit who had shaved off his beard, wore boots with high bootlegs and riding trousers. The Austrians had confiscated the local peasants' oxen and Misha Budnik drove them to Ruva-Russka, where they were loaded on freight trains bound for the Italian front. On the way back from Ruva-Russka, Misha smuggled tobacco from Galicia. He and his wife, Freidl, also a smuggler, had come to New York and looked me up, and a new friendship had grown between us. He and his wife were confirmed readers of mine. They had two daughters, both married. I had neglected these friends from whom I had received a standing invitation to occupy a room in their house whenever I wanted. Freidl cooked the old Bilgoray dishes for me, used the familiar "thou" in conversation, and kissed me often. Husband and wife had become anarchists in America.

"Misha!" I cried out.

"Arale!"

Misha tumbled out of the cab, threw his arms around me, and I felt his bristly beard on my face. He was six feet tall and known for his great strength. I heard myself saying, "It's a miracle! A miracle from heaven!"

"A miracle, eh? Where are you off to in the middle of the night?"

I began to explain my dilemma to Misha—a friend gravely ill in the Empire Hotel and the newspaper about to publish an outlandish blunder of mine. He stood and stared at me and shook his head. He snapped, "You are three blocks away from the Empire. Get in!" In less than a minute we pulled up in front of the hotel. He asked, "What's wrong with your friend? A heart attack?"

"He has problems with his prostate, but he apparently took suddenly ill."

"Come, we'll take him to a hospital. Is he a writer?"

"No."

"What is his name?"

"Max Aberdam."

Misha's black eyes bulged with anger. "Max Aberdam is in New York! Here in the hotel?"

"You know him?"

"He took five thousand dollars from Freidl and fled to Poland to the Bolsheviks."

"I didn't know you knew him," I stammered.

"I wish I didn't. He took Freidl's nest egg from her."

"Misha, the man is gravely ill!"

We entered the hotel lobby. A clerk sat behind the desk, dozing, and opened a pair of sleepy eyes. "Yes?"

"What is the number of Max Aberdam's room?" Misha Budnik asked.

"Whatever the number, you cannot visit him in the middle of the night." The clerk spoke the words through his teeth.

"Max Aberdam is ill. He suffered a heart attack!" Misha Budnik half shouted.

"As far as I know, no one here suffered any attack." The clerk opened a large book, consulted it, and said, "There is no one here by that name."

At that moment I remembered that Max Aberdam was registered in the hotel under a different name. He had told me what it was, but I had forgotten.

Misha Budnik stood and stared at me. "Really, I don't understand the whole thing," he said. "Were you joking, or what?"

"It may look like a joke, but unfortunately it's true."

"Max Aberdam is here?"

"Yes. He became ill abroad and flew here to see the doctor."

"It is dangerous for him to come here. His victims will tear him limb from limb. They curse him a thousand times a day. For the first time since I've known Freidl, I saw her cry. Five thousand dollars is no small matter to us."

"The thief was not Max."

"Well, all hell will break loose. A man must be heartless to cheat Nazi victims out of their money."

The clerk called out. From his angry expression and because he pointed to the door I understood that he wanted us to leave. I signaled Misha to wait and I approached the clerk again.

"Excuse me," I said, "but a young lady had taken a room for me earlier tonight. The man who is ill is a friend of ours and we wanted to stay with him."

The clerk shrugged his shoulders. "What is the young lady's name? What's yours?"

"A young lady, not tall. Her name is Miriam Zalkind."

"Zalkind? We have no one here by that name," the clerk said.

Misha Budnik came up to the desk. "Mister," he said, "this man is a writer. He did not come here to make up lies."

"You probably want another hotel. You must leave or I'll be forced to call the police."

We went outside and I tried over and over again to remember the name Max had given me, but I hadn't the vaguest idea what it might be. Misha said, "Well, everything will clear up tomorrow. The young lady will call you at home or at your office. Now what about the blunder in the text of your novel? The whole thing is not clear to me."

Again I explained the composing-room problem as simply as I could, and Misha said, "If you want, I can take you to the paper."

"Only if you let me pay you like any passenger."

"Are you crazy? Get in!"

The taxi pulled to a stop on East Broadway. We climbed out and found that the entrance to the *Forward* was open. The elevator man remembered me from the thirties, when I used to drop off my articles late at night so as to avoid meeting the regular contributors, those who received full salaries and belonged to the Peretz Union. Misha and I rode up to the tenth floor. The composing room was open and lit by a single light bulb. The metal frame with the latest installment of my novel was on the composing stand, and over it lay a discarded proof sheet. I removed the paragraph containing my error—fortunately, it was at the end—and threw it into a trash can. I crossed out the paragraph on the proof sheet, noted in the margin that it had been deleted, and asked the printer to insert some filler. Praise God, in a single moment the impossible had become an accomplished fact.

On the way back I begged Misha in the name of our long friendship to keep Max's presence in New York secret. After complaining and arguing, Misha finally agreed. Misha Budnik was actually my oldest friend. He had known me in the days when I wore red sidelocks, a velvet hat, a *khalet*. His wife, Freidl (it was she who had turned Misha into an anarchist), had a secret affair with me. Freidl and Misha both believed in free love and considered the institution of marriage obsolete and hypocritical.

Freidl had refused to be married by a rabbi. They had obtained a civil certificate in Cracow only because without it they could not enter America. In her letters to me Freidl had signed herself Freidl Silberstein, her maiden name. In that sense she had gone even further than the well-known Emma Goldman.

It was just then that I remembered the name Max had used when he registered at the hotel—Sigmund Klein.

At nine o'clock in the morning I telephoned Sigmund Klein, and Miriam answered. When she heard my voice she shrieked, "It's you? You are alive? I was going to inform the police that you disappeared in the middle of the night. What happened to you?"

In the midst of speaking she burst into tears. I tried to explain what had happened, but she was too upset to understand the weird details. "I'm coming right away!" I shouted, and Miriam put down the receiver. I went to the Empire unwashed and unshaven and took the elevator to the eighth floor. Miriam, wearing a robe and a pair of slippers, looked pale, disheveled. There was a look of alarm in her eyes. I barely recognized Max. He lay in bed, his head supported by two pillows. His beard had grown white. When he stretched out a thin and yellowed hand to me, I noticed he no longer wore a signet ring on his forefinger. I bent down and kissed him. He took my shoulders in both hands and kissed me. He said, "I must recite the 'Blessed be He who restores the dead to life' over you. We were both beginning to believe that you met with an accident. What happened to you? Sit down."

I told Max about my blunder involving a *Yizkor* on Rosh Hashanah, and about my unexpected encounter with Misha Budnik. Max's eyes filled with laughter. "*Nu*, now you'll have something to write about. I, my friend, am not well. But, thank God, I am not ready yet to give up the ghost. Everything went wrong, from the very beginning. It was as though a *tzaddik* or a sorcerer had cursed me. I know now why you and Miriam did not appear at Chaim Joel Treibitcher's party, but at that time I could not imagine what happened to you. Matilda claimed that you simply ran away and left me to stew. We arrived in Warsaw literally ill, both of us. In Warsaw they have already forgotten that Jews exist. That I survived their operation is one of God's miracles, and then they came to tell me I needed a second one. Soon Matilda was dead and I no longer wanted to stay abroad. Here at least I have Miriam and you. Word came of Hershele's suicide. When I heard that, I was convinced that my own end was near."

"Max, you'll be cured here, you'll be strong as an ox," I said.

"Butterfly, don't let him become resigned," Miriam cried out. "Millions of men suffer the same illness as he and they come through it healthy and strong!"

"Maybe I will and maybe I won't. Nothing lasts forever. Arale, I can't stay here, not another day. I lie here and think about those people whose last few dollars I took and I want to die. I hope you told no one where I am. If they find out, they'll come flying like locusts and bury me alive. I know that Priva is moving heaven and earth to find me. How long can it all go on?"

"Max, everything will end well, you'll see," I said. "I suspect that you were left without money. I have some, not much, but it's better than no money at all."

"And how did you come to have money?" Max asked. "Did you rob a bank?"

"I have four thousand dollars."

"I owe a quarter of a million dollars, not four thousand," Max said.

"I offer you the money not for repayment of your debts but for a doctor and a hospital."

"What do you say to that, Miriam?" Max asked. "Overnight he's a philanthropist, ready to give away his last penny."

"Miriam is in the bathroom," I said.

"Why should you give me what little you've managed to save?" Max asked. "Do you expect me to send you a check from the world beyond?"

"I expect nothing. You will recover, that is all that matters."

"*Nu*, it was worthwhile to come back and hear words like these," Max said. "How does the saying go? 'Sell your pants if you must, but have a friend you can trust.' I will not take your money. What I must do now is find a doctor and a hospital— not here in New York, but far away, California perhaps. In my condition at present I can bear no more than two persons, Miriam and you."

Miriam emerged from the bathroom. "I want to comb my hair but I can't find my comb."

"Your comb is in my bed. Something jabbed me in my side, and it was your comb." Max pulled it out from under his pillow. Miriam snatched it from his hand and promptly returned to the bathroom. Max followed her with his eyes.

"She is also a victim," he said. "All these years I've done but one thing—search for victims so I could heap misfortunes on their heads. But you, Butterfly, while there is still time—fly! You must do your work instead of trailing an old man who's getting ready to breathe his last. I am saying this to you as a friend, not a foe."

"You no longer want my friendship, is that it?"

"I do want it, I do, you are dear to my heart. That is why I implore you by all that is sacred to flee from me as from a plague."

NINE

I
T SO HAPPENED that Max's doctor in his younger days in Warsaw, Jacob Dinkin, together with the urologist Irving Saphir, both now in New York, decided that Max had to recuperate before he could undergo a second operation. Not only was his prostate ailing but his kidneys were disfunctional and he was beginning to show signs of uremia. They prescribed antibiotics, as well as liver extract to prevent anemia. Misha Budnik had promised to keep our secret and I did not believe he broke his word. It was probably Miriam's neighbor on Central Park West who disclosed Max's return, the same man who told Morris Zalkind I had spent the night with her.

The scandal which Max had feared never took place. When the refugees learned that Max Aberdam was seriously ill and needed surgery again, they stopped knocking on Priva's door, phoning and threatening her. Only the day before Max's presence in New York became known, Priva had boarded a small Jewish ship which took nearly a month to reach Israel—stopping in Marseilles and Naples. Max told me that Priva had a hefty nest egg of her own, derived from monies he had given her and from a one-time payment she had received from the Germans.

Priva owed three months' rent for their apartment on Riverside Drive, and the owners had applied for an eviction order. Doctors Dinkin and Saphir both felt that Max would benefit from several weeks' stay in the country, away from the sweltering New York heat. Miriam cabled her father in Rome asking for a loan, but Morris Zalkind replied that as long as she was involved with that charlatan, Max Aberdam, he would not give her a penny. Max, now penniless, was firm in his refusal to take my money, but I persuaded him to borrow three thousand dollars from me. This was not nearly enough to cover the cost of surgery or a hotel in the country, but then something turned up which Miriam said was nothing short of a miracle. Lynn Stallner was preparing to fly to Mexico with her friend Sylvia. She asked Miriam to look after Didi in her absence. Lynn had a house near Lake George which she had named The Chalet, with a peaked roof and a balcony of the sort one often saw in Switzerland. She proposed that Miriam spend the time with Didi in that house. Lynn and Miriam always confided in each other, and when Miriam asked whether she could bring Max and me along, Lynn answered, "Bring whomever you like."

Everything proceeded quickly. Lynn Stallner had met Max and had even read the novel of mine which had appeared in English. The house had every possible convenience, even a small motor boat, which was docked on the lake. A caretaker looked after it and the grounds. Two days later Lynn handed Miriam a check to cover her and Didi's expenses and another to cover her salary. Lynn packed into her station wagon every conceivable article that Didi might require in the coming weeks, as well as his toys and a stroller. Miriam had been looking after Didi since he was four weeks old and was even more attuned to his needs in many ways than his mother. Over fourteen months old now, Didi was already trying to talk. He crawled and was even able to stand on his feet. He called his mother Mama, and for some reason he called Miriam Nana. He had even begun to recognize me and liked to ride on my shoulders. Lynn had engaged two pediatricians for Didi; one was available in Brooklyn and the other at Lake George. She, Lynn, would telephone from Mexico every two days. The house in Lake George had a garage and a car which Miriam was free to use.

That morning Max, Miriam, and I met Didi and Lynn in the lobby of the Empire. I sat with Miriam and Didi in the back seat, while Max sat in front next to Lynn Stallner, who drove. Among ourselves Max, Miriam, and I had scarcely had any occasion to converse in English. Now I listened as Max spoke English to Lynn with a heavy Polish-Jewish accent, but at the same time with a rich vocabulary. Despite his illness he cheerfully flirted, joked with her, paid her compliments, and Lynn responded.

During our six-hour ride to Lake George, I was astonished to learn how versatile Lynn's interests were and how precise was her language. It was generally accepted by Polish Jews that native Americans did not receive a thorough education but emerged from high school and college almost illiterate. This young woman with her mane of red curls and a face sprinkled with freckles knew a great deal about stocks, securities, banks, insurance, real estate, politics. She mentioned the names of governors, senators, congressmen whom she knew personally. She showed expertise in Jewish matters, knew all about the newly established Jewish state, its conflict with the Arab nations, its political parties and their platforms. Looking back over her shoulder she conversed with me about literature, mentioning writers and critics whose names I had never heard. The opinions she expressed about my own book astounded me. "Where and when did she learn all this?" I asked myself. From time to time Max turned and threw me a look which seemed to ask, "What do you say to that?" I heard him saying, "Mrs. Stallner, you should be a professor."

"As a matter of fact I was a professor," she answered. "Not a full professor, but an assistant, a lecturer or, as you call it in Europe, a docent."

"What did you teach?"

"Political economy."

"Is that so?"

"Yes, just so. This is America. Here a woman need not spend her life peeling potatoes and washing dishes. While I often peel potatoes and wash dishes, I know that a well-organized person can find time for everything."

She drove the car at extraordinary speed, often with only one hand on the wheel and a cigarette in her lips. If the cigarette went out, she signaled to Max to light it with the lighter. She blew the smoke out not through her mouth but through her nostrils. I had been raised on the old views of Schopenhauer, Nietzsche, and Otto Weininger that women had no sense of time or logic and were always guided by their emotions. But Lynn Stallner made her decisions in a fraction of a second, and a certain resoluteness accompanied everything she did or said.

We arrived at Lake George precisely at the hour Lynn Stallner had predicted. She called her house a bungalow, but to my eyes it seemed a palace. There were five or six rooms on the ground floor and as many bedrooms above. The kitchen had the latest equipment and all the cooking was done by electricity. Lynn kept account of every detail in the household and showed Miriam exactly what needed to be done.

Max lit a cigar, but Lynn sternly warned him never to smoke a cigar in the house. For that there was a garden, with a hammock and with lounging chairs. It also turned out that Lynn spoke Yiddish. She had spoken Yiddish to her grandmother even before she had learned English. Max said to her, "You are truly an *Eyshes Chayil*. Do you know what that means?"

Lynn answered, "Yes, a worthy woman."

"All you lack is a man who will sit at the gates and praise you to the elders of the city."

"I've already had that with Didi's father," Lynn answered. "And it had no value whatever—none!"

When Lynn finished her chores, she took her leave of us. She embraced and kissed Miriam, then Max. She turned to do the same with me, but for some reason I was shy. She said, "A yeshiva boy still!" And she gave me a small, firm hand. She sat down at the wheel, and in an instant her car was gone. Max took the cigar out of his mouth. "Only in America," he said.

THAT EVENING MAX spoke to us openly. He had temporarily— at least until the next operation would restore them—lost his masculine functions. The doctors in Poland, the *shkotsim*, had come close to castrating him. But he had no intention of playing the role of a jealous eunuch. On the contrary, he wanted us to enjoy each other. He, Max, was happy to have our close friendship. Over and over again he repeated how old he was—old enough to be my father and Miriam's grandfather. But Miriam spoke out, "Maxele, you are not my grandfather, you're my husband. I will love you and stay with you as long as I live."

"You mean as long as I live," Max corrected her.

"No, as long as *I* live."

"Max, we came here to look after you, not to conduct orgies," I said, surprised at my own words. "Nothing is more important than your health."

" 'What does *shemittah* have to do with Mount Sinai?' " Max said, quoting a passage from the Gemara. "What does one thing have to do with another? We came here to enjoy ourselves, not to recite Psalms. If you and Miriam are happy, I am happy. I am not an idol for whom you should sacrifice yourselves. The truth is that I foresaw all this, and that is why I brought you together. I lay there in the hospital in Warsaw, in agony, surrounded by drunks, degenerates, lunatics, and I had but one thought to comfort me: you two were in America and you loved each other. Since my own daughters have perished, you are my children."

"Maxele, I am your wife, not your daughter. Now that Priva has gone to Israel and you are ill, my place is with you. Am I making myself clear?"

"Well, well, suddenly she has become a saint, a second Sarah Bas-Tovim," Max said. "You probably read about it in a Polish novel and now you want to ape the heroine. Nonsense, I am approaching the end of my life while you are just beginning yours. My advice to you is this: Divorce that Stanley and marry Aaron. You are a fitting pair, truthless and luckless." Max chuckled at his own joke. I felt my face reddening. Miriam threw me a quick glance. "Max, you've become a matchmaker now?"

Miriam moved closer to me. "Max and I will sleep in Lynn's bedroom, where I've put a cot for Didi."

"Yes, Miriam, thanks." I took her in my arms. She kissed me on the lips and lingered for a while. Her face was pale. "I love you both, but Max's health is most important now."

"Yes, you are right."

IN THE CAR I had been so tired that I could barely keep my eyes open. But now sleep eluded me. "Yes, we are actors," I said to myself, "a troupe of Purim players. Who knows"—the thought flitted through my brain—"God Himself—if He exists—may be an actor, too." I was reminded of the verse in Psalms, "He who smiles down from heaven," and I thought, God sits in heaven and laughs at his own comedy.

I slept for several hours, then woke up again. The luminous dial on my wristwatch showed twenty minutes to two. As often happened, I could not immediately remember where I was. I sat up in bed, then promptly put my head down on the pillow again. Max had refused to take the loan of my money at first. But for some reason I had grown stubborn and held my ground, and finally he had accepted it. Those four thousand dollars were always a source of comfort to me. I knew that whatever happened at the Yiddish newspaper, for at least a year I was provided for. I had my conflicts with the editor. In my articles I often mocked his calls for a united proletariat in the fight for a better world. One co-editor greeted me every morning with the news that he had defended me the evening before—a sign that others had attacked me. It was comforting to know that at least for a year all my expenses would be covered. What more did I need? Books, thank God, the library offered free. My women companions demanded no luxuries from me. They required neither the theater nor the movies. I also knew that Stefa and Leon wanted me to stay at their home, where they had set aside a room for me.

Suddenly I had casually given away three-quarters of all that I had in the world to a squanderer, a dissolute man, a man who was bankrupt to boot. I had become involved with a woman who by the time she was twenty-seven had undergone every possible adventure. For all her devotion to Max I was well aware that she had constructed her plans around me, not him. She had made known her dream of having a child with me, and her father even wanted me for a son-in-law. Deep inside I doubted I would ever give my name to Miriam. Old-fashioned masculine pride still breathed in me, the kind which separated a mistress from a wife, an affair from a marriage.

As I lay that night in Lynn Stallner's house, I tried to take stock of myself, and at the same time a sort of literary inventory. How, for example, could I tell my present story to the reader? What would I say if a reader should come for my advice—a person my age, in more or less the same circumstances? As a rule I pronounced judgments like an oracle, even before I heard out their stammers to the end. I had even convinced myself that I could predict a person's malaise merely by looking at him, hearing his voice, or from the tenor of his words. I had reread "The Death of Ivan Ilyich," again admiring Tolstoy's story, and I asked myself, What if a flesh-and-blood Ivan Ilyich came to me, would I have the patience to listen? No. We enjoy works of literature precisely because they demand no responsibility from us. We can open and close the book whenever we like. We are not called upon to comfort the sufferer or to lend him a hand. How many victims of Hitler had come to our editorial office whose stories we were not willing to hear? In recent years the editor almost stopped printing the memoirs of survivors of Treblinka, Maidanek, Stutthof, other concentration camps. I heard him explain to an author of one such memoir: "We no longer publish these things. Our readers don't want to read them . . ." The reader preferred anonymous suffering, tailored in such a way as to provide him with a certain entertainment.

I fell asleep, then woke up again. I could no longer sleep, and slowly my thoughts turned to reality. What was Miriam doing now? Was she really sleeping? And Max—was he really impotent? Could surgery destroy the eternal relationship between male and female? No, it existed in so-called inanimate objects. I believed that God is a novelist who writes what He pleases, and the whole world has to read Him, trying to find out what He means.

THE NEXT DAY was sunny but not hot. Max, Miriam, and I were having breakfast, while Didi was quickly mastering the art of walking. He stumbled from one chair to another, occasionally throwing us a glance as if to ask, "See what I can do! See how clever I am!" From time to time he burst into tears and Miriam picked him up, kissed and consoled him: "*Sha*, Didi precious. In time you'll manage everything. Someday you'll be a great big boy, you'll play football, run a mile in a minute." Max sat Didi on his knee and bounced him up and down. He spoke to Didi in Yiddish, English, Polish. He said, "Be glad, Didi, that you were born in Uncle Sam's land and not in Russia. They would call you a cosmopolitan, a saboteur, a chauvinist, and they would write in your passport the word *Yevrey*." Didi clutched Max's beard. He even tried to put it in his mouth, to see how it tasted.

Miriam heard Max's words and laughed. "It's time to go for a walk!" she announced.

Miriam put Didi in his stroller and we set out together. We took a long walk around the lake. Other passersby, mostly elderly couples, refugees from Germany, followed us with their eyes. The men regarded us with disapproval. We were speaking Yiddish, and the *Ostjuden*'s language did not belong here in the Adirondacks. It was the language of the Catskill hotels. Miriam had put a copy of the *Forward* in Didi's stroller, and it was eyed with distaste. These German refugees believed in assimilation —the Jewish minority should blend into the majority, not saddle itself with the East European *Golus*. From the pockets of these men's coats protruded copies of *Aufbau*. Max blurted out, "Why are they staring, the *Yekkes*? How did their assimilation help them in Germany, huh?" They remained what they were before, *Yehudim*, whose shred of Jewishness consisted of a visit to the synagogue on Rosh Hashanah and Yom Kippur to listen to their *rabbiner*'s sermon. What, when all was said and done, did Max's Jewishness consist of—or Miriam's, or mine? We had all severed ourselves from our roots. We were what the Cabala called "naked souls," remnants of a spiritual holocaust. And the modern ex-Christian was not much different from the modern Jew.

After our walk Miriam prepared lunch, with Max and me

helping in the kitchen. In the hours between lunch and dinner Max lay down and slept, Miriam continued work on her dissertation, while I wrote for the *Forward* and corrected the chapters of my novel. Once I heard Miriam say, "If I could have my way, summer would never end and we would stay here until eternity."

Every other evening, between eight and nine, Lynn telephoned from Mexico. The conversation was always the same: Miriam announced that Didi was fine, the weather was good. Lynn sang the praises of Mexico, its beautiful sea, its mountains, the relics of the Aztecs, the primitive nature of the Mexicans. Lynn had bought an embroidered shawl for Miriam, a cigar holder for Max. She asked to speak to me, telling me about a professor she had met who combed Central America for traces of Marranos, the hidden Jews who long ago had fled the Spanish Inquisition. In Mexico City she had run into Jews from Poland who put out a Yiddish magazine.

Every day Max assured us that he was feeling better, coming along nicely. But Miriam told me that he did not sleep well at night, and that his urine was bloody. That evening there was no phone call from Lynn and we all wondered what might have happened to her. Close to eleven o'clock, as I was bidding Miriam and Max good night, the telephone rang. Miriam picked up the receiver and I heard her say, "Who is this? You want Max Aberdam? Who is calling?"

Whoever the caller was, I had no wish to intrude and slowly walked up the stairs to my bedroom. I could hear Max speaking on the phone. Had the secret leaked out? And who was calling Max? Soon I heard heavy footsteps climbing up the stairs. My door opened and Max stood on the threshold. He was breathing with effort and looking at me with his big black eyes.

"Aaron, a miracle happened, absolutely—a miracle!"

"*What* happened?" I asked. My throat was so dry I could hardly speak.

"I'm flying to Israel. Chaim Joel Treibitcher has found a doctor for me."

Max staggered and I sprang up from my bed and helped him to a chair. He leaned on me so heavily that I nearly fell.

"Who telephoned you? How did they know you were staying here?"

"It was Tzlova, Priva's maid. I introduced her to you that day when you paid us a visit. Remember?"

"Yes, I remember."

"A long cable from Tel Aviv arrived at the apartment. It was from Chaim Joel Treibitcher. He met a doctor with whom I was acquainted in Warsaw and who is now a well-known urologist in Israel. Chaim Joel offered to pay all my expenses to fly to Israel. I'll be able to return your money to you. I'm beginning to believe that there is a God somewhere who does not want me to depart His world just yet. Priva, as you know, is on a ship bound for the Holy Land. It seems that I'll be there before her ship arrives."

"How did Tzlova know that you were here?" I asked, and my own voice sounded strange to me.

"It's a long story. When Tzlova received the cable she realized that I must be in America, not Switzerland. Miriam left our telephone number here in Lake George with her superintendent, and when Tzlova went to look for me at Miriam's, he gave her the number."

Max was shivering while he spoke. He blurted out, "Maybe I was destined to lie buried in the Holy Land."

"Max, no one is burying you yet. You'll be alive and well," I said.

"Miriam is all excited now. She wants to fly to Israel with me, but how can she? She is stuck here with the child. I want to fly out as soon as possible. I grew worse here, not better. If you want to accompany me, I'll take you along at our wealthy benefactor's expense."

"I don't have a passport. And a visa will also be required," I said.

"I didn't think of that. All I have at the moment are my First Papers."

"You can travel out of the country and return to it with your First Papers. But you'll have to take out a permit at the Emigration Office. What happened to your Polish passport?"

"I had my Polish passport extended."

The door flew open and Miriam cried out, "Butterfly, it's a miracle, a miracle! I hesitated whether or not I should leave our number with the superintendent. At the last moment I decided yes. Why it occurred to Tzlova to look for Max at my place and why John gave her the number I will never understand. I want to fly with Max, I can't leave him alone in his condition. But what will I do with Didi? As if to spite me, Lynn did not call tonight. I even think that Didi is not well. I touched his forehead and it felt warm to me. Lynn left us a thermometer, but I put it somewhere and now I can't find it. Ah, I'm going mad!"

Miriam burst out crying. I stood up from the edge of the bed where I had been sitting and Miriam threw herself into my arms. Her face was hot and wet with tears.

"Miriam, don't fall into hysteria," Max called to her. "Everything will straighten itself out. And even if it doesn't, the sky will not fall. Did Lynn leave you a telephone number in Mexico?"

Miriam tore herself out of my arms. "Have you lost your mind, or what? I'm tired. I can't go on. Go, fly to Palestine by yourself. Women of my kind exist even in Jerusalem. I no longer need men, I'm tired of them all. They repel me. I'll lie down somewhere and wait for the Angel of Death to come for me. I have but one friend left—death!"

Miriam ran out and slammed the door. At the same moment the telephone rang. Max said, "Please take the call, Aaron. I can't stand up."

I grabbed the receiver. "Mrs. Stallner?"

A young voice spoke with a Spanish accent. "Miss Sylvia is calling from Mexico City. Will you accept the charges?"

"Yes, yes, of course!"

I heard an unfamiliar woman's voice, hoarse and rasping: "Is this Mr. Greidinger? Sylvia speaking, Lynn's friend. Forgive me for calling at this hour. I have bad news for you, unfortunately. Lynn had an accident. She is in the hospital."

"An accident? What happened?"

"She was driving her car and a drunk ran into her. I was not with her, she was driving to her hairdresser. She broke her arm and has several other lacerations. May I speak with Miss Miriam Zalkind, please?"

"Just one moment."

I put the receiver down on the night table. The door burst open and Miriam rushed in. "Who is it—Lynn?"

"Miriam, don't be frightened. Lynn had a car accident."

Miriam remained standing in the center of the room. She said very softly, "I knew it. I knew it all the time."

I went into the bathroom and sat down on the cover of the toilet seat. How strange it was, I thought, that the good news of Max's prospective doctor and his journey to Israel had plunged Miriam into turmoil, while the bad news of Lynn's accident had been received calmly. One thing was certain: Miriam could not fly with Max to Israel.

I stood up and, intending to brush what was left of my teeth, opened the medicine cabinet. On the middle shelf lay a thermometer, which I picked up. Miriam's telephone conversation was over. She was sitting on the edge of my bed talking to Max. I heard her say, "Take only your summer suits and your rain-coat."

I said, "Miriam, I found the thermometer in the medicine cabinet."

Miriam nodded her head. "I'll use it later. Let Didi sleep now, the little darling."

TEN

I T WAS ALL over—the packing of Max's valises, the bus
ride from Lake George to New York, the arrangements for
quickly obtaining a permit to leave and re-enter the United
States. Miriam remained behind with Didi while Max and I took
the bus to New York, where we stayed in Max's apartment. The
very same refugees who had struck at Priva and stolen her jewelry
now telephoned Max to wish him goodbye and a speedy recov-
ery. Chaim Joel Treibitcher, in a cable to Max, had announced
his intention to compensate the victims of Harry's swindles, and
the news spread quickly among them. The probity and gener-
osity of this righteous man impressed everyone.

During the days we spent in New York, Tzlova and I became
friendly enough to address each other by the familiar "thou."
In Warsaw she had managed a lingerie shop for an ailing elderly
couple who were childless. They had entrusted Tzlova with their
business and at their death she was to inherit it. Predictably,
Tzlova told me her life story. She had been born in a small town
in the province of Lublin, and had been orphaned early in life.

She taught herself sewing and embroidery. She had worked for a corset maker and become a specialist in fitting undergarments for women whose busts were uncommonly large or small, and for those who had undergone breast surgery. "The *alte*," as Tzlova dubbed her employers, often suffered from ill health and traveled to foreign spas or to the villa they owned in Otwock. Tzlova looked after the household details of their large apartment as well as their business affairs. Customers came to her from every corner of Poland, and she supplied all their needs. During the war she had been thrown into a concentration camp; later, in a DP camp in Germany, she obtained a visa to America. Her friendship with Priva had begun while they were living in Warsaw. Priva had become involved in occultism, and had witnessed several séances by the famous Polish medium Kluski. When Priva turned out the lights and Tzlova laid her hands on the little table, it rose on its hind legs and gave correct answers to all the questions put to it. Tzlova became expert with the Ouija board. She assured me that long before Chaim Joel Treibitcher's cable had arrived to announce his finding a new doctor for Max, she had foreseen the event in a dream. Tzlova was also alleged to have seen in a dream that Max would live with Miriam in a house near a lake. When Tzlova asked me to show her the palm of my right hand, to read my future, she said, "A great fire burns within you."

"Is it God's or the devil's?" Max asked.

"A mixture of both," Tzlova answered.

Max often ridiculed Tzlova, making fun of her visions and dreams and accusing her of raising the table with her foot, of deceiving herself and others. He said, "How is it that all these spirits of yours did not protect you from the Nazis?" Yet I could plainly see how close they were to each other. Tzlova was forever telling Max what foods he could or could not eat. When he lit a cigar, she literally pulled it from his mouth. She packed his linen, his underwear, his medications with the practiced hand of a wife. She herself smoked three packs of cigarettes every day and I overheard Max warning her, "You are committing suicide, Tzlova. You may get to the world beyond long before I do."

"Then I'll prepare a reception for you."

"What sort of reception?" Max asked, not without curiosity. And Tzlova said, "I'll sit you in a golden chair, and for a footstool I'll give you that tart, Miriam Zalkind."

On the day before Max's departure, when Tzlova went to buy him things he might need for his journey—pajamas, socks, an enema syringe, a nail clipper, pills to prevent constipation, and other useful items—Max revealed his secret (which I had easily guessed): he had once lived with Tzlova. He knew that this young woman with the white teeth of a gypsy and with a Tatar's slanted eyes had deceived her employers in Warsaw and her mistress in New York. Max said to me, "I can't help myself. I was born a hog. You've inherited Miriam from me and you can also have Tzlova. You belong to my sort. I, my friend, am bound for the scrap heap."

"You'll get well and have a lot more 'hogging' left to do," I said.

"From your mouth to God's ears."

Max spoke the very words I often used to women of my acquaintance: "Is it my fault that I can love more than one woman at a time?"

"The whole idea of monogamy is a big lie," Max said. "It was invented by women and by puritanical Christians. It never existed among Jews. Even our great teacher Moses craved a Negress, and when his sister Miriam spoke ill of him she was struck with scabies. Where is it written that I must be saintlier than Moses or the patriarch Jacob? As long as I had my sexual powers, I enjoyed myself. Now that I'm preparing to make my exit, it is time for you to take over.

"My first wife," he went on, "may she rest in Paradise, was a proper Jewish daughter—but without a spark of imagination. I tried to awaken her by every means at my disposal. I let her read Maupassant, Paul de Kock, even our own Polish Gabriela Zapolska. But her thoughts were entirely immersed in dresses, baubles, expensive furs. Buttermilk flowed in her veins, not blood. I even tried to take her dancing at a cabaret. But anything like a little squirming and wriggling she called by one name— smut. When a man is impotent he is dragged before the rabbi and forced to give his wife a divorce. But when a wife is frigid, as cold as ice, she is praised for being chaste. My wife had one redeeming virtue—she was utterly faithful to me. With Matilda, may she rest in peace, everything was a matter of prestige. If the *grandes dames* of Paris had lovers, then she had to have lovers, too. Chaim Joel, may he forgive me for saying this, was epicene not only physically but spiritually. His passion always was, and still is, money—and thank the Lord, he made more than enough to reimburse all the refugees. If a woman is born who does have hot blood, the whole world rises to condemn her. She is nothing but a whore. Not only the women, the men, too—womanizers. You know very well whom I have in mind."

I felt my face turning white. "Miriam told you everything?" I asked.

"Everything."

"You know her past?"

"Yes."

"What would you call her, then?"

"I would take her as she is."

"Would you marry her?"

"If I were your age, yes."

"She wants to have children. How would you know if they were yours?"

"I wouldn't mind at all if they were yours."

"They could be the mailman's."

"No." Max laughed. "What's the use of talking? But there is one thing I want you to do—don't deceive her."

"I don't deceive her."

"You do. She is pinning her hopes on you. As improbable as it may sound, when it comes to real love, she is a virtuous virgin."

EARLY THE NEXT morning Tzlova and I accompanied Max to the airport. During the taxi ride back, Tzlova pressed her knee to mine. I said to her, "I know everything about you."

"I know that you know," Tzlova answered, "and I know everything about you."

"What do you mean?" I asked.

"First of all, I know that Max can't keep his word. He is like a person who is drunk: if it's on his mind, it's on his tongue. Second, I see things sometimes when I'm awake and sometimes in a dream. When Max first brought you to Priva, I saw a glow around your head."

"What sort of glow? What does it mean?"

"That you'll be mine."

"No, Tzlova. This time you guessed wrong," I said with a tremor in my voice.

Tzlova put her hand on my knee. "Not today. Today I'm menstruating. When you return."

I HAD TOLD Miriam that I wanted no children, neither with her nor with anyone else. The papers and magazines were filled with reports of the population explosion. Malthus had not been as wrong as the liberals claimed—there was simply not enough food for billions of people. The Hitler and Stalin catastrophes demonstrated that humanity's dreams of permanent peace and a united mankind were unreal. Dozens of new nations had sprung

up, and everywhere there was strife and warfare. The world's
hatred of the Jews did not diminish even after Hitler's Holocaust,
and Israel was encircled with enemies. What was the sense of
bringing a child into this world? Why increase the sum of human
suffering? Miriam partly agreed with me, but still she argued,
"If only the wicked multiply, what hope does humanity have?"

"There is no hope, no hope at all."

"Then how did a monkey give rise to a man? How did a
Spinoza come to be, or a Tolstoy, a Dostoevsky, a Gandhi, an
Einstein?"

"I don't want to play this lottery."

We kissed one another and continued to argue. All that remained for us to do was to snatch a few moments of pleasure
before we collided one with the other and, like the bubbles we
were, burst. Both Miriam and I could neither be together nor
stay apart. We did not deny God nor could we serve Him. Serve
whom or what—the technician of gravity and magnetism, of
universal explosions and cosmic beams, who neither accepted
our prayers nor rejected them? We lay in bed at night and confessed our sins, both those committed and the fancied ones, both
the comic and the tragic. And we had so much to say to each
other that the night was often far too short.

Miriam spoke to me bluntly: she could not remain in America
as long as Max was in Israel. He was still recovering; he required
her help and her love. She proposed to me that I accompany
her abroad. The truth was that she did not have sufficient money
even for her own expenses. I offered her the thousand dollars
left of my savings. What would I do in Israel in any case? Not
Yiddish but Hebrew reigned there, the proud language of the
patriarchs, not the jargon of exile. Those who continued to wage
the ancient battle with the Philistines planned to erase from their
memories two thousand years of expulsions and ghettos, inquisitions and pogroms. They wanted to be a nation among

nations, the same as all the others. I intended to visit the land someday, but not just yet.

Something had happened with my novel—I had reached an impasse. I had to rewrite dozens of pages, to retrieve parts of a manuscript already sent to the typesetters. The truth was that I lived in a state of permanent crisis, in danger of forgetting the plot, weakening the characters, diluting the suspense. I was battling demons who put stumbling blocks in the author's way, numbing his memory, intoxicating him with smug complacency. I had my own methods of expelling the evil spirits; I knew their mischief and their pranks. But that was not nearly enough. Like deadly microbes that become immune to medicine and find ever new means of attack, so did the imps of literature never give up the fight. They persistently searched for frailties, vulnerabilities. The more work was accomplished, the more weary the creator became and the more brazen these destroyers grew. One had to be constantly on one's guard. Even the great writers, the classical ones, the masters, had had their failures. Perhaps the human brain was so constructed that man was ingenious at seeing others' faults and naïve and blind as a child about his own.

A trip to Israel would rob me of my energy and time. I had to keep in close touch with the editors, to read proofs, to be ready to correct my text. I often remembered the words of the Cabalists, that man was sent to this world for the sake of *Tikkun*. We were continuously asked to mend our errors. Even in the sphere of *Atzilut*, the world of emanation, the vessels were shattered and divine sparks were scattered down on the abyss below into the world of the *Kelipah*. Art had a good deal to learn from those ancient mystics and from their symbols.

THREE WEEKS PASSED and Lynn Stallner returned, one arm in a cast and the other bandaged. With her were Sylvia and a

Mexican maid. Miriam cried when she took leave of Didi, and I felt my own eyes growing moist. The little boy kissed me and called me Daddy.

Soon an airmail letter arrived from Max saying that he was feeling better but had been greatly weakened by so much surgery. He missed both Miriam and me. He sent me a check for the three thousand dollars I had lent him, and another to Miriam for her expenses. Both checks were signed by Chaim Joel Treibitcher. Chaim Joel also sent me a letter in Hebrew sprinkled with flowery biblical expressions and quotations from the Gemara. He enclosed several friendly lines in Yiddish for Miriam. He had begun to repay all the thefts that his nephew, Hershele or Harry, had left behind him in America by defrauding helpless clients. He intended to return to Miriam the five thousand dollars which her father, Morris Zalkind, had given her and with which Max and Harry had speculated in stocks.

Miriam began to dance and clap her hands when she read the letter. She threw herself upon me with kisses and exclamations. But I had to tell her that I was not prepared to fly to Israel. The crisis involving my serialized novel-in-progress had grown worse. For the first time the editor had tried to eliminate entire chapters without consulting me. I called him up and told him that if he did not reinstate the missing parts, I would abandon the novel. Our feud was scheduled for discussion at a meeting of the paper's managing committee which could not take place for several weeks because the manager and some committee members were either away on vacation or abroad until Labor Day. Not only my novel but my very positions as a journalist and an adviser were also at stake. I had kept all this from Miriam in order to spare her worry, but now I had to reveal the entire situation.

It so happened that Miriam was to fly out three days before Rosh Hashanah, first to Paris and then to Tel Aviv. I wanted to buy her a gift, and when I asked what she wanted she said, "A Bible."

"Israel is crammed with all sorts of fancy editions of the Bible," I said, and suggested a fountain pen instead.

But she said, "A Bible is what I want and what you must give me. If you don't, I'll have to buy one myself."

She had never spoken to me in this fashion before. I asked her, "What happened? Have you turned religious overnight?"

And she answered, "Yes, religious."

I saw a small Bible in a shop window on Broadway, bound in wood, with an engraving of the Wailing Wall on the front cover, and I bought it for her. The shopkeeper threw in a small mezuzah in a bronze sheath and a Hanukkah dreidl. I took all these to Miriam. To my amazement she brought out from somewhere two silver candlesticks, which she said her mother had given her when she married Stanley.

"What are you planning to do?" I asked, astonished.

And Miriam answered, "Be so good as to open the Bible to the *Toykhekhe* chapter for me."

"How do you know about the *Toykhekhe*? What are you going to do?"

"I know about it from a story of yours."

"What are you trying to accomplish? I don't remember any such story."

"Open up. I remember."

I opened the Bible to that chapter, while Miriam lit the two candles.

"What sort of prank is this?"

"Be still and wait."

Miriam covered her hair with a white kerchief. From under her blouse she took a sheet of paper and began to read: "I swear by God in heaven and by the souls of those dear to me, the martyrs who perished at the hand of Hitler, may his name and memory be obliterated, that I shall have no other man in my life besides Max and you. If I should break this sacred vow, may all the curses of the *Toykhekhe* descend on my head. Amen."

Miriam read the words in a sort of singsong chant, recalling the Kaddish to me, or the *El Male Rachamim*, or the lamenting chant of pious women when they buried the dead. She lifted up both her arms and turned her eyes toward heaven. I wanted to interrupt her, but something in her gaze stopped me. When she finished she kissed the Bible and closed it.

I said, "What foolish melodrama. Really, Miriam, this is excessive. It's tasteless. How can you take such an oath? I am twenty years older than you are, and Max forty."

"I know that. But whatever happens between us, I don't want you to lie awake at night thinking that I'm deceiving you with others."

"What value does this oath have, coming from someone who does not believe in God?"

"I believe in God."

"May I put out the candles?" I asked.

"Let them burn."

"Should I also take an oath like yours?" I asked, astonished at my own words.

"No, no, no. You owe me nothing. I am going away from you, not you me. I'll be with Max, and you may have whomever you please."

There was something awesome and ancient in Miriam's voice and in her manner. A lump rose in my throat. All at once I remembered my parents, as well as my uncles, my aunts, my cousin Esther, all of whom perished at the hands of the Nazis. These two candles, lit in the middle of the day, reminded me of the candles placed at the head of a corpse. I tried to tell myself that the entire ceremony was theatrical, a display of female hysteria. But I stood, instead, and stared at Miriam and at the two little flames which played in the pupils of her eyes. She still wore the white kerchief on her head. It seemed to me that she had grown years older during these few moments.

Once again I heard Max's words: "When it comes to real love, she is a virtuous virgin."

"How long do you want these candles to burn?" I asked.

"Until they go out by themselves."

That evening Miriam forbade me to turn on the electric lights. She performed all her chores by the dim glow of the two candles: she cooked supper for us in her kitchenette, then packed all her things into three large valises she planned to take with her to Israel. With the white kerchief on her head, she resembled my mother when I was a small boy who went to Fishl, the *dardeke melamed* in Radzymin, or to Moshe Itzchak's *cheder* at 5 Grzybowska Street in Warsaw. On the bridge table Miriam laid out plates and silverware, all in silence, as if I were her youthful ward and she a newly married Hasidic bride. I could not take my eyes off the two little flames, which burned quietly, as if giving the lie to the tumultuous civilization outside—the culture of the nonbelievers, the countless machines and inventions wrought in the last two hundred years. "How can two candles costing pennies so alter the moods of a man and a woman?" I asked myself. We ate differently than we had before, spoke less, lowered our voices. It was strange, but it seemed to me that Miriam's hands had grown more delicate, her fingers longer and finer. From her eyes, encased in shadows, a certain nobility radiated, such as I had forgotten existed. It was years since I had looked into a holy book or stepped inside a sacred place. But the glimmer of these flames recalled to me the houses of study and the Hasidic *shtibls* where I had first begun to study a page of the Gemara. The first *mishnah* in the tractate of *Berakhot* surfaced in my memory, and I began to murmur and chant, "When is the Shema recited in the evening? From the time the priests come in to eat of their offerings, said Rabbi Eliezer. And the Sages say until midnight. Rabbi Gamliel says until the rising of dawn . . ."

"Did you say something?" Miriam asked.

"Something from the Gemara."

She went into the bathroom to brush her teeth. I lay down on the bed and she came to me wearing a lace nightgown I had not seen before. She said, "*Slub* in Polish means marriage, and *slub* is also an oath."

"Yes."

"Today I married you," she announced.

We put our arms around each other and we lay silent. Miriam squirmed in my arms; her body was hot and her breathing rapid, as in a fever. She said, "Don't worry. I won't force you into anything. I married you, not you me. I know that I am sinning gravely against God, against you, Max. In the old days I would have been ostracized, or even stoned. But what concern of God's is it what little people do on this planet? He has many myriads of worlds in the universe and other creatures, other souls everywhere. Even here on earth not all living creatures follow the same laws: we had a dog once who mated with its own mother. Wait, let me see if the candles are still burning."

Miriam got out of bed and went to the living room. She returned, saying, "One candle is out and the other still flickering."

We fell asleep and awoke exactly three hours later. Waking up was a relief for me, because I dreamed that I had been invited by a writer to an apartment on the top floor of a high building. I brought someone with me who both was and was not Miriam. I had forgotten to bring my hosts a bottle of wine and I left, telling them I would soon return. I began to descend numerous flights of stairs—there was no elevator—and when I finally reached the street I saw to my amazement that I was not in New York but in a *shtetl*, with small wooden houses, unpaved side-

walks, with rivulets and puddles of water as though after rain.
Goats meandered about and chickens pecked among kernels of
corn. "How can this be?" I asked myself. In one little house a
door was open and I went in to ask where I might find a shop
selling wine. To my astonishment there was a whole party of
young men and women whom I had known in Warsaw. They
all greeted me, and one girl, dressed in a tattered dress and
shabby shoes, berated me for having abandoned her. She stood
and read a poem that was familiar to me. "Where am I?" I asked.
"Is this New York? I was invited to the home of a writer and I
came down for a bottle of wine." "What is the address?" they
all asked. "What's the writer's name?" I realized then and there
that I had forgotten both. "It's somewhere on Broadway," I said,
"but not in Manhattan, in Queens." They all stared at me,
unable to understand my words. I was back in Poland, but how?
Besides, Poland was now empty of Jews. And what would my
host say? At that moment I heard Miriam's voice: "Butterfly, are
you sleeping?"

"No."

"What time is it?"

"Twenty after two."

"Oh, Butterfly, I can't leave you. I already miss you. I want
to stay here with you, but Max is waiting for me. He is my
father. He is very ill. I'm so frightened!"

"Of what are you frightened?"

Miriam did not answer. She touched her lips to mine.

I MOVED INTO Miriam's apartment for a while, but I did not
give up my room on Seventieth Street. Now that Max had repaid
me the three thousand dollars he had borrowed, I felt I was rich.
I received three invitations for the holidays. Freidl Budnik reminded me that the first night of Rosh Hashanah belonged to

her. She wanted me to come on the second night as well, but I had already promised to spend it with Stefa and Leon Kreitle. Tzlova also telephoned me. With Priva at sea, bound for Israel, Tzlova was utterly alone. She had struck up no friendships in America. She had not learned to speak English properly. She said, "Since your last visit here with Max, I have not spoken to a living person."

We arranged to meet for lunch at two o'clock on the day before Rosh Hashanah. Although the buildings in the Seventies, Eighties, and Nineties between Broadway and Central Park West were filled with Jews, there was no sign of the High Holidays. Broadway looked exactly as it did the other days of the year. In New York grapes, pineapples, and pomegranates were not special fruits reserved for Rosh Hashanah. The sound of the shofar was not heard in the synagogues during the month of Elul. No one tried to frighten Satan off, to stop his denouncing of the people of Israel. The constant honking of horns and the clatter of subways would have muffled even the sound of the shofar announcing the Messiah. I bought a box of chocolates for Tzlova with a golden inscription reading *L'shanah tove tiketeyve*, and I walked over to Riverside Drive, where Priva and Max had their apartment. On the way I stopped and bought a copy of the *Forward*. Between solemn articles devoted to the coming holidays and New Year greetings from assorted Jewish organizations, as well as from the Presidents of Israel and the United States, the latest installment of my novel brought a touch of the workaday world into the paper—the scene happened to take place in a Warsaw jail.

I rang her doorbell and almost immediately Tzlova appeared, wearing an apron and slippers. I had asked her to prepare a light lunch, since later that evening I was to dine with Freidl and Misha Budnik. Although Freidl considered herself an anarchist and atheist, and believed that religion was the opiate of the masses, on the holidays she prepared her meals in accordance with the old ways—on Passover there were matzohs, four cups of wine, bitter herbs, *kharoses*; on Rosh Hashanah she served radishes, apples with honey, carrots, and a carp's head. She always provided a decanter of sweet Jewish wine. Freidl's blintzes, dumplings, Hanukkah pancakes, Shavuos babkas, and Purim hamentashen were first-rate. For Hoshana Raba she baked a challah and sliced the carrots into "rounds." The Purim challah she braided on both sides and covered it with saffron. Freidl was descended from generations of pious Jews and Hasidim.

When Tzlova opened the door, the aromas of our lunch wafted from the kitchen. She embraced and kissed me. When I handed her the box of chocolates she exclaimed, "Spendthrift!" The table in the dining room was already set. Tzlova had assured me that the refugees had smashed Priva's china and her fine crystal, but the table was fit for a banquet. After a while we sat down to eat. I had learned that those who lived alone, men and women, experienced an inordinate need to talk. No sooner had we sat down to the vegetarian chopped liver, the tomato soup, the kasha varnishkes with mushrooms, and the compote with tea and lemon and preserves than Tzlova began to retell the story of her life, complete with fresh details and incidents. She ate, smoked, and chattered.

I sat at the table and vowed not to begin an affair with Tzlova. Miriam's oath before her departure and her remarks on the way to the airport were fresh in my mind. I began to question Tzlova about her occult powers, and she embraced the subject with enthusiasm. She said, "I've had these powers from childhood. As a child I dreamed that someone died, and days later they carried him past our window on a stretcher. Several times I told my parents what I had dreamed, and my mother scolded me. She said, 'These dreams alarm me. May all your dreams fall upon our enemies, body and soul.' My father was a teacher of

Gemara, and he told me that if I came to him once more with my dreams, he would whip me. He had a whip made of six straps nailed to a hare's foot. He used it to whip the boys who did mischief and refused to concentrate on their lessons. He grabbed me by my hair and dragged me to the room where we kept our tools—spades, brooms, troughs. He said to me, 'Your dreams come from an evil source; it's nothing but sorcery.' I didn't know what 'source' meant, or 'sorcery,' but the two words struck me with such fear that even today I shiver whenever I hear them.

"I swore to my parents that I would hold my tongue, but still I continued to have 'visions,' sometimes while awake and sometimes in a dream. I had a younger brother named Baruch David Alter Chaim Ben-Zion. Who, after all, has five names? He was named Baruch David, but years before he was born my parents lost a pair of twins, a boy and a girl, to scarlet fever. When Baruch David was born, my father traveled to his rabbi in Kuzmir and the rabbi instructed him to add the other names—Chaim (that he may live), Alter (that he may reach old age), and Ben-Zion (that he be spared from evil). The rabbi told my father to dress the boy in a little white caftan, white pants, a white hat, to make the Angel of Death believe that he was already dead and wearing shrouds. At home we called him by only one name, Alterl. My mother and father fretted over him as though he were a treasure. The other children were afraid to play with him. He had a good head on his shoulders, and his *melamed* predicted that he would grow up a prodigy. My father did not earn a living from his teaching, and so my mother helped out by selling milk. She also baked buckwheat *pletzels*, and the yeshiva boys used to come and buy them. When I was a child of nine, my mother fixed my hair in two braids. I don't know why, but those yeshiva boys always looked at me, devoured me with their eyes. In those days I was afraid of men.

• *165* •

"I was eleven years old when I dreamed one night that Alterl was lying on his bunk and a black fire was curling upward over his head. How can fire be black? But that was how it looked to me. I woke up knowing that Alterl was going to die. He slept in the bunk next to mine, and I went over to take a look at him. He was fast asleep, but his little face was all lit up, as if the moon, or a lantern, were throwing its light upon him. And over his head I saw that black fire, made as if by the bellows which our blacksmith, Itche-Leib, kept in his workshop. I quickly put on my clothes and fled from the house. I walked and walked until it was daylight. It was after Succoth then and the road was one long track of mud. The muds of Izevice were famous through all of Poland. Let me be brief. That day my little brother died.

"Soon afterward my father suffered a stroke. He collapsed and they could not revive him. My mother languished a year longer. It was in Izevice, in fact, that I became a seamstress. About Warsaw you already know. Why am I saying these things to you? For this reason: I have been seeing visions until this very day."

"What do you see in me?" I asked.

Tzlova examined me for a while and then she said, "You are not the same."

"What do you mean 'not the same'?" I asked.

"Don't be angry," Tzlova answered. "I mean no harm."

"Tell me what you mean!"

As if trying to gauge me, Tzlova said, "You have done something which you now regret."

"What have I done?"

"Got married, perhaps?"

"I did not get married."

"You've done something. This Miriam is a witch. Wait, I'll bring more tea."

———

EVENING FELL AND still we sat and talked. I kissed Tzlova, kissed her face, her lips, even her breasts, but I went no further. I had sworn not to betray Miriam. My watch now showed six o'clock and I told Tzlova that I had to go, the Budniks were expecting me.

She said, "I'll accompany you to their house."

"What are you saying? It means a long ride on the subway, an hour or more."

"I have plenty of time. I have never been alone on Rosh Hashanah. Not even in the concentration camps."

"I would ask you to come along, but you know how women are."

"I know, I know. They hate me, all of them, because I am younger and because Max was once mine. They unleashed all their rage on Priva and me. They berated her and cursed and spat on me. Why was she to blame or I? She knew nothing of Max's plots and schemes. And why did she run off to Israel? Come, let me go with you."

"Tzlova, it makes no sense."

"It makes perfect sense. When I am by myself I begin to think too much."

"Do you miss Max?" I asked.

"Yes, and now I'll miss you, too."

We left the apartment; Tzlova fastened the two locks on the door. In the elevator we bumped against men and women on their way to the synagogues, dressed in their finest clothes, prayer books in their hands. The subway was nearly empty— the onset of Rosh Hashanah was plainly in sight. The Gentile passengers, spread out in the sparsely occupied train, sat reading the English-language afternoon papers, which showed a photograph of a white-bearded Jew in a *tallis* blowing into a shofar. It had all been prepared for the press in advance. Tzlova and I sat down in a corner of the last car, and we watched the rails flying backward. Tzlova took my arm.

"He isn't worth my missing him. Max had affairs with everyone. He was like a Turk. He should have had a—what do they call it?—a harem. But he is sick, sick. One day he was as strong as an ox, the next as weak as a fly. And yet he never stopped questioning me: Whom did I have, how many did I have?"

"How many did you have?" I asked.

"Now *you* want to know? I didn't count them."

"Twenty?"

Tzlova did not speak for a long time. "Not even ten."

"Where? In Warsaw?"

"All in Warsaw. Here there was no one but Max."

"What happened in the concentration camps?"

"They were not allowed to touch a Jewish girl. '*Rassenschände*,' they called it. We were all crawling with lice. Ah, if only the subway could run and run and never reach its destination."

"Where would you like it to run to?"

"Israel, China—as long as I'm with you. What will I do alone at home?"

We sat without speaking, and Tzlova leaned her head against my shoulder. She must have fallen asleep, because suddenly she gave a little snort and sat up. "Where are we?"

"On Simon Avenue."

"Where is that?"

"East Bronx."

"I won't know how to go back home."

"Tzlova, I can't take you up to these people. They've invited me, not you."

"No, no, no. I wouldn't go even if they had invited me."

"Stay on this train until the end of the line and wait until it goes back. Then get off at Seventy-second Street."

"The train may stay at the end of the line all night."

"There will be another train."

"I'm afraid to do that."

"What do you want to do, then?"

"Wait for you."

"Have you gone mad? I'm spending the night with them."

"You didn't tell me that. Will you spend the night in bed with your hostess?"

"They have an extra room for me."

"What is the woman's name?"

"Freidl."

"She is in love with you, huh?"

"Don't speak nonsense."

We got off the subway and I showed Tzlova the way to the train that would take her back to Manhattan. Tzlova said, "Wait here. Don't go until I come up the stairs opposite and see you. I want to be sure I am not lost."

"All right."

I stood and waited and still I did not see Tzlova. Two downtown trains arrived and departed on the opposite platform. "What could have happened to her?" I asked myself. I was suddenly seized with hysterical laughter. We had just become acquainted and already she clung to me like a wife. "What's become of her?" I asked myself. At last I saw her and shouted over to her, "Why did it take so long?"

"I didn't have change and the man would not accept a ten-dollar bill. What are you doing tomorrow evening?"

"I have another invitation for tomorrow evening."

"When will I hear from you again?"

Before I could answer her, a train arrived and Tzlova boarded it. She called out something and gesticulated. I went quickly down the stairs and began to walk toward the Budniks' apartment. Here in the East Bronx Rosh Hashanah was much in evidence. The stores were all shut and the streets were dimly lit. Darkness fell from the sky. I was reminded of the sentence in the Gemara: "On what festival is the new moon hidden? On

Rosh Hashanah." Yes, where were the dead? What became of the hundreds and thousands of generations which once lived on this earth? Where were their loves, their pains, their hopes, their illusions? Were they all gone forever? Or was there an archive somewhere in the universe where they were all recorded and remembered?

All at once I realized I could not go to the Budniks' empty-handed. I set out to look for stores that might still be open and began to lose my way in the streets of the East Bronx. A fine, needle-sharp drizzle began to fall. I stopped passersby to ask where a wine shop might be found. Several would not answer me; others said that all the stores had closed by now. Suddenly I was in a well-lit street where a liquor store materialized. I bought a bottle of imported champagne, spotted a taxi, and climbed in. Several minutes later I knocked on the Budniks' door.

Freidl had dressed up for the holiday and had lit some candles. She was a small woman, her hair was dyed as black as her eyes, and a Jewish-Polish joy radiated from her small face. She may have made Misha an anarchist, but in recent years she had begun to admit that life was not precisely as Bakunin, Sternen, or Kropotkin determined that it ought to be—the Jewish state, for example. I ate challah with honey and recited, "May the coming year be good and sweet." I ate the carrots and recited, "May our merits and virtues increase and multiply." This last wish was bound up with the Yiddish language. Surely the Sephardic Jews did not recite it. I did not touch the carp head, because I was a vegetarian, but when Freidl sat down to eat it I recited for her, "May we henceforth be heads and not tails." These customs had arisen after Jews had begun to speak Yiddish, in Germany or perhaps later in Poland.

Misha turned his back on all the prayers and the blessings, but not on the food. He devoured everything with relish, while heaping abuse and invectives on Jewish reactionaries of every camp: on the General Zionists, on Poale Zion, on Orthodox and Reformed Jews, on Conservative Jews, as well as on Jewish socialists and Communists. He said they all had but one wish —to amass privileges for themselves and to exploit others. They concealed their greed behind flowery phrases and hypocritical slogans. In the last twenty years the anarchists had officially renounced terror as their method. But Misha was doubtful whether the anarchists' goal could be achieved without it. "How would the revolution come about?" he asked. "Will the militarists, the Fascists, the Stalinists suddenly decide to grant the masses their freedom? Nonsense, wishful thinking!" Freidl smiled, shook her head, and reminded Misha of his promise not to spoil my visit with political talk. But Misha was eager to draw me into a debate. He said, "I read your pieces in the paper. You write well, it would be better if you didn't—but what will the masses learn from your articles? Love, love, and more love."

"What should I write about—hate?"

"Go into the factories and see how the workers are exploited. Go to the coal mines and see what's going on."

"No one wants to read about factories and coal mines, not even the workers themselves."

"Misha, will you let him eat?" Freidl said. "He can't change the world. How long ago was it that he did not even have a nickel for the subway? Do you remember, he was as white as chalk? He had gone without food that entire day."

"I remember, I remember. But he has forgotten."

"You, Misha, have also forgotten," I said. "Remember the stories you used to tell us in the *Bet Midrash* at night. The one about the little woman, the dwarf, who threw you a pinecone and caused you to faint."

"Those were just stories, tall tales."

"Misha, you told me the same story. It was even before we

decided to live together," Freidl broke in. "And remember the gypsy woman you met in Ruva-Russka, the one who could name all the members of your family? She predicted when and where you'd meet me, and other things as well."

"Freidl, what is it with you? Have you also joined hands with the parasites? You yourself taught me that property was theft. Now you've gone and changed your mind."

"Misha, there are more mysteries in the universe than you have hairs on your head, more than the grains of sand by the sea," I said.

"What mysteries? There is no God, there are no angels, no demons. These are all fairy tales, much ado about nothing. Freidl, I'm going."

Her eyes bulged in their sockets. "Where are you going?"

"Where I go every night, to my taxi. Rosh Hashanah means nothing to me. God does not sit down on His fiery throne to inscribe in His book who should live and who should die. This night for me is no different from others."

"You ought to be ashamed of yourself, Misha. A guest like Aaron and you run out? We don't need what few dollars you'll make dragging yourself around all night. It's raining outside."

"Ah, it's not the money. What's money? In a free society money will not exist. People will swap what they produce. I slept during the day, and now I won't sleep a wink all night. I like to drive my taxi at night. It's quiet. The types who come crawling out at night are interesting to me. The other night I stopped for a well-to-do couple, a gentleman and a lady. No sooner did they sit down than he began to beat her. He slapped her face, punched her, shouted abuse at her. I stopped the taxi and said, 'Sir, my taxi is for riding, not for fighting.' She began to scream, 'Driver, mind your own business. Just keep on going where you were told to go.' They lived on Fifth Avenue. Perhaps they were husband and wife. He gave me ten dollars and told me to keep the change. I saw she had left her purse in my taxi.

I ran and gave it to her. She said, 'You are an honest bum.' That was her thanks."

"Misha, you make me ill with your stories!" Freidl exclaimed. He kissed her and left.

Freidl said, "He is a madman. I'll never know what he is and what he wants. I've lived with him for some thirty years, and sometimes I think that he is as naïve as a child."

"He is not so naïve. He was a smuggler for many years. And when he married you, he knew you were not a saint."

"During the war, how could I have done otherwise? We were hungry, my family and I, and I became their breadwinner. It was as the saying goes: 'Bread or dead.' My mother pretended not to know. My father sat in the Hasidishe *shtibl* all day long. Cholera was rampant then—the Austrians brought it with them—and there was death in every home. One day you suffered cramps; by the next day or two, everything was over. Who gave a thought then to what one could or could not do? I had found a book by Kropotkin—in the Jewish library, in fact—and I simply devoured it. When he, Misha, met me and fell in love with me, he knew nothing. He could read the prayers in the prayer book, but he could not read a newspaper. I had to teach him everything. Our daughters went to college, but sometimes they speak as if they are children. They take after him. Well, there's nothing more to say. I hear that Max is in Israel."

"Yes."

"And where is that girl—what is her name—Miriam?"

"She followed him to Tel Aviv."

"Well, well. Must be head over heels in love with him."

"Yes."

"A tramp."

"According to Emma Goldman's *Shulhan Arukh*, it is not a transgression," I said.

We stood without speaking, and finally Freidl said, "Sometimes it seems to me that the whole world is one vast madhouse."

ELEVEN

INASMUCH AS THE world is insane, I thought up an insane
plan—to travel to Israel with my closest friends, Stefa and
Leon, Freidl and Misha, and Tzlova. I told them what I
proposed to do and they all accepted the plan. I knew that people
from travel agencies, and even rabbis, led groups of people to
the new Jewish state. Many Jews in America yearned to visit
Israel, but they were reluctant to travel alone since few of them
spoke modern Hebrew, with or without a Sephardic pronunciation. I first presented my plan to Freidl on the eve of Rosh
Hashanah and she said, "I know whom you mean to see there,
but I will go with you just the same. Max Aberdam lost five
thousand dollars of our money, but we can still afford the trip."

Between us Freidl and I convinced Misha that there were
anarchists even in Israel. I also explained to them that Chaim
Joel Treibitcher was prepared to make restitution for his nephew's losses and debts. Irka Shmelkes had already received repayment from him: Chaim Joel did not intend to sit by and see
the Treibitcher name besmirched.

When I told Misha about this, he talked like an anarchist: "Where did he get so much money? It must be from fraud and theft."

"If it is," I said, "you will still be happy to accept it. Chaim Joel is a just man and no thief ever returns stolen money willingly. Why don't you get him to contribute a million dollars to the *Voice of the Free Worker?*"

Freidl chuckled and winked at me. I left after breakfast and looked for a drugstore not owned by Jews. I spotted an open one with several telephone booths and called Tzlova. I knew I could not spend this entire day by myself.

"Tzlova, did I wake you up? Forgive me."

"Is it you? I lay awake all night and thought of you. Really, I'm afraid that until Priva returns—if she decides to return—they'll put me away in the madhouse!"

"Tzlova, we're going to Israel!" I cried out.

"When? What are you saying?"

I repeated my plan to Tzlova and told her about the other four I meant to take along.

"Arale—may I call you Arale? I'll go with you wherever you go and with whomever you go. From this day on I am your slave. Yes, I am!"

"Don't talk nonsense, Tzlova."

"You saved me from death. I was already searching the ceiling beams for a hook from which I could hang myself. God is my witness. Where are you?"

"On Tremont Avenue, not far from my *landsleit.*"

"Come on over now!"

I SPENT THE day with Tzlova. We strolled along Riverside Drive and had lunch in a Chinese restaurant. We walked past a synagogue as the cantor's singing drifted outside. Tzlova tried to demonstrate her skill at levitation, but the little table refused to rise. She said, "It's because you don't believe in these things."

"I believe, I believe."

"What are we going to do with our apartments, you with Miriam's and I with Priva's?"

"We'll lock them up securely while we're abroad."

Tzlova showed me her bankbook. Apart from the money she had given Max to invest for her, she had nearly three thousand dollars. Tzlova also had some war bonds and a quantity of jewelry. She would settle on a kibbutz and begin a new life for herself. She brought out all her trinkets and baubles, showing them off to me the way my childhood friend Shosha used to do when I was a small boy.

We embraced and kissed. There was no love on my part, not even lust, but what else was one to do with a pretty woman like Tzlova? We lay down together on Priva's bed and Tzlova said, "She'll know about this, she'll know everything. There are no secrets between us. She is not jealous of me."

"Priva knew that you had relations with Max?"

"She knew everything."

"Did Max tell you about Miriam?"

"Every detail."

"To what depths will people sink?" I wondered, and Tzlova answered, "Great depths."

Soon Tzlova rose and I heard her bustling somewhere in the large apartment—in the kitchen perhaps. She returned wearing an ornate nightgown and slippers, carrying a tray with cookies, two wineglasses, and a decanter of red wine. She said, "Let's drink to the new year. Just so. *L'chaim!*"

I FELL ASLEEP and dreamed of Miriam. In my dream it was also Rosh Hashanah. My parents were alive and we were all going to the *Tashlikh* together. Was it in Bilgoray? The river was too wide to be Bilgoray's. No, this was the Vistula. The men led the way, dressed in satin *capotes* and in *shtreimls*. I myself did not go to the *Tashlikh* but looked out of a window of the Trisk *shtibl*, which stood on a hill. My father was bent over my brother Moshe, speaking to him. In a little while the girls and the women appeared, all decked out in their holiday finery. Old Genendele wore an ancient costume called a *rotanda*. "Genendele is alive?" I asked myself. "She must be over a hundred now." And then I saw my mother. She wore the gold-colored dress she had worn at her wedding and which she always wore on the Days of Awe. Over her wig she wore a white silk shawl. In her hand she held a prayer book with a brass clasp. *"Mameshi,* are you alive?" I cried out in my dream. A frail nobility emanated from her pale and narrow face. Had the Messiah come? Had the resurrection of the dead begun? My mother had died in Dzhambul, in Kazakhstan. Suddenly I saw Miriam standing near her. She held my mother by her arm. "It's a dream, a dream!" I shouted out. I opened my eyes and the bedroom was dark. Twilight had fallen. Tzlova was bending over me.

"Arale, it's a quarter to six. You must go you-know-where."

I sprang out of bed. I was expected at the Kreitles' at six-thirty. I dressed quickly, with Tzlova's help. She picked up my shoes, shirt, and tie, which I had scattered in disorder, as was my habit.

I found a liquor store and again I bought a bottle of champagne for my hosts. This time I did not need to take a taxi. Both the store and the Kreitles were nearby. The Kreitles lived in a skyscraper with two spires on Central Park West and Seventy-second Street. I was ready to present my plan for a journey to Israel to Leon and Stefa. As I stood in their spacious lobby and waited for the elevator, it became clear that again I had plunged myself into a predicament, woven myself into a tangled web. But why did I do these things? Was it a form of masochism?

I rang the bell and Stefa opened the door. She wore an ex-

Isaac Bashevis Singer

quisite silk dress, and her hair was freshly brushed and combed. But she did not look well, having gained both weight and wrinkles. She looked me up and down, and from her expression I knew that my own appearance was lacking. But soon a smile lit her face, she threw her arms around me, and we kissed. She cried out, "Look, champagne!"

Leon appeared and we embraced each other. To overcome my embarrassment and the uncertainty I felt over my own plans, I exclaimed, *Mazeltov!* We're going to Israel!"

"Who is this 'we'?" Stefa asked.

"You, Leon, I, and several others of my old guard."

"What old guard?"

"Ah, *landsleit* of mine, simple people but good souls."

Stefa shrugged her shoulders. "My mother used to say: 'He is hatching a plan without consulting the boss.' "

"Why sit here in New York when over there a new Jewish state is springing up?"

"When do you expect to go?"

"As soon as possible."

I could see in Stefa's face that she liked the idea, and I said, "By Succoth we'll be there."

"Leon, are you listening?"

"Yes, I'm listening. We should have done this long ago."

"How is your business doing?" I asked.

"My business is taking care of itself," Leon answered. "They write in the papers about a hidden inflation and it is true that things are becoming costlier, not cheaper. But in my business the less one tampers, the better."

"Leon, it's a holiday!" Stefa interrupted him.

"The Angel of Death cares nothing for holidays. In my father's town there was a woman who had her own shrouds. She used to lend them to anyone who died on a holiday. It is permitted to bury a corpse on the second day of a holiday, but one may not sew shrouds for it."

· *178* ·

"What happened if the person who died was a male?" I asked.

"It is permitted to bury a man in a woman's shroud. The dead are all of the same gender," Leon said.

"Why all this talk of death?" Stefa asked. "For the time being we are alive. Yes, we'll go to Israel with you. Why do you need these *landsleit* of yours?"

"It will be livelier with six of us."

"Well, give me a little time. How long is it to Succoth?"

"Exactly two weeks."

We ate, drank champagne, and Stefa's eyes glistened with youthful fire. Yes, the impossible was possible—that would be my motto in the future. We sat and talked until a late hour, when both Leon and Stefa urged me to stay the night. Franka's room was still waiting to receive me, and this time I allowed myself to be persuaded. Leon knew all the details concerning Max Aberdam, Harry Treibitcher, and his uncle Chaim Joel. Leon said that years ago Chaim Joel Treibitcher had bought lots in Miami Beach which were now worth millions. This former Hasid was so rich he could not and did not know the exact extent of his wealth. He, Leon, also owned real estate in Miami but, he declared, "in comparison with him, I am as a fly is to a lion."

After Leon retired to bed Stefa said, "How did you suddenly come to plan this trip to Israel? Do you have a mistress there?"

"Maybe."

"A new one? An old one? You can tell me the truth. I am not jealous. Who are these *landsleit* you plan to take along?"

"An elderly couple and a friend of Priva's."

"From the old country, huh? And who is paying their expenses?"

"They are paying for themselves."

"Well, that does not concern me. Come, I'll fix your bed," she said.

We walked into Franka's room. The room was shrouded in darkness. I took Stefa in my arms and we stood locked together in a long kiss. Stefa said, "Don't worry, Leon is asleep. He falls asleep immediately, then wakes up two hours later unable to drop off again. He awakens me, too, and so we lie together immersed in our troubles. When one lies awake all night," Stefa added, "the brain becomes a storehouse of madness. Good night!"

DURING THOSE DAYS —the ten Days of Repentance between Rosh Hashanah and the Day of Atonement—I sensed that my tension was at its height and that I was in danger of bursting. Yet I proceeded with our arrangements according to schedule. I had secured the tickets with which, on the day after Yom Kippur, we would board a ship bound for Cherbourg. We would spend several days in Paris, then fly from there to the land of Israel. We would be in Israel the day following Simchas Torah.

On the ship the Kreitles would travel first-class, while the Budniks, Tzlova, and I had tickets for tourist class. Stefa asked me to join her and Leon, at their expense, in first class, but I could not consent to such a proposal. I had never taken anything from anyone, other than a meal, and even then I always remembered to bring my host a gift.

I left two weeks' worth of copy for my serialized novel with the editor. The subsequent installments I was to send from Israel by air. I recorded several weeks' advice for my radio broadcasts. I gave everyone the same advice—the would-be suicide, the disillusioned Stalinist, the betrayed husband, the woman ill with cancer, the author without recognition, and the inventor whose patent had been stolen: This world is not our world, we did not create it, we are powerless to change it. The Higher Powers gave us but one gift: choice, the freedom to choose between one woe and another, between one illusion and another. My advice was, Do nothing. I even made up my own motto: "Nothing is as good as nothing." After all, most of the Ten Commandments begin with "Thou shalt not." I cited the Gemara: "Sit and do nothing is preferred." I instructed my listeners to swap, for the time being, one passion for another, one kind of tension for another. If you are unsuccessful in love, I said, try to channel your energies into business, or a hobby, even into some kind of amusement. Why commit suicide when inevitably one dies anyway? Death could not stop the human spirit. The soul, matter, and energy are made of the same stuff. Death is only a transition from one sphere to another. If the universe is alive, there is really no death within its framework. How could there be an end to what was infinite? The very thing that filled the living with terror—death—could well be a source of boundless bliss.

As I talked so glibly on the radio, I realized that I often contradicted myself. But to whom would it cause harm? Surely somewhere a power existed which blended together all contradictions and made of them one truth. I quoted Spinoza's saying that there was nothing in divinity which could be called a lie. Our lies were bits of truth, smashed tablets of the law, where the "Thou shalt not" remained etched on only one fragment of stone. All that we could do was to avoid, as much as we could, inflicting pain on ourselves and on others. I advised my listeners to take a trip, to read a good book, to take up a hobby—never to try to change this or another system, this or another government. The problems of the world are beyond our powers. We could bring our free choice to bear only on trifles, on matters which touched us personally. I embellished my "sermons" with quotations from Goethe, Emerson, the Bible, with tractates from the Gemara and the Midrash. I myself felt greatly comforted after I had finished.

Yiddish journalists often wrote disparagingly of those who played cards, but I did not agree with them. If cards could inject a measure of tension and enjoyment into an individual's life, they were beneficial, not harmful. The same could be said of theater, films, music, books, magazines. Whatever killed time was good. Time was a void which somehow or other had to be filled.

I promised no permanent peace, no cure for humanity's neuroses and complexes. On the contrary, I warned my listeners that no sooner did one free oneself of a neurosis than another rushed in to take its place. The neuroses were waiting in line. Life was one protracted crisis, one long-drawn-out struggle. When the crises ceased, boredom came—the worst anguish of all. I quoted Schopenhauer, my favorite philosopher, although I did not agree with his assertion that the World-Will was blind. I was certain the World-Will, like the Angel of Death, had a thousand eyes.

OUR SEA VOYAGE was leisurely. By the time we arrived in Paris, at the hotel our travel agent had booked for us, night had fallen. I did not recognize the city. The Paris I remembered from the mid-thirties on my journey to America had been elegant, gay, clamorous—virtually a carnival. Paris after World War II seemed drab, shabby, desolate, beset with nocturnal gloom. Rain fell and a chilly wind blew. Even the Place de la Concorde had lost its beauty; it was covered with old-model cars as if it were no more than a giant parking lot.

When we finally arrived at our hotel on the Place de la République, we were told that its restaurant was not in operation. The waiters had gone out on strike. In fact, almost everything in France seemed to be in a state of strike. The trade unions threatened that soon the trains would cease to run, airplanes would not fly, and taxis would disappear from the streets. Anxious as I was, I could not resist a dig at Misha. "You must be happy," I said. "After all, this is what the revolution wanted."

Only Freidl kept her head. She went down to the lobby, and although she spoke not a word of French, she managed to find a bearded American officer who turned out to be an Orthodox rabbi, a chaplain. This hotel "Intellect" swarmed with American Jews. When Freidl explained that she was accompanied by an ailing eighty-year-old man, and that she was traveling to Israel with the Yiddish writer Aaron Greidinger, everyone offered help. The rabbi said he was a confirmed reader of mine. Although he could never accept my view of Jewishness, he respected the knowledge I had acquired in the Old Country. A young man who had joined in the conversation volunteered to take us to a restaurant nearby. Pockets of the black market still operated. Prices were higher, but one could order whatever one liked, even *cholent* with *kugel*, and they often stayed open late at night. The young man—short and broad, with a full head of hair as curled as a sheep's—showed us the way to the restaurant. In a dimly lit alley we climbed up two dark flights of stairs. I could smell the aromas of chicken soup and chopped liver. "This boy is none other than the prophet Elijah," Freidl quipped. The darkness of Egypt reigned over the rest of Paris, but here Jews sat down to a late meal and Yiddish was spoken. A woman came out of the kitchen wearing a dress and an apron that reminded me of Poland. I even thought I detected a *shaytl* on her head. She told me she was a reader of mine and that the Paris Yiddish paper reprinted my articles and novels. She stretched out a moist hand and exclaimed, "If I were not too embarrassed, I'd kiss you!"

AFTER THE WAR the French municipal government had consigned a certain building in Paris to intellectual refugees—writers, painters, musicians, actors, directors. Most of the refugees had dispersed to America, Israel, and elsewhere, but some had remained. During our stay in Paris the Jewish Writers' Union invited me to a reception in that building. The leftists—Communists, quasi-Communists, and their fellow-travelers—arrived armed with complaints. The few Zionists among them were disgruntled because in my writings I had ignored political parties, the struggle against Fascism, the rebirth of Israel, the bravery of the partisans, the struggle of women to achieve equality with men. They all enumerated the political sins I had committed, and a Trotskyite reproached me for not having sided with Trotsky. I had grown accustomed to these literary gatherings during my days in Warsaw. They repeated the usual cliché: writers could not hide in an ivory tower while the masses stood on the barricades. Misha Budnik, who attended the gathering, asked for the floor and made a lengthy speech. Did the writers know that in Spain Stalin had murdered hundreds of anarchist freedom fighters? Were they aware that in the Soviet Union thousands of anarchists languished in slave labor camps and prisons? Had they read how Emma Goldman and others had been treated in Russia when they had gone there to spread the truth? He mentioned Sacco and Vanzetti and the four who were hanged in Chicago. Someone in the audience heckled Misha: "Did the distinguished speaker know that Machno had staged pogroms against Jews?" And Misha shouted back, "Machno was a hero!" A tumult erupted in the hall, and the chairman began to pound the table with his fist. He forbade Misha to continue his speech, and Misha was led down from the platform.

When my turn came I spoke briefly, saying that Nietzsche's theory of eternal repetition was true. Should I—some million years from now—again be a Yiddish writer, I would wage a literary battle both for the Zionists and for the territorialists, for nationalism and for assimilation, for Marxism and for anarchism, for Weizmann and for Jabotinsky, for the *Neturei Karta*

and for the "Canaanites," as well as for the Bund, the General
Zionists, the right-wing *Poale Zion*, the left-wing *Poale Zion*,
for *Hashomer Hatzair*, for the Folkists, as well as for the Luba-
vitch Hasidim, the Bobov Hasidim, the Orthodox, Conservative,
and Reformed Jews. I would write novels about them all, as
well as stories and poems in the styles of naturalism, realism,
and symbolism and follow the Futurists, the Dadaists, and all
the other "isms" and "ists." Several in the audience laughed
and applauded. Others grumbled and registered their protests.
Refreshments of lemonade and pretzels were served. A large-
bosomed, aging songstress sang folksongs and refused to relin-
quish the microphone.

When the entertainment was over I chatted with several
women who had lived through the war, some of them in ghettos
and concentration camps and others in Russia. I heard new variations of Nazi brutality and Bolshevik chaos—the usual stories
of midnight arrests, hunger, denunciations, overcrowded prison
cells, of packed trains left standing for days on end, black-market
commerce, of drunkenness, theft, plunder, hooliganism, and
prostitution. It was all so tragically familiar. I was told about a
well-known poet whom Stalin had liquidated: to the very day
when he was put against the wall to be shot, he had continued
to write odes to the great Comrade Stalin. One writer confessed
to me that, after a shot of whiskey and a candid conversation
with a friend, he had blurted out an unkind word about Stalin
and the other had done the same. When he sobered up, he was
overcome with fear and went straight to the political police to
inform on his friend. Apparently his friend was struck by the
same fear, because they collided at the entrance to the denun-
ciation chamber.

During our stay in Paris our group drifted somewhat apart.
Stefa and Leon visited museums, expensive restaurants, cafés.
They even made a bus trip to Deauville. Misha and Freidl went

searching for anarchists, who had their haunts in the Belleville quarter, not far from our hotel and from the center of Jewish radicals.

We were in Paris for only a few days, but it seemed like weeks. An old Yiddish classic poet, David Korn, invited me to his home. I asked Tzlova, who had no one in Paris but me, to go along. She clung to me like a wife. The poet, who earned his living as a correspondent for a Yiddish newspaper in New York, spoke with bitterness about all Jewish leaders—those on the left, the right, the Zionists, the anti-Zionists, and so on. He waged a private war on all modernists—they murdered literature, made it loathsome, boring, turned poetry to parody. Like the Chelm *melamed* who asked his wife to bake a cake without butter, sugar, raisins, or eggs, so the modernists tried to create poetry without rhyme or rhythm or music or love. David Korn apologized to me for not attending my reception. "I can't abide their ugly faces, their crafty eyes. A relentless bunch. Their phrases about justice are too repulsive to mention. As long as there was a Stalin, they flattered him and worshipped him as an idol. Now that the boor Dzhugashvili is dead, they will leave no stone unturned until they find a new Stalin. Slaves need a master."

His wife, younger than he, came to the table with a pill and a glass of water. In her old-fashioned clothing and in the manner in which she combed her hair, she reminded me of those young women who manufactured bombs for the revolution.

"Davidl, take your vitamin pill."

David Korn fixed a pair of angry eyes on her. His mustache twitched like that of a tomcat. "I don't need any vitamins. Leave me alone."

"Davidl, the doctor prescribed it for you. You must take it!"

"I must, huh? Those doctors are all swindlers, robbers, crooks. Their medicines are nothing but poison."

"Mr. Greidinger, do me a favor and ask him to take his pill.

He is ill, ill. He is barely alive. He must not excite himself."

"Friend Korn, do me a favor and take the vitamins," I said. "How does the saying go? 'It may not help, but it won't hurt either.' "

"Rubbish. Thieving druggists thought it up."

David Korn took the pill, threw it into his mouth, made a sour face, and drank half a glass of water. "It has the taste of Mayakovsky's poetry," he muttered.

WE BOARDED THE plane for Israel in the morning and late that afternoon arrived at the airport in Lod. In comparison with the enormous airports in Paris and New York, Israel's airport seemed provincial. The peace of the Sabbath rested on it. The plane on which we had arrived had been filled with Hasidim, yeshiva students, and women with wigs and kerchiefs on their heads. One passenger had prayed an early *Minhah*, a second had browsed through a volume of the Mishnah; a red-bearded rabbi had examined a young man studying to receive a *heter horaah*. As the religiously observant passengers disembarked, a throng of rabbis and other yeshiva students waited for them. I had not seen sidelocks as long and as curled as theirs, literally down to their shoulders, in many years. They exuded a freshness. Under their long *capotes* they wore short trousers, white stockings, and slippers, and their velvet hats appeared to be new. They were too young to have gone through the Holocaust as adults and too old to have been born in the DP camps.

The inspection of passports and baggage progressed slowly. Occasionally a customs officer opened a suitcase and began to shake out shirts, trousers, sweaters, other garments. The owner watched the scrambling of his belongings with apprehension. Finally we passed through customs. Misha carried not only his own valises but Stefa's, Leon's, Tzlova's, and mine as well. I tried to help him, but he snapped at me. All at once I spotted Miriam. It was she, but something in her appearance had changed; I could not determine exactly what it was. She wore a white blouse, and her slacks were black. She ran toward me with her arms stretched open. I had sent her a telegram from Paris saying that I would arrive with others, but I felt embarrassed at having arrived with so many companions. Miriam embraced and kissed me.

"Well, here you are," she said. "Butterfly, I brought along a car."

"Where did you get a car?"

"Mr. Treibitcher gave me his. He wanted to come himself, but I discouraged him."

"How is Max?"

"Better, but not completely well. You'll see him soon in Tel Aviv."

I introduced Miriam to the Kreitles and the Budniks. I said, "Misha Budnik is a childhood friend of mine from Bilgoray. And this is Freidl Budnik, his wife, a dear woman."

"I remember Aaron when he had two red sidelocks," Misha said, "and when he swayed over the Gemara in the *Bet Midrash*. Under the Gemara he was secretly reading a novel printed in *Moment*."

"Misha, enough," Freidl murmured.

Miriam greeted Stefa, Leon, Freidl. For some reason she did not hold out her hand to Tzlova, merely nodded her head. She asked Misha, "Were you also a yeshiva student?"

"I was a smuggler in those years. But I used to come to the *Bet Midrash* at night to chat. I loved to hear Aaron's fantasies."

Miriam left and returned in a large car, but it was not big enough for six people, our luggage, and a driver. Stefa proposed that she and Leon find another taxi, and no sooner had she uttered the word than a *nehag*—as drivers are known in the new land of Israel—presented himself. Stefa asked Miriam for the name of Max's hotel and Miriam answered, "Max is staying at a small hotel. But I don't believe that you, Mrs. Kreitle, will find it suitable. There is a larger and better hotel nearby, a more modern hotel, half a block away."

"Good. My husband is not in the best of health. He must have a private bathroom and all the rest. Is there a restaurant in the hotel?"

"An excellent restaurant."

"He also needs a doctor."

"There are more doctors in Tel Aviv than patients."

I could see that Miriam and Stefa took to each other. They immediately began to chatter in Polish. Miriam completely ignored Tzlova. Freidl asked, "Where are we staying?"

Miriam answered, "On Hayarkon Street. Many Jews arrived here for the High Holidays, but most of them have already gone home. There will be room for everyone."

"Lady, are we going or staying here?" the taxi driver asked.

"We are going. To Hayarkon Street," Miriam answered.

Miriam had already become an Israeli. Even her Hebrew was spoken with a Sephardic pronunciation. We were greenhorns. The taxi driver took off first, after helping the Kreitles settle with their luggage in his taxi. The Budniks and Tzlova got into Chaim Joel Treibitcher's car; I sat in the front seat next to Miriam. The luggage fit in the trunk, with several small valises on our laps. I asked, "Why did Treibitcher send along his car?"

Miriam answered, "Chaim Joel cannot do enough for Max. He is also an ardent fan of yours. If not for him, Max would have been finished here. He called in the best doctors and hired nurses around the clock for Max. Half of Warsaw is here. Max does not like Jerusalem."

"Why not?"

"It's too holy for him. He is as *meshugah* as ever, but also sweet."

The car sped along while I sat and looked out at the houses, palm trees, cypresses, and garages. Jewish soldiers—boys as well as girls—stood along the roadway, thumbs out, hoping for a ride. We were in the midst of a hot summer day, with the sky very blue and without a cloud. Everything shimmered in the sun, as though the light had grown sevenfold brighter than it had been during the Diaspora. I had arrived in the land of Israel, the land for which my ancestors had yearned for two thousand years.

STEFA AND LEON moved into two rooms in the Dan Hotel. The Budniks settled in a hotel on Ben Yehuda Street, one block from Hayarkon. Tzlova and I took rooms in the small hotel where Max and Miriam were staying. Max had changed utterly—he had lost nearly forty pounds, his beard had turned white, and his face had become sallow. Miriam slept near him every night. He told me that Priva was living in Jerusalem. Her ultimatum: either Priva or Miriam, and he had chosen Miriam. He said to me, "But I'm afraid not for long. I am more *there* than here." And he pointed his finger toward heaven.

I had made a monumental error when I decided to bring my five companions with me. Tzlova wanted to stay with Priva, not Max, and a few days after we arrived she moved to Jerusalem. She informed me that Priva had found a rich widow in Jerusalem who arranged séances. They planned to put out a journal, half Hebrew and half English. Priva telephoned to tell me that all her occult powers had returned to her in Jerusalem stronger than they had been before. She and her patroness, Mrs. Glitzenstein, had summoned up the spirits of Dr. Herzl, the Hebrew writer and martyr Y. H. Brenner, Max Nordau, and Ahad Haam. The most interesting had been Max Nordau. He, the noted materialist, who had scoffed at every religion and considered even the literary masters to be madmen and degenerates, now conceded that he had lived in error and that all his works, especially the two volumes *Degeneration* and *Paradoxes*, should be burned. In the higher spheres he had met the Italian-Jewish materialist Lombroso, who had written that genius went hand in hand with lunacy. Together they begged forgiveness from the spirits of those they had once attacked, among them the Polish medium Kluski and the Italian Paladina. Priva also informed me that she had contacted Max's dead wife and two daughters, who had died at the hands of the Nazis.

Freidl Budnik was captivated by Eretz Israel, but Misha managed to spoil her pleasure. From the day he arrived he complained and grumbled about the Jewish state. Nothing pleased him. He caused a commotion in a restaurant when the waiter refused to serve him coffee with cream at the end of a meal which included meat. When the proprietor explained to Misha that this was the law of the land, Misha hollered that such a law was Fascist. In Tel Aviv Freidl had run into *landsleit* of hers from Izevice, Gorshkaw, Krasnystaw. Several of them had already forgotten their Yiddish and spoke Hebrew among themselves, for which Misha attacked them. I invited Freidl and Misha to dinner at the new Dan Hotel, where Stefa and Leon were staying. During the meal Misha berated me for having brought him to a land which was ruled by theocrats. He wanted to know why in America Jews demanded the separation of church and state, whereas in Israel one was forced to eat kosher food and brides had to immerse themselves in a *mikveh* before their wedding? Misha banged his fist on the table. He asked to see the *mashgiach* and demanded that he, Misha, be served ham. At the end of eight days the couple returned to America. Freidl cried when we said goodbye. As for Misha: "It is as if a dybbuk had entered into him," she said.

Oddly enough, I myself now felt sometimes that I was not the same person I had been. What was the nature of the change and did it have to do with the climate? Perhaps it was connected with the thousands of years of Jewish history. Did the spirits of the ancient Jews—the priests, the Levites, the leaders of the various tribes, the heroes, the Hasmoneans, the Sadducees, and other unknown forces—hold sway here, forces that we Diaspora Jews had long ago forgotten or perhaps never known? Max had aged here.

Miriam had begun to use Hebrew words and expressions in our conversations. I suspected that she was no longer as interested in Yiddish as she had been in New York. She still called me Butterfly, still embraced and kissed me, but now that Max was ill and apparently impotent, she was no longer willing to submit herself to me. She always found an excuse. Was she carrying a grudge against me for my having brought Tzlova and the Kreitles along? Sometimes I felt as though Max's friendship had also cooled. The one who clung to me more than ever was Leon. He was forever inviting me to dinner or lunch. He continued to receive the newspaper for which I wrote and he wanted to discuss every installment of my novel. Leon's health had improved and he claimed that Tel Aviv's air was curative. He even voiced his desire to buy a home here and live what years he had left among Jews.

My room had a window overlooking Hayarkon Street and a balcony which faced the sea. In the evenings I often sat on the balcony and took stock of my life. I had flown to Eretz Israel to rejoin a beloved woman. I had taken with me three women with whom I had had affairs, but fate decreed that here, for the first time in years, I should be celibate. Miriam slept near Max, Tzlova was in Jerusalem, Freidl and Misha had gone back to New York, and Stefa was exceedingly devoted to her husband.

Polish Jews in Tel Aviv published a Polish weekly, German Jews a German weekly, Hungarians a Hungarian paper, and Romanians a Romanian one. In the shop windows on Ben Yehuda and Dizengoff Streets were displayed new editions of books in every language. Sometimes I would wake in the middle of the night, seat myself on a chair on my balcony, and gaze at the star-studded skies and the sea. In New York I had forgotten that there were stars in the sky. But over Tel Aviv there hovered the cosmos with all its stars, its planets, and the whole heavenly host. The air was fragrant with the smell of vineyards, of eucalyptus trees, of cypresses, and other aromas which seemed familiar to me and at the same time new. Warm breezes blew, carrying with them perfumes for which I could find no name.

This sea before my eyes was not some random body of water, it was *Hayam Hagadol,* or the Great Sea, the sea on which Jonah had fled from God to be spared prophesying the destruction of Nineveh. The ship which had carried Judah Halevi—the greatest Hebrew poet of the Middle Ages—to Eretz Israel had sailed on this sea. Here had sailed the merchant ships to which the Woman of Valor had been compared in the Book of Proverbs. The waves sparkled in the moonlight and God Himself watched over Tel Aviv. In the stillness one could hear the echo of the prophet's words: "Behold, the vision of Isaiah the son of Amos which he foresaw for Judah and Jerusalem in the days of . . ." Nearby Rachel still wept over her children and refused to be consoled. All around us lurked Philistines, Ammonites, people of Moab, Aram; Canaanites, Amorites, Hittites, Jevusites, Girgashites—all waiting to resume the ancient war against God and His chosen people.

ONE DAY A writer came to see me with a Hebrew translation of one of my stories. I edited the translation in his presence, and the writer asked me, "Since you seem to be so knowledgeable in Hebrew, why don't you write in Hebrew instead of Yiddish? As you must know yourself, Yiddish is becoming extinct, while Hebrew has come back to life."

"Becoming extinct is not a shortcoming in my eyes," I told him. "Ancient Greek became extinct, and so did Latin. Hebrew was a dead language for two thousand years. All of us who are alive today will sooner or later become extinct."

He opened his mouth as if to speak but instead said nothing. He picked up the manuscript and left.

He was not alone. I had heard the same sentiment expressed by other writers and scholars. I could have easily adapted myself to modern Hebrew and to the Sephardic pronunciation. But the answer I most often gave was the following: "My mother spoke Yiddish. My grandmothers and grandfathers spoke Yiddish, all the way back to *Siftei Cohen*, to Rabbi Moshe Isserlish. If Yiddish was good enough for the Baal Shem Tov, for the Gaon of Vilna, for Rabbi Nachman of Bratzlav, for the millions of Jews who perished by the hands of the Nazis, then it is good enough for me."

"Yiddish is 80 percent German and German was the language of the Nazis," someone once said to me.

"And Hebrew was spoken by our enemies—the people of Ammon and Moab, by the Philistines, the Medianites, and perhaps also the Amalekites. Aramaic, the language of the Zohar and the Gemara, was spoken by Nebuchadnezzar and Hamilcar," I replied.

IN ISRAEL THE rainy season had begun. Max's health improved and he could walk with the aid of a cane. We often sat with Miriam at a café table on Dizengoff Street drinking coffee and chattering. It looked as if Stefa and Leon would buy a house and settle in Tel Aviv. I myself could not remain here much longer. The final chapter of my novel in the *Forward* had been delivered, and for some reason I could not settle on a theme for a new work.

Chaim Joel Treibitcher was arranging for a housewarming party at his new house. Since Miriam and I had not attended his party in New York, we knew we could not miss this one. There were rumors that Chaim Joel had met a rich widow in Haifa, an American millionairess, and planned to marry her. His new house was situated on Rothschild Boulevard, and Max joked that the street would now be renamed Treibitcher Boulevard. Chaim Joel told Max all about the widow, Mrs. Beigleman, who was rolling in money. Her deceased husband, who hailed from South Africa, where he had owned a gold mine, had built sky-scrapers in New York, Chicago, Los Angeles, and Houston. Despite this good fortune, he had suffered a heart attack and died. Mrs. Beigleman had met Max and was entranced with his jokes, his charm, his flattery, and his stories of Warsaw. She recommended a doctor in New York who had operated on her husband. Mrs. Beigleman, who expected to be at Chaim Joel's party, was an immense woman, almost six feet tall, with a nose like a shofar and the teeth of a goat. When she spoke, her voice was a deep alto. Stefa whispered softly to me, "She could swallow up Treibitcher and no one would ever know it."

My creative drive seemed to have left me and I had not the least desire to begin a new novel. For the first time in years I felt a need to rest, to take a vacation. A weariness came over me and there was a twitch in my wrist—the well-known writer's cramp. I had also lost my desire for Miriam. For some reason which I could not explain, I was filled with dread whenever I thought of Treibitcher's upcoming party. Chaim Joel rang me up at my hotel and warned me to take special care about the party and not be late. I asked him why this matter was so im-portant and he answered, "I can't tell you now, but in a certain sense the party is for you. Don't be frightened. No one will crown you with a pumpkin and candles as was done to a hero in a story of yours." I wanted to scold Chaim Joel and tell him that he had drawn up his plans without consulting the person involved, but he repeated, "For God's sake, be on time," and put down the receiver.

It was raining in Tel Aviv and it turned cold. The papers reported that in the Negev rivers were suddenly overflowing. Places which a moment before had been dry land and sand had in an instant been overrun by raging torrents which swept away men, camels, sheep. Not far from Tel Aviv deep pools of water had formed which women and children, as well as the elderly, were unable to cross. Young men volunteered to carry passersby on their shoulders. Several times the electricity went out at night; Tel Aviv was plunged into the darkness of Egypt. Even at the Kreitles' hotel, which was new, for some reason there was no cold water. The telephone did not function properly; in the midst of one of my phone conversations with Leon, the lines were disconnected.

Priva now arrived in Tel Aviv with Tzlova, not to see her sick husband, but to attend Chaim Joel's party. As a result Miriam had to vacate Max's room to come and live in mine. In her resentment she threatened to boycott the party.

"We can't do that again!" I cried.

"*You* must go. Don't you know that you are to be presented with a literary prize?" It seemed that Mrs. Beigleman had set up an award of five hundred dollars in the name of her late husband. "Treibitcher is planning to add a similar award in Matilda's name, so your prize will be one thousand dollars!" Miriam chuckled at the thought. Then she said in a serious tone, "Butterfly, I've wanted to bring up this matter for days, but I've lacked the courage to do so. You have been good to me, but you are too young to be what Max is to me."

"Too young? I'm twenty years older than you are."

"I am approaching thirty and I would like to have a child before I lie dead in my grave. If I am to have a child, now is the time. Every month when my period comes I feel that my last chances are slipping by. No man can ever understand this. We all have our foolish fantasies. You once wrote a story—it was actually a memoir—about the mother of a friend of yours who every two years gave birth to a child, a boy. And to each little boy as she rocked him in his crib she would sing that someday he'd grow up to be a rabbi. Do you remember?"

"Yes, it was my friend Isaac's mother. Not one of her boys ever grew up. They all died in infancy, but she never stopped singing her song: 'Moishele will be a rebbele, Berele will be a rebbele, Chazkele will be a rebbele.' "

"I mention this story in my dissertation," Miriam said. "Why am I living, if not to produce someone who will be worthy of the name Man? To what end is all this sex and all our love and passion? What I feel inside me is stronger than logic. You may even tell me that I am being shameless. You once quoted an expression from the Gemara which I have now forgotten, meaning a woman who demands sex. You wrote that one may divorce this woman without a *ketubah*. Is this true?"

"That is what the Gemara says."

"Well, inasmuch as I am not your wife and I have no *ketubah*, you can't divorce me and you can't take away my *ketubah*. Remember the oath I swore to you?"

"I remember everything. But what will you do if you get a negative answer from me, look for another father?"

"I just told you that I will not break my vow to you. If I am destined never to be a mother, I want to know it and make my peace. There's no need for you to answer me now. Tell me only how long I must wait. I don't want to live in this kind of suspense year in and year out."

"We'll have a child."

We both sat still, without speaking. I was stunned by what I had said, and Miriam by what she had heard. She looked at me as if she was ready to laugh and to cry at the same time.

THE DAY OF the party finally arrived. According to Max, Chaim Joel had invited hundreds of guests, "half of Eretz Yisrael," and it would cost him a small fortune. I had taken my good suit to be pressed and I had also bought a shirt and a tie for the occasion. Miriam had gone shopping with me and had persuaded me to buy a new pair of shoes. Since Priva had returned, Max had no visitors, not even Miriam. Only Priva and Tzlova watched over him.

Chaim Joel telephoned to say that he would send a taxi for Miriam and me. For Max, Priva, and Tzlova he would send his own car. He enumerated a long list of notables he had invited, among them ministers, members of the Knesset, military officers, authors, editors, scholars from the universities of Rehovot and Jerusalem, and actors from Habimah and from other theaters in Israel.

The party was to open with a buffet supper. Although Miriam had consistently belittled the affair, she nevertheless prepared for it. She even had her hair done, something I had never seen her do in New York. Yes, Chaim Joel Treibitcher had elegant invitations printed, which mentioned my name and announced my literary award. He also ordered a sort of diploma, inscribed on parchment in both Yiddish and Hebrew, for the presentation of the award.

It had rained the night before, but now the rain had stopped and the sky had cleared. I went out on the balcony to look at the sun setting in the west. It seemed to me that the sun of Eretz Yisrael was not the same as that of Poland or America. It was awash with a gold which reminded me of Yom Kippur at dusk, before the *Neilah*. A sanctity seemed to hover over the waters. This was the sea of the Bible, of "those that go down to the sea in ships, that do business in great waters, these see the works of the Lord, and His wonders in the deep." It was the sea of the prophet Jonah, of the book of Job. Nearby were Tyre, Sidon, Tarsis. This was not an ordinary sunset, the likes of which I had seen in Bilgoray and Warsaw and on Riverside Drive in New York. This sun truly meant to dip in the waters of the sea, as it was written in the Gemara and the Midrash.

Chaim Joel's big house, located in a suburb of Tel Aviv, was filled with guests—room after room crowded with people who represented female beauty, male talent, civic distinction, and even philanthropy. I had never witnessed anything like it. Chaim Joel was still remembered for his receptions in Berlin, where he had lived until the year before the rise of Hitler. At that time the late Matilda was his hostess. This party or *mesibah* [gathering] seemed to be a free-for-all, a bit chaotic. Chaim Joel greeted me at the door for a brief moment, together with his wife-to-be. He was dressed in a tuxedo, which gave his short figure a comic appearance, not unlike that of a dwarf in a circus. The large woman next to him was covered with jewelry, in a dress that glittered with gold sequins, with her dyed red hair piled high like a tower. They greeted us pleasantly, but the deafening noise in the room swallowed up their words. Every language of the world could be heard—fragments and phrases in Yiddish, Hebrew, English, German, French, Russian, Polish, Hungarian. Miriam held on to my arm and together we were pushed on. Waiters and waitresses carried trays laden with delicacies. Groups of guests clustered near buffets groaning with food and drink. One stranger I saw bore an uncanny resemblance to Dr. Herzl —the same beard, the same eyes, the same pale aristocratic face. I bumped into men and women to whom I was apparently known. They greeted me, pressed my hand, shouted unintelligible words into my ears. From time to time someone tried to

shout over the crowd, to tap a spoon against a glass, to call for
order, without success. The air had turned warmer and the house
was now extraordinarily hot. Miriam spoke into my ear, "Let's
get out of here!"

We pushed our way from room to room until finally we found
ourselves in a bedroom. On two wide beds were heaped piles
of coats and jackets. On top of one pile perched the velvet hat
of a rav or a rabbi. I had earlier noticed several bearded men
dressed in long, coarse frocks, with skullcaps on their heads. I
had heard that, among other institutions, Chaim Joel Treibitcher
supported several yeshivas in Safed and Jerusalem. In this room
there was quiet and I went to a chair that stood against the wall.
Miriam exclaimed, "Butterfly, I'm hungry. I was foolish enough
to believe that they would seat us at a table and serve us a meal."

"Perhaps they will. Be patient."

"I must look for Max. You stay here."

"Don't forget to come back."

I sat down on the rose-colored armchair. I had put two fresh
handkerchiefs in the pockets of my pants, but they were already
wet from the perspiration on my face. Miriam threw me a kiss
and plunged into the confusion and bedlam. When she opened
the door, it was as though a thousand throats had lifted their
voices in a roar. The room was filled with shadows from a single
lamp. So, this is the millionaire's bedroom, I thought. Here he
will sleep with that huge woman a mere handful of months after
his wife has died. I was hungry, but at the same time it was as
if I was also stuffed. My stomach felt bloated and a sweet-and-
sour fluid filled my mouth. "How will they present me with an
award in the midst of this orgy?" I asked myself. "How will they
even find me?" It was good to be alone again. I wanted neither
their money nor their honor.

"To be married, to father a child?" my own dybbuk asked.
"To raise another Aaron Greidinger, another Max, another Mir-

iam, another Chaim Joel Treibitcher, or maybe even another dragon lady like his wife-to-be?" One could never know what the genes and their combinations might produce. I began to look for something to read, a book, a magazine, or a paper, to rid myself of my thoughts, but I could find nothing. I rested my head against the back of the chair and closed my eyes.

I lapsed into these black moods whenever I happened to find myself in a large crowd. One person, even two or three, I could easily tolerate, but an assemblage of people always struck me with fear. A crowd can turn ugly; mobs can launch wars, revolutions, inquisitions, expulsions, crusades. Even a group of Hasidim, or a crowd at a funeral, terrified me. It was a mob that cast and worshipped the Golden Calf; a mob had ostracized Spinoza; in 1905 a mob of Jewish revolutionaries had attacked and killed a shopkeeper on Krochmalna Street, alleging he was a capitalist. Mobs had burned Jews, heretics, and witches, lynched Negroes, set houses afire, robbed, raped, even murdered little children.

I had begun to doze off when the door suddenly flew open and I heard a medley of voices. It was Miriam accompanied by Chaim Joel Treibitcher, Max, and Stefa. I shivered and woke up. Max looked well in his dinner clothes. He had dyed his beard, because once again it was streaked with black. He shouted in a loud voice, "Why are you hiding yourself as if you were a shy bride? We've come for you!"

"You are, after all, our guest of honor tonight," Treibitcher cried out.

"He wants to show us how modest he is," Stefa said, and from her voice I could tell that she, too, was a trifle drunk. Miriam was holding a drink in her hand and an intoxicated bliss shone in her eyes.

Chaim Joel Treibitcher took my arm and began to lead me through his large house. The rooms were not as crowded as they had been before. The evening was warm and so the buffet and the drink tables had been carried outside. Chaim Joel's house had an enormous garden. Miriam handed me a plate of food and even found a chair for me. The outdoor lamps threw a mysterious light over the trees, the grass, the guests' faces. The air had a fragrance of both autumn and spring. We were no longer in Tel Aviv but in a royal court somewhere in India, Persia, or deep in Africa. It reminded me of the royal court where King Ahasuerus feasted with his slaves, his nobles, his ministers in Shushan. Merry with wine, he decided to show off the beauty of Vashti, his wife, while nearby lounged scores of his concubines, watched over by eunuchs. I ate, drank the sweet wine which Miriam brought me; guests—both men and women—came over to greet me. They assured me that they had read everything I wrote. Two of my books had been translated into Hebrew; my stories were published in Hebrew and Yiddish magazines, and sometimes even in the daily press. Tel Aviv was not New York, where a writer could live out his life, publish scores of books, and remain unknown. Here people read everything and kept abreast of everything.

That evening for the first time in my life I experienced a taste of fame. When my name was called, I was placed at a table among notables. Chaim Joel handed me a scroll inscribed and decorated on parchment and an envelope containing a check. He spoke about me briefly in Yiddish. Then someone spoke in Hebrew about my work. Miriam, Stefa, and Chaim Joel's wife-to-be kissed me on the cheek. I myself was growing tipsy. Nevertheless I managed to thank Chaim Joel and his guests and to say a few words about the fate of Jews and Yiddish, words which brought applause. I also remembered to mention my friendship with Max and with Miriam, the woman who was writing a dissertation about my work for an American university. It was the first time in my life that I had spoken before an audience.

After the presentation of the award, the assembled guests broke up into small groups. I heard old questions being discussed: What was a Jew? What role was left to Diaspora Jews now that a Jewish state had been created? A professor of Polish extraction complained that German Jews had complete control of the university at Jerusalem and that they kept out scholars whose origins were Polish or Russian. The political situation was also discussed. Small as was the number of Jews in Eretz Yisrael—a third of those living in America—still they were split into many political parties—half leftists, three-quarter leftists, even Communists. Although Russia had voted for the Jewish state at the United Nations, Khrushchev had begun to tilt toward Egypt, Syria, Jordan, even toward the Palestinian terrorists. The tiny nation was surrounded by foes on all sides. A white-bearded rabbi whose face was nevertheless young reasoned with several youths wearing yarmulkes: "The whole idea of Eretz Yisrael rests on the Bible, on our sacred books. But when faith in the Almighty and in Providence ceases—in what way are they Jews and Eretz Yisrael a Jewish land? They might just as well have chosen Uganda or Surinam. This worldliness of ours is nothing if not foolishness and ignorance. Rabbi Kook was speaking the truth when he said . . ."

I listened closely to hear what Rav Kook had said, but someone gave my arm a gentle tug. It was a short, broad, middle-aged woman. Her eyes were black. Even before she opened her mouth, I knew she was a Jewish woman from Poland and a victim of Hitler. She said to me in Yiddish, "Forgive me for disturbing you. I am a reader of yours . . . I must speak to you about a certain matter, but it cannot be done hurriedly. Can we sit somewhere and talk?"

"Come, let's find a place."

The rooms had gradually begun to empty out. We found a room that was free of guests and sat down in a corner. "The matter I want to discuss with you is very very important," she said. "I hesitated all evening whether or not to approach you. I am a cousin of Chaim Joel's wife, Matilda, may she rest in peace. My daughter attended the Gymnasium in Warsaw with Miriam Zalkind. My daughter, unfortunately, is no longer among the living. Miriam does not recognize me now—how could she? At that time I was relatively young, but now I am neither young nor well. I have only recently been discharged from the hospital after a serious operation."

"What is your name? Miriam will be glad to hear about you."

"I don't want her to hear about me. It's better that she doesn't recognize me."

The woman shook her head from side to side. With a tremor in her voice she said, "I beg you, don't be angry with me. What I want to tell you will not be pleasant for you to hear, but I feel it is my duty to speak to an honored Jewish writer."

I realized that the woman knew of Miriam's conduct, her licentious ways, perhaps also of her doings on the Aryan side. I said, "Yes, I understand, but I want you to know that we cannot judge those who have suffered through the Holocaust. I mean *I* cannot judge. You are probably also a victim of Hitler's."

"Yes, I lived through that hell, all of it."

"So did Miriam."

"I know, but . . ."

The woman paused. She opened her purse, took out a handkerchief, and touched her eyes. "What the murderers did to us, that God will judge someday. But those who helped the murderers and served them—for them I can have nothing but contempt."

"What do you mean?"

"Miriam was one of their *kapos*."

It was as though the woman spat out the words. A spasm
twisted her face. Everything in me grew very still.

"Where? When?"

"You must hear me out."

"Yes, yes."

My throat was so dry that I could barely pronounce the words.
The woman said, "Don't worry. I am not about to tell you all
I've endured at the hands of the Nazis. I was dragged from one
camp to another. I was a seamstress, and for that reason alone
my life was spared. I mended their uniforms, I sewed underwear
for them—for the officers, not the soldiers. The whole story will
never be told. Our refugees have written heaps of books and
I've read almost all of them. What they say is true. But the real
truth—that the pen cannot capture. For me, in any case, it is
too late. By the time I wrote about what happened to me—if I
could—I would be gone."

"You mustn't speak that way!"

"I want you to know that what I am doing now I do with a
heavy heart. I can't tell you exactly how at the end of 1944 I
was sent to Riga. We were dragged from one location to another
until I found myself in Riga with hundreds of other lost souls.
Some of us were still more or less healthy and others were already
nearing their end. One day they loaded us on a ship, a freighter,
packed us in like herrings in a barrel, and brought us to Stutthof.
That it was Stutthof we learned only because a few of us were
allowed to go on deck and see the light of day. Then they
transferred us to Marburg, which was to be our last station. It
was already clear at that time that the Nazis had lost the war.
But whether we would live to see our liberation was an open
question. Outside Stutthof we saw mountains of children's shoes,
clothes, articles of every description. The children themselves
had been burned or gassed, and their little garments lay in piles.
Now comes the part I want to tell you, because I feel compelled

to do so. Miriam paraded around Stutthof with a whip which only the *kapos* were allowed to carry. I saw her as clearly as I see you now. That is all I want to tell you. I believe you know that a Jewish girl did not become a *kapo* for her good deeds. The whip was meant to be used. With it she thrashed Jewish girls for the smallest sins, for being slow when called for work, for trying to steal a potato, for similar petty crimes. Some *kapos* even helped the Nazis to drag children to the gas ovens. Well, that's what I wanted to tell you. How does the saying go?—'The facts speak for themselves.' "

I sat in silence for a long time. "Are you sure that it was she?" I asked.

"There's no dodging it. She used to visit our home. I'd recognize her a mile away."

"Did she see you?" I asked.

"No, I believe she did not. And even if she had seen me, she would not have recognized me. We were, as they say, on our last leg, a group of skeletons. No, she didn't see me—I mean recognize me."

I thanked the woman and solemnly promised her to say nothing to Miriam. Just as I stood up to shake her hand, Miriam suddenly appeared. The woman grew even paler and hurriedly withdrew her hand. She swayed unsteadily on her feet and opened her mouth to speak but uttered not a sound.

Miriam asked me, "Where have you been all this time? I've been looking for you."

"I'm leaving. Good night," the woman said, her voice breaking as she left.

"Yes, good night, and again—thank you."

"Who is that woman? What did she want?" Miriam asked.

"A teacher. She needed some advice."

"You're dispensing advice here, too? Max and Priva have gone home with Tzlova. Before we go tell me, what did that woman want?"

"Ah, the eternal story—the husband, the children."

"She looks familiar to me. Why are you so agitated? Did she say something that upset you?"

"The eternal family tragedies."

"Let's go." And Miriam took my hand.

The night was not cold, but still I felt chilled. We waited for a taxi, a *sherut*, or even a bus, but thirty minutes went by and we had not found transportation. The countryside was nearly dark. The sky had clouded over, but between the clouds I could see the flickering stars. Miriam was wearing a light summer dress and soon she, too, complained of the cold. She said, "Where are we—in the middle of a desert? Ah, your hand is so cold! Your hands are generally warm."

"I'm not so young anymore."

"You're young, you're young. Maybe we should start to walk. It can't be far, but the question is, in which direction? All we need to know is, where is the sea?"

"Yes, where is it?"

No sooner did I utter those words than the supper I had eaten earlier that evening came gushing out of my mouth. I began to run and to vomit. I ran up to the lamppost and clung to it, knowing that I could go no farther. Waves of bitter fluid rose up into my mouth, then rushed out. In the midst of this outpouring my face was bathed in perspiration. I knew that I must take care not to soil my shirt, my suit, but I was no longer master of my body. Miriam ran shouting after me. She grabbed me by my neck and slapped it as if I were choking on food. A taxi passed us and Miriam called to the driver to stop. The driver shouted something back, probably his reluctance to have his taxi smeared with my vomit, and drove on. Flames danced in front of my eyes, my knees shook, and with all my strength I kept myself from collapsing. "I must not faint! I must not!" I kept warning myself. I realized I no longer had the scroll Treibitcher had given me and had probably lost the envelope containing his check. Miriam stood over me, wiping my face with a handkerchief. At that moment a taxi pulled up in front of us.

Only after I got into it did I see that Miriam had Treibitcher's award *megillah* in her possession. I also found the envelope with the check in my breast pocket. Miriam asked, "What happened? What did you eat that disagreed with you so? Everything they served was so fresh." My intestines had emptied themselves out, but my mouth, my palate, even my nose felt sour. This was the second time that I had vomited in front of Miriam, the first being the night when Stanley had broken in on us with his revolver. I was unable to give Miriam an answer.

I nevertheless remembered to take my wallet out of my back pocket in anticipation of paying for our taxi ride. The driver, in a talkative mood, asked Miriam a question in Hebrew. It was as if my ears had turned deaf. I could hear his voice, but I could not make out his words, which were spoken in the Sephardic pronunciation. Miriam spoke fluent Hebrew. I had given her money with which to pay the driver, and she said it was too much. We pulled up in front of the hotel, and climbing out of the taxi, I felt my knees shaking again. The night clerk, an elderly man, looked at me and asked, "What's the matter? Not feeling well?" There was no elevator in the hotel and Miriam led me up the stairs. As we climbed together, I felt for the first time in my life that pain of which old people complain, as though the veins in one's legs are clogged up.

Miriam helped me to undress myself, and she sponged my body with cold water. She fussed over me like a devoted wife and I began to think, I'll stay with her. Whatever she was before—it's all the same to me. Who am I that I should judge victims of Hitler? I had also heard that among the *kapos* there had been decent people who helped the inmates in the camps. What they all wanted was to save their lives. I was filled with great pity for this young woman who, at twenty-seven, had experienced so much of life's bitterness as a Jew, as a woman, as a member of the human species. She found my pajamas and she helped me to put them on. She tucked me into bed. A little while later she asked, "May I stay here with you?"

"Yes, my dear."

She went to her own room, where she lingered for a long time. I lay back in bed depleted and spent. My feet remained as cold as ice, not the ordinary cold which came from outside, but a cold which arose from within me. I had already begun to doze off when I heard the door open. Miriam came to me, and her body, too, was cold. She had evidently washed herself in cold water. She embraced me and a shudder ran through my spine at the touch of her cold fingers.

"Wait, I'll fix another blanket for you." She busied herself with the next bed. I heard her muttering, "All the hotels fasten the blankets so tightly around the mattresses that you must be a Hercules to pull them apart." She managed to peel off a second blanket, but it did little to warm me up. The Jew in me recalled the verse in the Bible: "And King David grew old and advanced in years, and they covered him with clothes, but he could not keep warm." Somehow I managed to fall asleep, and even in my sleep I felt the cold.

An hour later, I shivered and woke up, although Miriam continued to sleep. I could feel her breasts and belly pressed against my back. Her body had warmed up and I was being warmed as if by an oven. She probably slept with Nazis, I thought. I recalled Stanley's words, that Nazis had given her gifts snatched from murdered Jewish girls. Well, I seemed to have sunk into the deepest quagmire of all. The phrase "Forty-nine Gates of Uncleanliness" came to my mind. "A person can sink no lower than this," I said to myself, and for some reason I derived comfort from that. "Never will I be dealt a harsher blow."

ALTHOUGH IT WAS not the truth, I told everyone that I had received a telephone call from my editor and I had to leave immediately for New York. Stefa and Leon had flown back to America the day after Chaim Joel's party. Max was scheduled to return to the hospital and Miriam could not leave him alone. Before my departure I met Miriam's mother, Fania Zalkind, and her lover, Felix Ruktzug. She resembled her daughter, but she also differed from her: she was taller and darker and her eyes were black. She spoke a Warsaw Yiddish very rapidly and laughed a good deal—even when I saw no cause for laughter. She dressed in the manner of an actress, her makeup was excessive, and the heels on her shoes were the highest I had ever seen. She wore a huge hat and a dress that was of two colors: the left side was red and the right black.

When she spoke about Miriam it was as though Miriam were a younger sister or a friend, not her daughter. She said, "She is stubborn, terribly stubborn. She is clever, but for a clever girl she committed far too many follies. On bended knees I begged her to come with us to Russia. She showed promise at school, but between you and me—she fell in love with every one of her teachers. I cannot understand how her mind works. Clever, intelligent—and foolish like a small child. If someone says a kind word to her, she is ready to sacrifice herself for him. Sometimes she is sophisticated, especially when it comes to literature, and at the same time she is terribly naïve. I disapproved of that Stanley. One had to be blind not to see that he was, as they say in America, a phony. His poems were preposterous. You won't believe this, but he even tried to flirt with me. His physical appearance alone repelled me—he had the belly of a pregnant woman.

"About Max I'd better not speak. He is too old even for me. In Warsaw he had the reputation of a first-rate charlatan. After he squandered his father's money he lived off women. Someone told me that he literally sold a mistress of his to an American tourist for five hundred dollars. If he were younger and stronger he'd make a fine pimp. Miriam escaped from the arms of one rogue only to fall into the arms of another. I ask you, where is all this going to lead? I pictured you to myself differently—taller, darker, with fiery black eyes."

"My hair was red before I became bald," I said.

"Yes, I see. Your eyebrows are still red. They say red-haired people are temperamental. I like your voice. Miriam idolizes you. Well, I'd better not go into detail. What we've lived through turned everything topsy-turvy for us. I would really love you to see me perform. My friend Felix Ruktzug could adapt some story of yours for the stage. Naturally I would play the lead role. In his eyes I am the greatest actress who ever lived." And Fania Zalkind burst out laughing.

I also had occasion to meet Felix Ruktzug. He was short, dark, his shoulders broad, his belly flat. He had a thin nose and thick lips. He wore his trousers narrow and tight, sported a red tie, and on his fingers were two diamond rings—the typical gigolo. Felix Ruktzug remained a Communist, a Stalinist even. He was still contributing theater articles to the only Jewish journal left in Warsaw. Even the Marxists sneered at his stale phrases.

I spent only a few moments with Miriam's mother, who spoke mischievously, cleverly, joked, flirted. Miriam, in turn, watched her mother in amazement.

Everything was over—the farewells, the kisses, the promises, the vows. Both Miriam and Max accompanied me to Lod. On the way to the airport I peered at everything in sight, hoping to find those features peculiar to Eretz Yisrael, those which separated the old from the new. At first it seemed to me that nothing was left here of biblical times. But soon I began to spot images that bore an ancient charm—a Yemenite face, an olive tree, a cart harnessed to a donkey. Had this region belonged to Jews? Philistines? Miriam held my hand, pressing it from time to time. I had betrayed my parents' religion, but the Bible still held me spellbound.

Max was speaking: "Did I even for a moment believe that the Zionist dream would become a reality? No, I bought their *Shkalim*, contributed to the Jewish Foundation Fund and the Jewish National Fund, but never for a moment did I believe that anything would come of these fantasies. Even the Balfour Declaration left me unconvinced. But the Jewish state is here and I am here. Since I was destined to die I want to be buried in this ancient soil."

"Stop, Max!" Miriam called out.

"*Nu, nu.* For the time being I'm alive. We'll all be gone sooner or later. But a breath of something remains, I feel it. Come back, Butterfly."

"I'll go to New York later," Miriam said. "We'll all go back to America, and soon."

"Yes," said Max, and patted my back.

I SAT BY the airplane window. Next to me was a small gray-bearded man, a rav. He wore a long caftan, a small fringed shawl under the caftan, and held a volume of the Mishnah in his lap. Between the yellowing pages of the Mishnah lay a *Messilat Ye-sharim*, which kept falling to the ground and which the rav kept picking up and touching to his lips. He had put his hat down on a bundle together with his topcoat. On his head he wore a wrinkled skullcap. I had told him who I was—a grandson of the Bilgoray rav, a Yiddish writer living in New York. He was the rav of a synagogue in Haifa, which he said was populated by German Jews and atheists. Even on the Sabbath his synagogue could barely scrape together a *minyan*. He, the rav, had been invited to become a Rosh Yeshiva in Jerusalem and he had answered, "Jerusalem is filled with yeshivas and with Torah. It is Haifa that needs me." He had lost his wife and children in the Holocaust. People tried to marry him off. How could it be otherwise, a rav needed a *rebbetzin*! But he had told them, "I have already fulfilled the commandment 'Thou shalt be fruitful and multiply,' and that is enough for me." The rav was traveling to the United States to raise money to establish a yeshiva in Haifa.

He said to me, "I know all about you. I read about your arrival in the newspaper. Was your grandfather a Hasid?"

"My grandfather from Bilgoray used to travel to the Maggid of Trisk, not to the son," I said.

"I know, I know. We in Galicia used to travel to Belz, to Bobov, Garlitz, Shenyava, and to the Rizhyn line: Chortkov, Husiatyn, Sadagura. Trisk was in Russia, and people rarely traveled there. But I know, I know. *Divrei Avraham*. He used to favor *Noterakon* and *Gematria*. Every Master had his own way, and that is as it should be. You have a family, a wife and children?"

"No."

"A widower?"

"I never married."

Rav Zechariah Kleingewirtz scratched his beard. "How come? Since Hitler—may his name be blotted out—murdered so many of our Jews, it behooves Jews to raise new generations."

"True, but . . ."

"I know, the enlightened argue as follows: Why bring up new generations when Jews are always in trouble? They all say this to me. All year long my synagogue is empty. But on Rosh Hashanah and Yom Kippur they come. Not all of them, but many. What is the point of it? If there is neither judgment nor judge, how do the High Holidays differ from other days of the year? I talk to them, I ask them why they don't marry or why they have so few children, and they all have the same answer: 'For what? So that there'll be someone to kill?' The Evil Inclination has an answer for everything. On the other hand, a spark of Jewishness exists in every Jew, and a spark can easily become a flame. Who drove those youths from Russia, those who called themselves *Lechu Ve-nelcha*, to go to Eretz Yisrael? Why did they not adopt the thinking of the *Am Olamniks* and go to America instead? They came here and sacrificed themselves; they drained the swamps and fell ill with malaria. Many of them died. Take, for example, Yoseph Hayyim Brenner. In his own way he was a fervent Jew, he died a martyr's death."

The rav picked up the Mishnah and returned to his browsing and swaying. In a while he seemed to have fallen asleep. But soon he shook himself and sat up. He asked, "Do you at least make a living from all this writing?"

"Barely."

"What is it that you write about?"

Several moments passed before I answered him. "Ah, about Jewish life."

"Where? In America?"

"In America. Mostly from the Old Country."

"What do you write, novels?"

"Yes."

"I have glanced through such novels. 'He said,' 'she said.' What comes of all these romances? If he is licentious and she is licentious, what has love to do with this? It's hate, not love. They grow tired of one another. Each of these females is a *sotah*, an adulteress. In former days they were given the *mayim me'arerim*, the waters of malediction, but today they drink these waters themselves. The whole game is built on lies. Today he deceives her and the next day she him. Do you understand what I am saying?"

"Yes, Rabbi."

"And if this is what you write about, what is your conclusion?"

"I have no conclusion."

"And so it must stand?" the rav asked.

"When one lacks your faith, Rabbi," I answered, "so it must stand."

T W E L V E

I T WAS WINTER in New York and it had snowed. Leon and Stefa were preparing to fly to Miami Beach; Leon said he could not abide New York winters, and besides, he had business in Miami. He had become a partner in a new hotel venture. Stefa poked fun at him, and Leon said, "I'm a businessman. What should I do, study the Mishnah? As long as a person breathes he must do something. Aaron, am I right?"

"Absolutely right," I answered.

"Will you stop writing when you reach my age?"

"I am afraid I won't."

"When a person does nothing he thinks only of death, and that does him no good. When he is busy, he forgets. Arale, am I right?"

"From your viewpoint, yes."

"And from whose viewpoint am I wrong?"

"The *Musar* books are of the opinion that man must always keep in mind the *Yom ha-Mitah*, the day of his death."

"What for?"

"It keeps one from sinning."

"I don't need to be kept from sinning. I only wish I *could* sin," Leon joked. "At least I can read how others sin. The dead can't even do that."

"Leon, your remarks are misdirected," Stefa broke in. "Aaron believes that the dead go on cruises and carry on love affairs. You yourself read his article to me the other day."

"He writes these things only to play games with readers," Leon answered. "He himself does not believe them. The truth is that pious Jews and the *rabbaim* don't believe in life after death. When one of them is ill, he runs to the doctor. They swallow medicines and vitamins and what have you. If the righteous sit in Paradise on golden chairs and eat Leviathan, why tremble so about death?"

"They fear hell," Stefa said.

"Lies, self-deception, nonsense," Leon said. "They all know that after death it's all over. Even Moses didn't want to die. He kept begging God to let him live another year, another week, another day. Isn't it true, Arale?"

"That is what the Midrash says."

"The Midrash itself was also afraid of death."

"If everyone is afraid, why is it that in every generation hundreds of thousands, even millions, of soldiers go marching off to wars?" I asked. "The world is never at a loss for candidates who'll go to do battle for the merest trifle. Not long ago seven million Germans gave up their lives for Hitler. One million Americans risked their lives to fight Hitler and Japan. If some demagogue were to rise up today and call for war against Mexico, or for seizure of the Philippine Islands, there would be no lack of volunteers eager to follow the call. How can you explain this?"

Leon Kreitle knitted his brow. "Each one thinks the other will die, not he."

"*Nu*, so that is your explanation?"

"Somewhere within him man knows that something of him will remain."

"What will remain? Bones. Eventually even they will decay. Nonsense."

"War is an instinct," Stefa said. Our discussion was taking place in her kitchen, and all the while Stefa was pressing handkerchiefs and lingerie. She put the iron down on a metal plate and added, "If you don't go off to war, your enemy will come to you. Either way, you lose your life. Men are all crazy."

"Women are also becoming soldiers now—in combat, just like men," I said.

WHEN IT CAME time to say goodbye to Leon and Stefa, I kissed them both. A closeness had grown between us which no longer distinguished between husband and wife. Stefa often admitted to Leon that once she had had an affair with me. And Leon, in turn, declared that he hoped I would marry his wife after his death. He offered to have my work published in Yiddish, but I never accepted the offer. Yiddish had reached the stage where a book could not be published without a subsidy and it all seemed pointless to me. Before I left them, I gave my solemn promise to visit them in Miami Beach. In two years I would be fifty, and already I felt like an old man. I had lived through two world wars, my entire family had perished, women with whom I had been close had been reduced to clumps of ashes. The people I wrote about were all dead. I had become a fossil of a long-extinct epoch. When my publisher had introduced me at a literary party, the younger guests asked, "You are still alive? I thought that . . ." And they apologized for their error.

How quickly situations arise and how quickly they end. It was only a few months ago that I had had a love affair with Miriam. We were aflame with sexual fervor, but now in the month of

January it all seemed to belong to the distant past. It seemed
clear to me that Miriam would remain in Eretz Yisrael with Max.
He was alive, thank God, even though his heart was ailing.
Moreover, he now suffered from diabetes. Miriam could not,
nor did she want to, leave him alone in his condition. He would
have died long ago had it not been for Chaim Joel Treibitcher.
Treibitcher had literally taken Max into his home. I had heard
from Miriam and others that there was no harmony between this
generous man and his new wife, who was more often in America
than Tel Aviv. She had her own sons, daughters, daughters-in-
law, sons-in-law, grandchildren. She traveled to spas and managed her own business. The merger of her fortune with her
husband's never materialized. They both had their own methods
of conducting business. She had a host of heirs, but Treibitcher
planned to leave his money to the Jewish state and to various
charitable societies. In addition, his wife was constantly em-
broiled in lawsuits. Miriam informed me of all this in her letters.
She herself had applied to the university in Jerusalem, which
had indicated it might accept her dissertation and grant her a
doctorate. All that was required was that she take certain courses
in Hebrew and in Jewish history.

Miriam wrote me long letters and I answered in short notes.
As long as Max was alive she would not leave him. Their relationship had turned platonic and become closer than before.
Oddly enough, Chaim Joel Treibitcher in his own way had also
fallen in love with her, and now she had not one old man but
two. Miriam wrote:

> Don't laugh, Butterfly, but I am very pleased with this situa-
> tion. I've had enough sex and filth in my life. I have developed
> a profound affection for old men. They attract me more than all
> the students and young professors who try to flirt with me. Max
> is everything to me—a father and a husband.

But Chaim Joel also has his charm. He is naïve, incredibly naïve. It is impossible for me to imagine how he could have amassed millions and become the patron of famous European artists. And to this day Chaim Joel does not realize that the late Matilda had lovers. I have never come across a person whose soul is so pure. At the same time he has a sense of humor, always with a flavor of the Talmud, of Hasidism. He was acquainted with all the rabbis, the *rabbaim*, the rebbetzins, he knew all the secrets in their courts. But he sees everything with innocent, childlike eyes. To hear him and Max in a discussion is a rare treat. Their Yiddish is such that sometimes it's difficult for me to catch their meaning. They mix in words from the Holy Tongue, the Gemara and other books. It seems that for such Jews everything derives from the Torah, even their jokes.

The thought that all this will vanish with their generation is very painful to me. In the eyes of the Sabras, they are considered idlers, *shmageges*. They often say that you are "steeped" in Jewishness, which makes me fear that my dissertation on your work is superficial. To me you are a modern man. I live with but one dream: to see you here. But when?

PRIVA HAD RETURNED to New York with Tzlova. Both women telephoned and invited me to supper. They told me that Chaim Joel Treibitcher had given them all the money they had lost, with interest. Priva had come to New York with a plan: to establish a Jewish Psychic Society. Jews who spoke Yiddish did not read occult journals and could best communicate their experiences in Yiddish. Priva reminded me that I had printed many readers' letters of this kind and had written that if these experiences were true, we would have to rethink all our values. She had collected many such stories herself. Holocaust survivors had been saved through miracles and had neither the courage nor the wish to tell their stories to psychologists and scientists. They had to be handled in a friendly, familiar manner. I discussed the matter with Priva and Tzlova, and two weeks later my article appeared. Soon letters began to arrive.

I had never received so many letters in response to what I had written. Those interested in psychic research, like Dr. Rhine, complained that they could not obtain the funds needed for their investigation. But the Jewish Psychic Society needed no funds. We created our society somewhat like pious Jews had once set up *cheders*, Hasidic *shtibls*, *yeshivot*—without benefit of permits, secretaries, typewriters, mailings, stamps. We needed no office space. Those who had something to report could write a letter, or call me at the *Forward* or call Priva at home. The editor gave me freedom to write whatever I wished and to print what letters I chose. My article said that psychic research could never become a science. How could it? The researcher was forced to rely on people in his research, on their memories, their honesty. I had quoted my father's words: "If Paradise and hell were in the middle of the marketplace, there would be no freedom of choice. One had to believe in God, in Providence, the immortality of the soul, in reward and punishment. Everyone could see God's wisdom, but one had to have faith in His mercy. Faith in turn was built on doubt."

The greatest saints had had their doubts. No lover could be absolutely sure that his beloved was faithful to him. As proof that the Almighty demanded His due, I quoted the verse: "And he had faith in God, and it was counted up as credit to him." I pointed out that even the so-called exact sciences were no longer sure. Gases believed to be fundamental to all electromagnetic phenomena had been all but consumed years before our time. The atom, long believed unsplittable, had certainly been split. Time had become relative, gravitation was a sort of "wrinkle" in space, the universe was fleeing from itself after an explosion believed to have happened twenty billion years ago. The axioms of mathematics had ceased to be eternal truths, having been transformed instead into definitions and the rules of a game.

I had begun to visit Priva in the evening, because my room on Seventieth Street was often cold. I had resumed my Sabbath visits to the Budniks, but most of my weekday evenings were spent with Priva and Tzlova. I often invited the two women for supper at the Tip Top Restaurant on Broadway. Sometimes Tzlova cooked my favorite Warsaw dishes for me—scalded soup, noodles with beans, kasha and fried onions, potatoes and mushrooms, sometimes even my mother's grits, which consisted of pearl kasha, potatoes, sugar beans, dried mushrooms. Tzlova never had to ask me what foods my mother cooked. She found them in my stories.

At first Priva had forbidden me to mention Miriam's name. She called Miriam "that *treyf* girl." But when we sat with the Ouija board or around the little table, Miriam's name often crept in. The planchette which ran over the letters informed us that Max was disappointed with Miriam and that she had betrayed him (and also me) with Chaim Joel Treibitcher. Priva exclaimed, "Don't be so shocked. A slut remains a slut."

Priva and I still addressed each other by the formal "you." Tzlova and I, on the other hand, had become so informal and committed so many slips of the tongue that Priva announced, "Children, enough of this playacting. I am not a fool. You've let the cat out of the bag."

The table, the Ouija board and tarot cards had, in a sense, legitimized our relationship. One evening, when all the lights were out and only the little red light bulb we used for séances flickered in the darkness, the planchette informed us that Miriam had been a *kapo*. Priva asked, "Where?" and the planchette shaped the word "Stutthof." Priva went on to ask how Miriam had conducted herself (she posed the questions in a solemn voice), and the planchette began to leap with extraordinary speed and formed the following words: "Whipped Jewish girls, dragged children to the gas chambers." The planchette further revealed to us that Miriam had been the mistress of an SS officer named Wolfgang Schmid. I had never really believed in the occult powers of the table or the Ouija board, because I had felt Tzlova lifting the table with her foot. More than once her knee had bumped mine. How those two women maneuvered the planchette and made it move at their command I shall never know. I had always agreed with Houdini that all mediums, with no exception, cheated. Priva's hands often shook; she suffered from Parkinson's disease. How could a woman in her condition manipulate a planchette over a lettered board? That evening the planchette hurried across the board in zigzag fashion, as if propelled by its own power. I closed my eyes, and in the red-tinged darkness the figure of Wolfgang Schmid materialized before me: a giant Nazi, his face pockmarked, a swastika emblazoned on his sleeve, a pistol on his thigh, and in his hand a whip. His eyes were beady, a scar was spread across his forehead, his closely cropped hair bristled white and stiff like a pig's. I heard him shouting at Miriam in a rasping voice. I had the peculiar feeling that I had seen and heard all this before, either while awake or in a dream.

DURING THE NIGHTS in which I slept alone, I often was awakened by worry about my literary work. Several stories and a novel which had appeared in the paper were deposited in my suitcases. But what publisher would publish a long novel by an unknown beginner who was approaching fifty? My earlier novel in English had received favorable reviews, but it had not sold well. I had spent my advance on rewriting the manuscript. I had included an episode set in Switzerland, and my conscience did not allow me to write about a country I had never seen, so I had traveled to Switzerland before turning the book in. The journey cost me three times as much as I had received in royalties. The publisher had refused to issue a second edition of the novel. He even told me that the plates had been "tossed on the scrap heap."

The thought of beginning the whole process anew, with all the complications entailed in translations from the Yiddish, struck me with terror. One voice in me said, "It's too late, it's no longer within your powers." I was in the midst of writing another novel, which demanded every ounce of my literary energy. Thirty or forty thousand readers were reading it every day, most of them Polish Jews acquainted with every town, street, and house I described. The most minute error brought scores, sometimes hundreds, of letters. My descriptions of sex or the underworld brought protests from rabbis and community leaders, who claimed that I poured oil on the fire of anti-Semitism, embarrassed and dishonored the victims of Hitler. Why should the Gentile world know of Jewish thieves, crooks, pimps, prostitutes, when they had all been martyred? Why not write instead of righteous Jews, rabbis, Hasidim, scholars, pious women, virtuous maidens? True, I had also written about so-called positive types, but the times demanded—so the letter writers argued—that a Jewish writer stress only the good and the saintly.

I also touched upon matters which were all but banned in the Jewish press. I did not fit in, either in fiction or in journalism. The articles I was printing now—on telepathy, clairvoyance, daydreams, premonitions—aroused readers who considered themselves rationalists, socialists, radicals. Why bring back the superstitions of the Middle Ages? they asked. Why awaken the old fanaticism? The Communist paper took every opportunity to point out that my writing was opium for the Jewish masses, to make them forget the struggle for social justice, for a united humanity. Even Zionists demanded to know where in my writing was the rebirth of Jewish history witnessed by our generation?

The dawdler in me, the pessimist, argued: "Success as a writer is beyond your power. Give up!" I fantasized about becoming an elevator man somewhere in Brooklyn or a dishwasher in some cheap restaurant. All that I, a vegetarian, required was a slice of bread, a piece of cheese, a cup of coffee, and a bed to sleep in. I could still get by on less than twenty dollars a week, I could go on relief, I could always commit suicide. But another voice argued: "You have genuine works of literature lying in those suitcases you drag from one furnished room to another. Don't leave them to disintegrate. Forty-eight is not exactly old age. Anatole France was forty when he first began to write. There were even those—what were their names?—whose literary careers began in their fifties. For the time being you have a job, and for as long as you have it, devote yourself to it. Begin tomorrow!"

I got out of bed, turned on the light, and opened the drawer where I kept my notebooks and several old diaries. God in heaven, I had begun to treasure the gift of freedom of choice when I was quite young, not even twenty. FREE CHOICE OR DEATH I had written on a page in my notebook, and then underlined it three times: first in green, then blue, and finally red. I had written this little motto more than twenty years ago in a hotel in Otwock, when I was nearly twenty-seven. At that time I suffered the same crisis as now. In the still of the night I raised my hand and swore that this time I would keep my word.

HAVING MADE THAT solemn promise, I could no longer sleep. On one slip of paper I read the following verse: "Smuggle your way through wrongdoing and dread / Hide in your hole and gnaw on your bread." The lines evoked countless associations. I had long ago formed the theory that freedom of choice was strictly individual. Two people together had less choice than did one;

the masses had virtually no choice at all. A man who had a family had less choice than a bachelor; one who belonged to a party had less choice than his unaffiliated neighbor. This went hand in hand with a theory of mine that human civilization, and even human culture, strove to give mankind more choice, more free will. I was still a pantheist, not of Spinoza's school, but partly of the Cabala's. I identified love with freedom. When a man loved a woman it was an act of freedom. Love of God could not take place by commandment; it could only be an act of free will. The fact that almost all creatures are born of a union between male and female was proof for me that life is an experiment in God's laboratory of freedom. Freedom could not remain passive, it wanted to create. It wanted countless variations, possibilities, combinations. It wanted love.

My bizarre fantasy concerning freedom of choice was also bound up with a theory of art. Science was, at least provisionally, the teaching of constraint. But art was in a sense the teaching of freedom. It did what it wanted, not what it had to do. The true artist was a free-willed man who did as he pleased. Science was the product of teams of investigators: technology required a collective. But art was created by a single individual. I had always considered erroneous the art theories of Hippolyte Taine, as well as those of professors who wished to transform art into a science.

During these sleepless nights, I let my thoughts run free, lest when I fell asleep I entered the realm of absolute compulsion. In sleep every choice ceased, or so I thought when I awakened from my nightmares.

One morning I opened my eyes and outside there was daylight. Something had gone wrong with the heating and it was as cold in my room as it was outside. I touched the radiator, which was not even lukewarm. My nose was stuffed and a cough was brewing in my chest. I had forgotten to wind my wristwatch and it had stopped at a quarter to four. Despotic causality was still ruling the universe. Bathing or taking a shower in this chill was out of the question. But I did need to shave. I turned on the faucet and moistened my shaving brush in cold water. I decided to warm up in Miriam's apartment, since I had a key and it was too early to go to the newspaper office. I put on my clothes and set out for Central Park West and 100th Street. When I reached the house the doorman greeted me: "I'm glad you're here. I have a cable for you."

He handed me an envelope. I opened it and read, "Max died tonight in his sleep. With love, your Miriam."

WINTER WAS NEARLY over and soon it would be spring. Fania and Morris Zalkind proposed to make our wedding a lavish affair, but Miriam and I insisted on a small ceremony, with only the two of them in attendance. In a sense it was a double celebration, because Miriam's mother had returned from Eretz Yisrael having broken with Felix Ruktzug, and Morris had taken her back.

That early morning in April had started out to be sunny, but by the time we were ready to ride to the City Hall in Brooklyn snow had begun to fall. Soon it turned into a snowstorm. Fania had bought a magnificent straw hat for Miriam, but Miriam would not wear it in the snow. Morris Zalkind had given me a check for twenty thousand dollars. I thanked him, and promptly tore the small paper to shreds. I had taken my three valises, two of them packed with manuscripts and newspaper clippings, and moved into Miriam's apartment. She had had a photograph of Max enlarged and framed, and had hung it in our bedroom above our bed. Our wedding consisted of a civil ceremony, since neither Miriam nor I relished being married by a rabbi. After the ceremony the Zalkinds invited us to lunch at a vegetarian restaurant. After the meal they drove to their house in Long Island and

Miriam and I took a taxi home. Morris Zalkind had said to me, "That was the quietest wedding since the one between Adam and Eve."

In the taxi Miriam leaned on my shoulder and sobbed. She said she could not keep from crying. As soon as we entered the apartment, the telephone began to ring. The proofreader at the *Forward* had found an error in one of my articles and asked for my permission to correct it. I said to him, "You need not ask permission. For this very purpose you were born: to correct writers' blunders wherever you find them."

Miriam's apartment never lacked for heat. Steam hissed in the radiators, the snow had stopped falling, the sun broke through the clouds, and Max's face in the photo on the wall was flooded with light. His eyes gazed upon us, smiling with that Jewish-Polish merriment which death could not extinguish. Miriam had stopped her crying. Sprawled on top of the bed she said, "If we have a child, we'll name him Max."

"There will be no children," I said.

"Why not?" she asked.

"You and I, we are like mules," I answered, "the last of a generation."

TRANSLATOR'S POSTSCRIPT

Meshugah was serialized in Yiddish in the *Forward* under its original title, *Lost Souls*, from April 1981 to February 1983. After I had completed a draft in English, at Mr. Singer's request, he decided to change the title and wrote the word MESHUGAH in ink on the first page of the typescript.

I first met Isaac Bashevis Singer in 1975, after a teacher of mine in graduate school, who edited *The Jewish Spectator*, asked me to interview him for her journal. At our second meeting I presented him with my translations of two stories he had written many, many years ago—in Hebrew. He snatched the pages from my hands, saying that he did not want "this ancient work" circulated anymore. "But," he added with a smile, "why not help me to translate my Yiddish work?" I said I would love to do some of his Krochmalna Street stories, since my father, Josef Kratka, had grown up on the very same street in Warsaw and could help me with the translation. Isaac—as he asked me to call him—seemed pleased with this knowledge of my background, and we shook hands.

Working with my father brought unexpected rewards. Immersing himself in Isaac's world, my father began to recall relatives and friends of whom I'd never heard. Small details in the novel jarred long-forgotten memories. When I was confronted with an unfamiliar Yiddish word regarding food, my father produced not only a translation—"pan-browned grits"—but the recipe as well: Boil the potatoes until they fall apart, add fried onions and browned flour, mix well; best eaten with two slices of bread. It seems you had to live in a certain neighborhood and reach a certain level of poverty to appreciate such a delicacy.

In May 1982 Isaac asked me to meet him at the American Restaurant on Broadway and Eighty-fifth Street to discuss his current serial, *Lost Souls*. Despite his years (he was seventy-eight) Isaac approached at a fast clip, wearing sunglasses and with the brim of his hat pulled down over his eyes. In the restaurant he explained that he had set out to write a novel about a young woman who was genuinely in love, first with an old man and then, simultaneously, with a middle-aged man who had entered the picture. "That in itself is a strange situation," he said, "with lots of promise." He was writing about events that had occurred in the 1950s in and around New York. He said he wanted the reader to see the contradictions and conflicts within each of the three principal characters. I assumed that his fictional creation drew on events that had actually occurred, as well as on aspects of people he had known. It seemed obvious to me that the first-person narrator, the author Aaron Greidinger who wrote for the *Forward*, was based on Isaac himself, though he never directly said so.

Working with Isaac in his and Alma's spacious apartment on Eighty-sixth Street, off Broadway, had its ups and downs. He made corrections by hand in black ink. Once he typed a paragraph on his Yiddish typewriter and then wrote it out in English by hand. He had a "clippings suitcase," in which he kept installments of the novels as they were serialized in the *Forward*, to be doled out to trusted co-translators. He stressed the fact that the English translations, not the Yiddish, provided the basic texts of all his foreign editions, and that was why he involved himself in the translation process. Behind one door in the apartment lay what he called the Chaos Room. It was stacked not only with typescripts and copies of the *Forward*, but with books, gifts, plaques, medals, honorary doctorates, the certificate of his Nobel Prize for Literature, the National Book Award, and similar honors. If Alma herself had not cleared a narrow path through the accumulated material, it would have been almost impossible to enter the room.

Once while we were working on the script and Alma was not present, he answered a phone call in the next room. It was a newspaper reporter and I heard Isaac say, "Now you won't have to call me anymore, you'll be calling Milosz instead." That day the poet Czeslaw Milosz had been announced as the new Nobel Prize winner. When Isaac returned he said, "In this world it does not take long to become a has-been."

I also worked with Isaac on the translation of *The King of the Fields*, his novel about Poland in its primitive period of history. It was published in 1988, during his final illness, when the publisher was unaware that I was co-translator of this work. I am glad to know that the publisher will give me credit in future editions of the book.

At dinner one evening at our house, Alma told the story of having traveled—on Isaac's behalf—to Dusseldorf to accept the Buber-Rosenzweig Medal for his work. It was a tale of missed connections, canceled flights, and unplanned-for complications as harrowing as "The Lecture" and "The Briefcase," Isaac's stories about the nightmarish adventures that befall a traveling Yiddish writer. This was a favorite theme of Isaac's: In life, despite the best-laid plans, one can never be sure of anything.

"Sometimes," he told us, "I lie awake at night and wonder, Did I really give that lecture or is it still to come? In the morning when a friend calls to say what a fine lecture I gave—only then do I know for sure."

One morning I arrived at his apartment thoroughly discouraged and told him that everything—the daily routine, the daily struggle—seemed so pointless. Isaac sighed and agreed—yes, he had days like that, too. But what can one do? One accepts it and continues to work. "I'd like to believe that all this is evolving toward some good," I said, "toward something higher." Isaac hoped so, too. "But who knows?" he said. "We are in this world to learn to become wiser, more compassionate, to grow. But if we know in advance how it will turn out in the end, how can we learn and how can we grow?"

He was glad when I phoned one day. "I meant to call you," he said, "but I've been going through a terrible crisis, a literary crisis." He was due to leave for his summer hiatus in Switzerland and he could not decide which way the novel, still being seri- alized, should go. The next day the crisis was over. "I've dis- covered how to end the novel," he said. "It was the kind of crisis that does not kill you. On the contrary, it makes you think, makes you create. The creative process is nothing but a series of crises."

—NILI WACHTEL